The Strings of Life

Y. A. Picker
&
Rand Soler

Publisher: Archean Enterprises, LLC

Y. A. Picker & Rand Soler

The Strings of Life

.

Published by: Archean Enterprises, LLC

Suite #3173, 1321 Upland Drive
Houston TX 77043
United States

Cover Design by: Archean Enterprises, LLC

.

ISBN: 9780999281734 (Paperback Edition)
ISBN: 9780999281741 (Ebook Edition)

CONTENTS

Deep in the mists of time, when Earth was young, and life had not yet appeared, a probe appeared in the night-time sky, emerging from the termination of a wormhole and hovering in a low planetary orbit. Sent by a civilization now long past and forgotten, it pelted Earth's ancient seas with its entire supply of small cannonball-sized projectiles. As each sphere sank into the Archean oceans' murky depths, its organic payload was released into the cold salty waters, infusing Earth with life.

During routine geological fieldwork on Greenland's southwest coast, graduate student Susan Calder finds dense, mysterious objects embedded in four-billion-year-old rocks. She shares the find with her mentor Mat Dover, but the secret is not theirs alone, and other shadowy groups actively pursue the same prize. Mat and his lifelong friend Mark work to stay one step ahead and uncover the mystery behind the spheres, and they stumble upon the exotic origin of the seeds of life.

....

Thank you Melissa for your help with editing.

Not Quite Right (Mat)

Two o'clock in the morning is not a great time to hear my phone vibrating on the bedside table, but it is not an entirely unknown event either. I glanced at the screen to check out who was calling and figured the caller believed they were reaching me in Portland, Oregon. The call was coming in from a grad student in Greenland. Susan was calling me at 11:00 pm from Nuuk to contact me at 6:00 pm in Portland, but waking me up at 2:00 am in Orkney. So goes life.

"Susan, still seeing some daylight in Nuuk?"

"Affirmative, Mat. I thought I would catch you before dinner."

"You should have called about eight hours ago. I'm spending the week in Orkney."

In the silence over the phone, I could hear her doing the mental math. "Sorry," she said.

"Not a problem. What's up?"

Susan had been in the Nuuk area for part of the summer doing work on the Isua Greenstone Belt. The geologic formations she was interested in are composed of an ancient set of mafic and metasedimentary rocks generally considered to be 3.7 to 3.8 billion years old.

"I just wanted you to know that I have about finished the work in the Isukasia Terrain," Susan told me.

The Isukasia Terrane within the Greenstone Belt, lies just north of the Ivinnguit Fault. The fault itself cuts a southwesterly line that runs almost straight through Nuuk, carving out the winding coastline of the Godthab Fjord.

7

"Have you seen any more signs of bugs in those rocks?" I asked, and Susan sighed.

The bugs I was referring to were not bugs at all but stromatolites. These structures in the rock are fossilized remains of what used to be large colonies of cyanobacteria, blue-green algae. Their fame in the Isua formations came from a 2016 report that identified stromatolites in the sedimentary portions of the rocks. A team working with an Australian based research project made the find.

Almost as soon as they found the evidence, though, there was someone disputing it. Claiming that the scorched black and copper banding was the result of nothing more than inorganic alterations of the rock fabric, or purely geological processes that have nothing to do with living creatures.

Technically, Susan was not looking for more bugs. Instead, she was following some previous work identifying isotopically light carbon hidden deep within the Isua rocks—something that can only be produced by organisms that eat, grow, and reproduce. In short, evidence of early life.

Light carbon or stromatolites—finding either in these rocks would quite possibly make them the oldest indications of life on the planet. It would most certainly push the origins of life back past 4 billion years, not too long after the earth formed from a collection of cosmic debris. While the broader geological interest in the Isua Greenstone Belt extends beyond the origin of life, Susan's slice of the research pie was limited to her current project.

"I might not have seen any bugs," Susan continued, "but I am getting some interesting leads from the samples I collected. That's not why I called, though."

"Oh?"

"Mat, I've been out here all summer, and we both know it's a freaking lonely place. Your chances of running across another person are slim to none. But I've met four geological teams in the past four weeks, and these aren't amateurs or academic dudes. One of the teams was carrying around about a half-million dollars of shiny new equipment. Hell, one of the groups had that much invested in ATVs alone. They didn't buy them in the country, so they must have flown them in. They were also using private unmarked choppers to get inland, so you know there is money involved. I didn't recognize all of the equipment, but I did see miniature mass specs, high-end electron scopes, and some weird scanning device."

I was wide awake now and curious. "Were the groups working together?"

"That's the strange thing," she said. "It looked more like they were competing with each other from the way they talked. They wouldn't tell me anything about what they were researching, but people like that don't come to Greenland to sightsee."

It was deja vu for me. I had almost the exact same conversation with another colleague of mine three weeks ago, Bruno Vandorff. The only difference was that he was working in Australia, not Greenland. It didn't feel right, and Susan was correct, she was working in a freaking lonely place.

"Let me ask you another question," I ventured. "How interested were these guys and gals in your work?"

"Very interested, actually." I heard her shifting over the phone. "They had a lot of questions about some low-grade slate and cooked mudstone that I located last summer. I don't know how they even knew about the find unless they attended my presentation at the symposium last February."

"What did you tell them?"

"Not much. I may have mentioned some of the weird inclusions I found in the rocks. Several really dense objects, but I don't have any idea what they are. I guess we'll find out when we get them back to the lab, huh?"

"So you say you're wrapping things up?" I asked, and Susan hummed in affirmation.

I paused. "Look, Susan. You know I don't usually tell researchers working with my grant money how to run their projects. But that being said, I am anxious for you to wrap it up tomorrow. Get out of Nuuk and fly back to Eugene. There's a plane to Reykjavik that leaves around 6:00 or 6:30 tomorrow evening. I want you to be on it. I'm setting you up with business class tickets on my dollar. Just go to the cargo terminal at the airport and find Joseph. He can get the samples and mobile lab equipment shipped."

"What about the helicopter contract?" she asked.

"Don't worry, one unused day on the contract won't make any difference."

"Why the hurry?"

I leaned forward and rubbed my temple. "To be honest I'm not completely sure, but you just told me a story similar to one I have already heard. Suffice it to say, it didn't end well. No dead bodies or anything, but creepy nonetheless. Do me a favor and clear out of there as soon as you can tomorrow."

"You're the boss Mat. I guess I can forego one set of samples I was going to retrieve tomorrow."

"Thanks Susan. Just leave the last samples and clear out tomorrow evening. We'll speak when I am stateside."

"Alright, I'll catch up with you when you get back to Portland. Bye, Mat." There was a click as the line went dead, but instead of rolling over and going back to sleep, I forced the phone back up to my ear and called Joseph. One short conversation and one big headache later, Susan's travel plans were set and the sun was starting to peek through the shades of my hotel room. Woodwick House was located on the northeast side of Orkney's main island, overlooking the waves churning, frothing, and eating their way into the coastline. It offered a magnificent view, but one I was too groggy to fully appreciate.

A Nespresso coffee machine sat ready and waiting on the counter top, so I loaded up one of the dark purple arpeggio capsules to wake myself up. I set it to lungo and watched the cup fill halfway, popped a second capsule in, and waited until coffee was nearly brimming over the edge. Nespresso gave me the best home-away-from-home packaged morning coffee I could get. The individual capsules are hermetically sealed as soon as the beans are ground. Fresh oxygen is a lousy curse for freshly ground coffee. It immediately starts drawing off the volatile components and hence drawing off the flavor.

The air outside was crisp, so I took my coffee to the patio hoping that the fresh air would help me think. I couldn't seem to get Susan's call out of my mind. There were countless parallels between her story and the one Bruno Vandorff told me not three weeks prior, and they were too significant to be mere coincidence. He had been working in the East Pilbara region of Australia, delving into marine sediments along the Mosquito Creek Belt. If the rocks Susan dealt with were ancient, then the samples Bruno studied were positively primordial. Some sat close to the 4 billion year mark; almost too old to be conceivable.

Bruno was as enthusiastic about sample collection as Susan, and he called me almost immediately when he stumbled across something strange. Two odd samples of slightly metamorphosed shales, both with dense, wedge-shaped fragments embedded in them. Just like Susan, his research team ran into several other well-equipped groups who, while reluctant to discuss their work, were very interested in hearing about his. Nothing seemed suspicious until the entire set of samples Bruno had collected disappeared from a storage warehouse without a trace. The whole affair was a complete mystery to him. The loss of the shale samples was especially unfortunate, since he had been looking forward to investigating their composition and the high density inclusions.

What Susan didn't know is I had recently run a zircon age dating analysis on rocks from her shale and mudstone sample location, and the analysis had placed the age of the rocks at around four billion years old. The thing is, there aren't many players in the field of early Archean geology, and those that publish are well known. The four billion year age-date placed Susan's rocks at the beginning of the Archean period. The sudden appearance of well-funded teams of unknown researchers reeked to me of commercial or government activity. I had organized and sometimes funded enough research expeditions to know the equipment these guys were using required some deep pockets. Why were they interested in these very old rocks? Something stank, and I wanted to know what.

I thought it through and decided to cut my vacation short and travel to Houston. I wasn't keen on leaving the Scottish countryside, but, fortunately, I had already spent a day exploring the western side of the island including the Skara Brae ruins, the Ring of Brodgar, and Maeshowe.

Neolithic cultures have always interested me, and the wealth of ancient activity still visible in the Orkney Islands is what attracted me there initially. The restored village of Skara Brae, nestled on the water's edge, was like a picture frozen in time. Five thousand years of history still hewn and chiseled into the land. The village had remained untouched until the mid 1800s, when a massive storm swept away the coastal sands to uncover the treasures hidden below. The stone circles and chambered tombs like Maeshowe hold a level of architectural sophistication, which offers vivid acknowledgment of human genius.

The pre-booked tour for the Highland Park Distillery would have to wait for another trip, though. I booked the earliest flight I could manage, departing at 7:30 in the morning from the little town of Kirkwall. As much as I'd been looking forward to a tumbler of 18 year Highland Park single malt, I had more pressing matters to attend to.

Joseph (Mat)

Joseph Sebastiao sat in the evening sun, his chair propped up against the east wall of the cargo terminal at the Nuuk International Airport. The airport, located just east of town, nestles into a flat area at the base of a 400-meter hill. From where Joseph sat, the main terminal was out of sight. The two-story building at the front of the airport was a gray, boxy, angular structure with two rows of dark windows breaking up the monotony. Hills backdropped the building to the east and south, exposing a patchwork of brambles and rocky slopes—a real study of gray on gray.

The air was cool, but the sun was warm, and Joseph closed his eyes as he took in the damp, organic smell of the ocean nearby. The scent reminded him of the shantytown in Luanda, where he grew up along the coast of West Africa. A lot of water had passed under the bridge since then. There were lots of smart kids living in the slums of Angola, and the city of Luanda was no exception. Joseph still marveled that the gods of fortune had spun the roulette wheel in his direction.

The city of Luanda was founded by the Portuguese explorer Paulo Dia de Novais in 1567. Like other coastal ports on the African continent, it served the human trafficking markets of imperialist empires built by powerful European countries. Luanda was a gateway to misery for slaves shipped to Brazil and other Portuguese colonies.

It wasn't until the 1970s that Luanda earned its independence. Immediately following the 1974 Carnation Revolution and the fall of the Estado Novo regime, Portugal let go of its stranglehold on most colonies. The people of Luanda gained their freedom, but independence

13

is a two-edged sword. It wasn't long before the bloodletting began. The ensuing 27-year civil war left over half a million people dead and over one million internally displaced. The freedom fighters then became the oppressors in a savage struggle to control the remaining wealth. "Follow the money" is the best guide to understanding these human tragedies.

The communist People's Movement for the Liberation of Angola (MPLA) was eventually defeated by the National Union for the Total Independence of Angola (UNITA) in 2002. The end of the war allowed the victors to start the process of pillaging the natural resources in pursuance of vast fortunes for the few. The process left the rest of the population living as serfs in the mosquito-ridden slums.

Joseph technically counted as one of the many internally displaced Angolans, but he was too young to remember how he got to Luanda. The city streets were the only childhood he knew.

Minerals and oil were Joseph's savior, and through blind luck, his teacher spoke to other teachers, who spoke to civil servants, and Joseph was noticed for his exceptional mind. The country lacked a viable intelligentsia, and its rulers resented the reliance on foreigners for extracting wealth from the earth. Selected students were sent abroad to study geology, with the intent they would return and form a technical working class to assist in the government's exploitation of the oil and mineral deposits.

So it was, at the age of eighteen, Joseph found himself in the Canadian town of Sudbury, a stranger amidst the sea of students flocking back for their next semester at Laurentian. Joseph was academically brilliant and also a social creature who had learned the subtlety of dealing with his fellow human beings in the slums of Luanda. He made friends quickly and soon added English and French fluency to his repertoire.

Joseph's real break came in a first-year lab taught by a geology graduate student, Matthew Dover. Mat and Joseph found themselves to be of kindred spirit, and it wasn't long before Mat found himself taking Joseph under his wing. With Mat's help, Joseph became the top student in his class. He got his undergraduate degree in geology along with a second degree in business management.

It's no secret governments are not known for their critical thinking skills. Grand plans are not generally formulated by the best and brightest, and when those plans try to control the best and brightest, the chance of failure is high. When the Angolan government started its international education program, it made the fatal assumption that these newly trained minds would have no choice but to flock back home with their newfound skills and generate wealth for their oligarchs. The fact that these young men and women would have globally marketable skills did not seem to figure into the bureaucratic planning.

Mat had recently started a small energy exploration business in the Powder River Basin when Joseph graduated. The business was small, but Mat's plans weren't, and he immediately hired Joseph on as his Chief Operations Officer. Mat had attracted enough money from investors to finance his first drilling venture, so he could at least provide Joseph with a living wage.

Joseph worked for Mat over eight years, helping to create and build a business that eventually sold for 40 million dollars. Mat cut him a sizable check from the sale, and Joseph started a logistics consulting business for mineral and energy companies. His combination of deep business skills and an even deeper geotechnical knowledge kept him in high demand.

Mat and Joseph kept in close touch after the company sold, and Joseph was not surprised when Mat came out on top of the bitcoin craze in 2017. On a whim and in true Dover style, Mat started buying a then-unknown and unproven cryptocurrency product called bitcoin back when it first appeared in 2009. In just two years, he had accumulated a massive investment for pennies on the coin. Joseph didn't know exactly how much, but Mat referenced that he spent about $40,000 in total. Joseph translated that into something like 100 to 300 thousand bitcoins in the early days of cryptocurrencies. In November and December of 2017, he sold it all at an average price of over $10,000 per coin. The math was staggering, but it truly put Mat in a position to pursue his passion in early earth geology.

Mat currently had his fingers in almost a dozen university research projects via funding grants, and he was also underwriting scholarships for more than two dozen graduate students. With lots of spoons in the pot, he convinced Joseph to go on retainer to handle logistics for a variety of projects around the world. Joseph never once considered saying no, even though it meant he had to hire two more ops managers to cover the gap created when working for Mat. Truth be told, he probably would have done it for free if Mat asked.

Joseph snapped out of his thoughts at the sound of a car engine. He turned his head to the left as Susan's car came around the corner. He had only met Susan once, in Greenland last summer when he arranged helicopter, security, and equipment logistics for her fieldwork. She was a damn good geologist and had a passion for being in the field. She could take care of herself as well, so no babysitting required.

Susan stood a little over five and a half feet tall and kept her hair pulled into a tight auburn ponytail. Her shoulders were on the broad side, and her muscled arms reflected a fair amount of weight training. Joseph remembered her mentioning regular kickboxing sessions when she wasn't in the field. She was sporting dark green, deep-pocketed field pants, hiking boots, and a gray tee-shirt underneath an unbuttoned plaid flannel shirt.

She gave Joseph a firm handshake and opened the back of the rented vehicle to reveal a jumble of boxes and equipment. She shot Joseph a quick smile. "Why don't you let me help you unload, Joseph?"

Joseph was rolling a pallet truck behind the car with one large, empty wooden pallet on it. "We'll put it on the pallet, and then you take off," he said. "I don't want you to miss that flight."

"Why does Mat have a wild hair up his ass about clearing out so quickly," she said as she placed the first sample box at the back of the pallet. Truth be told, he was just as curious as she was. This current project was an odd one. Joseph had never known Mat to be this cautious with rock samples. However, he just gave her a shrug as he hauled down a box.

"Oh, you know the boss," Joseph replied. Susan scoffed.

"I don't, actually. But you certainly do." She stood up and scrutinized him with striking hazel eyes. Joseph paused and held her gaze. "He doesn't always divulge everything," he admitted. "But on the other hand, he didn't make a fortune in bitcoin by telling people what he was doing."

She gave a "Humm..." and went back to unloading.

Joseph told her to leave the car in the parking lot by the terminal as he wheeled the pallet into the warehouse. He had arranged for a private space in a bin to the left of the door. Joseph settled the pallet on the gray polished concrete floor and went to work.

Joseph had a set of custom-made crates ready. Each crate was constructed with a false bottom into which he transferred the rock samples. The individual samples were already packaged, labeled, and ready for transport, so the process went quickly enough. The original sample boxes were then repacked with decoy rocks collected from the beach that morning, all wrapped and tagged with labels identical to the real thing. Even Joseph couldn't tell them apart. He set the original crates aside for normal delivery to the USA.

Scientific field equipment was packaged, cushioned, and loaded into the tops of the new custom-made crates. Even if someone went looking, they'd be hard-pressed to find the false bottoms under all of that heavy gear. The custom crates were then nailed shut and labeled for delivery to an address in Goose Bay, Canada, a nondescript self-storage unit near the airport. Joseph and his pilot would accompany the crates there, but then deliver them to a second unlabeled storage unit, and then he was back off to his home office in Denver. To the casual observer, they were nothing more than a logistics company working on behalf of their client to store field equipment for the next season.

Hot in Houston (Mat)

My plane touched down at approximately 4:00 on a Wednesday afternoon at IAH, otherwise known as George Bush Intercontinental Airport. Houston is not at its finest in July. My iPhone weather app pegged the temperature at 105 degrees, and the air was so thick it was like breathing through a wet towel. Squeezed up against the Gulf of Mexico, the city is primed for scorching temperatures and stifling humidity. With my body accustomed to Scotland's chill, the heat made it feel like I had run into a brick wall as I stepped out of the departure door and looked for my driver.

I was in a full sweat by the time I hopped in the back of the town car waiting for me. I slid my old, leather computer bag and a medium-sized, waterproof duffle across the seat and stuck out my hand to the driver.

"Jay, long time no see." I had started using Jay's service when I was running Dover Exploration and had to frequent Houston for meetings with my investors. The metropolitan area is home to over six million people, and the majority of them are on the road at 4:00 in the afternoon. Having a driver was the best way to solve that problem.

"Mr. Dover, always a pleasure. Are you headed to your usual?"

"You got it, Jay."

My "usual" was the Post Oak Hotel at Uptown. A comfortable place in the Galleria area immediately off the I-610 West Loop. The location was particularly attractive since it placed me close to Morton's Steakhouse on Westheimer Road and Brenner's Steakhouse on the Bayou. Since I had met Jenara, red meat was a rare treat for me.

She threw herself body and soul into fighting the destruction of the Brazilian rainforest for cattle pastures. I figured the least that I could do was forgo the occasional burger. I guess I'm just weak, though, because I sure wanted an 8 oz filet mignon for dinner this evening. Not having eaten for fourteen hours was also weakening my resolve.

I caught up with Jay on his business and family as we trudged across Houston's rush hour traffic. His oldest son, Stephen, was two years into an undergraduate petroleum engineering degree at the Colorado School of Mines, while his youngest daughter was just starting Middle School in the autumn. I told him to have Stephen contact me when he got closer to job hunting, and I would help him get a foot in the door at some quality companies. Even in a downward trending business cycle, there was a demand for talented young scientists. Starting salaries were still considerably north of a hundred grand per year.

Once I had settled into the Post Oak, I flipped open my laptop and looked at my schedule. I had a meeting set up the following afternoon with John Patchett, a long-time oil business buddy of mine. He was well connected within the oil and gas industry. More importantly, he also had his finger on the pulse of everything ranging from equipment supply chains to specialized personnel recruiting. We were meeting at the West End Public House on Thursday to knock back a few beers while we caught up.

I saw my calendar reminder that Jenara was due back in Portland next Tuesday and fired off an email informing her of my latest change in plans. She had been in Brazil for the past month on both business and pleasure. She had family in Sao Paulo, which was the pleasure side of the trip. After Sao Paulo, she had traveled west to the Peruvian border to continue her research on the indigenous Rohodi tribe. She first connected with the tribe many years ago as part of her doctorate in anthropology, living amongst them for six months. Over the years, she had continued to keep in contact with the tribe, getting a first-hand look at the environmental and human effects of climate change. As a professor in the anthropology department at Portland State, she had no trouble splitting her time between graduate-level teaching and her research.

My travels were catching up with me, so I decided to skip the trip to Morton's Steakhouse and settle for a cobb salad at the hotel. By the time I returned to my room, I had a message from Joseph confirming Susan had departed on time, and the samples were packaged and sent as planned. I pondered the nuances of our particular situation as I lay in bed. Something was amiss, but there were too many missing pieces for me to bring things into focus. It was only after a quick dram of Glen Dronnach I was finally able to drift off into a fitful sleep.

I caught up on some research papers the next day and left for my 4:00 pm meeting. It was a typical Thursday afternoon in Houston, and the first of the after-work crowd gathered around the bar at the West End Public House. The craft beers were flowing, and I ordered a Breakside IPA, bringing a little bit of Oregon to the Houston bar scene. John had procured a table on the far side of the bar, so I sat down and asked about his kids. Other than dealing with the usual teenage mood swings, things seemed to be going well. His wife Nancy was still active in local theater groups, and his dog, Pablo, gave him the least flack of all the family when he worked late.

We were well into our second beer before we got past the small talk and moved on to more pressing issues. John listened while I recounted Bruno's story from Australia and my more recent conversation with Susan. I didn't mention anything about the dense fragments in the rock samples, though. As much as I trusted John, something about those samples nagged at the back of my mind.

John listened through my story without comment. "It's an odd story, Mat, and I don't have any real idea of what is at the bottom of it," he said. "What I can tell you is about six months ago I saw a flurry of recruiting for hard rock geologists. No clue what it was about."

The oil business splits geologists out into soft rock and hard rock players. While the hard rock geologists are looking for just that—rocks—the soft rock geologists are more interested in the absence of rock. If that doesn't make any sense, just think of sandstone. Sure, if you drop it on your foot, it's just as hard as any other rock. Take a look under the microscope, though, and you'll see a labyrinth of sand grains all pressed and packed together to make a single stone, but there are spaces between the grains. It might almost look like a sponge if you didn't know any better.

All of those holes and tunnels winding their way through the rock are known as pores. And, for soft rock scientists, those pores are everything. While most people labor under the misconception that oil resides in underground lakes and rivers, really, it's the pores in the rocks that hold the oil.

Hard rock geologists, on the other hand, couldn't care less about pores. They spend their days with igneous and metamorphic rocks, where porosity is little to none. Gold mines, diamond mines, silver, and copper are all the products of hard rock exploration. No oil there, but still a lot of money to be made. The ancient Archean rocks I was currently interested in fell primarily into the hard rock category. The rocks Susan and Bruno had sampled were low-grade metamorphic shales. Metamorphism is the process of subjecting a rock to enough heat and pressure to alter its characteristics. One of the by-products of the pressure is it collapses the pore spaces. A shale starts as a sedimentary rock, but squeeze it and heat it enough, and you may get a slate.

I needed a bit more information from John. "Did you find out anything else about them, John?" I asked. "What level of experience were they looking for?"

"Deep experience. They were only looking for seasoned professionals. Word has it that the contracts were paying up to $30,000 per month, with a sign-on bonus of $200,000. That's some serious money for most people."

"What else?"

"Well, I didn't think anything of it before, but I've also noticed a lot of orders for cutting edge analytical equipment. Most of it was

22

compact and field-ready, which doubles the asking price. But it must have been a one-time buildup because the hiring and buying activity stopped after about three months. I guess they got what they needed."

"Who is 'they' in this process?" I asked.

"It's hard to say, Mat." John shook his head. "The whole thing was very hush-hush, and I understand that some heavy-duty non-disclosure agreements were required to collect the big bucks. If I had to guess, I would say government or government-sponsored groups. I can tell you there were several groups because the recruiting sucked up multiple people with the same skill sets. Hell, at one point, multiple offers were being made to just a few individuals."

"Anyone I might know?"

He thought for a minute and said, "Duncan Mercer."

I did know Duncan, and I had hired him to consult on several projects where his particular skill sets were of value. Duncan was more of a crystallographer than a geologist, and he had carved out a niche for himself in the area of crystal lattice memory storage. The field is a hot area of research because once data is encoded into the crystal lattice, it is permanent. A billion years from now, the data can be retrieved intact down to the last line of code.

I had what I needed, and we shifted the conversation back to some projects we worked together several years ago. We parted ways after another beer, and I made a mental note to send him a couple of bottles of Pappy Van Winkle Family Reserve 23. I am not much of a bourbon drinker, but I heard John rave about this particular bourbon more than once. One of Jay's drivers got me back to the hotel by six o'clock, so I had time to collected my thoughts.

It was about seven o'clock when I placed a call to Steve Leblanc in Montreal, Canada. Steve was another researcher I worked with regularly. His primary focus was on the Nuvvuagittug Greenstone Belt at the northern end of Quebec, right along the shores of Hudson Bay. These are some of the oldest rocks on the planet, clocking in at 4.28 billion years old. They formed during the Hadean Eon. A time when the earth was newly minted and barely cool enough to hold liquid water. A time before the first specks of life had appeared. If there was anything happening on the ground around Hudson bay, Steve would know.

I missed him on the first call but managed to catch up with him thirty minutes later. Talking with Steve confirmed my suspicions, ancient rocks were currently a hot commodity. He told me several handsomely funded research groups had been on his turf all summer, and he had taken the time to actually talk with two of them. Both seemed to have an international mix of technicians and scientists, he said, though one was backed by Americans and surrounded by what he could only describe as a security detail. Apparently, the lead geologists in both groups quizzed him about the possibility of remnant, metamorphosed deep water shale deposits. Both groups were familiar with the banded iron formations in the area but considered them to be of shallow-water origin.

I drifted off that evening with the scientist in me listing what I did know:

Lots of money was being put into geological expeditions researching some of the oldest rock on earth.

The expeditions were each looking for deepwater shales or their metamorphic equivalents.

Whatever was going on was sensitive enough to have security personnel.

Samples with odd fragments embedded in them were important enough to steal.

Crystalline lattice memory experts were necessary for the job.

Someone knew something very interesting that I was unaware of.

I had booked tickets back to Portland on Saturday morning, leaving Friday free to meet with a firm I employed for personal financial management. A smart group of men and women who got paid well to look out after a portion of my investment portfolio. Two of them, Kristin and Jagat, were dedicated solely to my account. It turned out to be a long day with a lot of discussion on some venture capital opportunities they wanted to pitch to me.

I flew home to Portland Saturday, arriving so early that the sun had barely begun peeking over the horizon. That afternoon I received a call from Joseph. The decoy sample crates he had packaged and sent never made it to their final destination. He could trace the crates to the port of entry in Atlanta, but there the trail went cold. US customs claimed they never received the shipment. The samples were definitely on the flight when it left London but never arrived in Atlanta. You didn't have to have a sensitive nose to smell some bullshit there, because there's no way those samples were hijacked in mid-flight. I quickly added another note to my mental list:

Samples with odd fragments embedded in them were important enough for the US government to steal.

I was still pretty sanguine about the whole affair until Saturday evening, when I received a phone call from Susan's partner, Brad. I was settling back into my condo and checking to see if Jenara was still on schedule when I heard my phone buzzing in the other room.

I didn't know Brad well, but my gut instinct told me that he was a pretty solid, straight-up guy. A good match for Susan. In a rush, he told me that Susan had arrived back home in Eugene on Wednesday evening without an issue. In typical Susan fashion, she headed out to the University the next morning to polish off some work. She had taken off Friday and then returned to the University Saturday morning. When she wasn't home by 3:00, Brad had called her and been sent straight to voicemail. By 5:00, he was worried enough to make the drive down to campus. He spoke with six different students, all of whom had been at the geology lab that day, and none of whom had seen Susan.

As he grew more panicked, he had combed through the parking lot and found her car abandoned there. It was unlocked, and her cell phone was turned off and on the floor. I felt a knot grow in my stomach as I realized that we were all getting in way over our heads. I told Brad I was on it, and for him to file a missing person report. I hung up and quickly punched in the number of a lifelong friend of mine. I had known him since our mothers put us in the playpen together to keep us out of trouble. With everything going on, I wasn't sure who to turn to. But if anyone would be able to help me, it would be Mark.

The Phone Call (Mark)

The sun had melted behind the high hills in the Okanogan-Wenatchee National Forest, just to the east of the Cascades. Total darkness would not fall for another hour. The forests surrounding me were still mostly dead, scorched matchsticks standing a hundred feet high. They were a stark reminder of the wise words from Smokey Bear: Only you can prevent forest fires.

There was a bit of greenery amongst the carnage as mother nature clawed and struggled her way back to the surface, just as she always does. The record-breaking massively-devastating fires in the western United States in 2018 would only be surpassed by, well, every subsequent year. Due to the activities of the industrialized nations over the course of recent history, known as the industrial revolution, things had gotten hotter and dryer for longer periods of time, rendering the forests ripe for incineration.

I had left the State Highway 97a and driven up WA Highway 2 along the Entiat River three days earlier and parked my rig on the edge of a dead-end National Forest dirt track. The spot sat up above and to the west of a closed and empty Spruce Grove Campground. Perfect for my four-by-four Landcruiser.

The truck sat six inches off the ground, gunmetal paint dusty and scratched beyond repair; knobby off-road tires dug down into the dirt. I'd first gotten the truck from a guy named Lefty from outside Ghost Ranch, New Mexico, years ago. It could go for days without stopping, assuming I could too, with buttery-smooth suspension and enough gadgets to keep me amused until the sun burns out.

In the front rested a 2,500-pound winch, mounted there just in case. Sometimes, it seemed that everything in my life was earning the name "just in case."

Earlier that day, I had been fishing for trout using a beat-up old 6'8" bamboo flyrod I had purchased for a song years before at an antique store outside Chase City, Virginia. An older Orvis reel hung from the butt of the rod, with floating double-taper line and a tapered tippet dropping down to two-pound test to complete the rig. The end of the line held a small nymph, submerged and drifting under the fallen logs dangling above the river. The nymph was a reasonable facsimile of the hatch that was evident all around me. The gear had seen better days, but it was still capable of serving its purpose. This was evidenced by the 12" Cutthroat I managed to drag up on the gravel. It went straight into the game pocket on the back of my hardware store fishing vest, stuffed down next to the three other fish already hanging out there.

The stark beauty of the burned forest was not lost on me as I watched the sun continue its descent. I remembered reading about bigfoot, yeti, and other creatures when I was a kid. The thought made me look up, around, and up and around again. I realized I was dead in the middle of Sasquatch country and was, at best, a torn artery too far away from medical attention. What a comforting feeling. I had always felt most at home out in the wilderness.

I am no daredevil. I just don't like people very much. Country to country, around the globe—there's so many different places I've been, and yet, the people are always the same. So I seek out those places where elbow room is plentiful. I had not seen or heard a human in several days, but that was fine with me.

By the way, my name is Mark. I'm 6'3", 200 pounds, physically fit and somewhat mentally fit, with gray hair slipping to my shoulders and a gray beard I sometimes let someone trim. Years ago, I became involved in something folks today call black ops—all civilian work with no backup, making what we did completely deniable by various governmental agencies. These days, I don't look for trouble. Even if

I did, the baddest of the bad usually recognize the steely glint in my eyes. We'll call it mutual respect. I am a guitar pickin' semi-scientist and sometimes ne'er-do-well according to the handful of folks I call friends.

I sat on the gravel along the east side of the river to clean my fish. I was singing softly to myself the old Taj Mahal song "Fishin' Blues." My faded khaki cargo shorts were wet from the wade, as was a faded blue fishing shirt. Old gray Mizuno tennis shoes wrapped around my bare feet. I tugged them off, rinsed out the sand, and laced them on again. I gutted the trout, flicking away the entrails before rinsing the nine-inch blade of a Rapala knife I am quite fond of. I slipped the knife back into its black leather sheath and then tucked it safely away inside my vest. From another pocket, I retrieved a well-worn True 8-ounce stainless steel flask, unscrewed the cap, and had a taste of 16-year old Lagavulin. I massaged my gums a bit and slowly swallowed the Scotch, leaving the taste of smoke lingering in my mouth. Glancing around the nearby, and then scanning further, I said to myself: "It don't get no better than this."

The first taste of Scotch was so good I decided another taste was in order. It was about then that the hackles went up on the back of my neck. Years of wandering the wild had taught me to trust my instincts. Was it a bear, or a mountain lion, or Sasquatch himself that had kicked in my sixth sense? I sat perfectly still and slowly surveyed all three hundred and sixty degrees. The view up the river was obscured by the next bend, perhaps a hundred yards north or so. It was from there I heard the slight splash of hoofs echoing through the trees.

The young elk made it across the river, stopped, and looked over its shoulder. Mama had held back but then started her crossing as well. Mid-way across the 100-foot wide stretch of river, she glanced downstream. I felt the breeze in my face as we stared at each other. The breeze was a good thing because it meant she could not smell me. Sitting perfectly still, including not blinking or picking nymphs out of my eyes, was equally important. Mama did a few slow back and forth glances between me and the little one, snorted, and in three splashy bounds, she was across. They disappeared northward into a slot canyon. Damn. That was a bit close, I said to myself. If I had been a little further upstream, I probably would have been stomped to extinction by mama. So it goes.

It was dark when I stood under the canopy rigged from the rear of my Landcruiser. I pulled a Lagunitas from the built-in cooler, popped the top using the church-key, and pulled my old 12" black cast iron skillet from the built-in storage unit. I fired up the right-hand burner on the Camp Chef Pro standing nearby, placed the skillet on the grill surface, and sipped on my beer. When the skillet heated to sizzling, I threw in diced potatoes and some fresh-chopped onion. By the time they were crisp and browned, I could hear my stomach growling over the crackle and hiss of cooking oil.

As the vegetables cooked, I settled into my old folding camp chair, slowly sipping on my beer. Not a care in the world but right there, right then. As the air began to chill, I fired up my rig's custom heating system, warming the water in the tank nestled in the roof area. As the water warmed, I quickly put together the portable shower arm and head assembly. If I can't have a shower when I come to in the morning and before I crash at the end of the day, I get cranky. I ate an amazing supper, showered, and picked a couple of old tunes sitting naked before the camp stove. By the time the stars came out in full force, I was sleeping like a baby in the back of my rig.

It had been several years since I was last settled down. She decided she wanted to be with a pop/rap music producer. The chance to sit at some Hollywood awards bash, see her man stand up front, winning a gaudy golden trinket—that was just too much for her to resist. So I walked away from a half-million-dollar home and a Beemer. From what I hear, it took less than a month before the guy just laughed and went back to his last wife. Not long after she lost everything, a lucky Powerball ticket saw me rolling in almost 300 million dollars of untouched, untapped cash—more than enough to fund a retirement far, far away from the drama of society. So it goes.

It wasn't long after that I found myself sitting in a bar in Five Points, on the outer edge of midtown Atlanta. I was having drinks with an old friend and entrepreneur named Jessica, both of us sipping on something cold and local, shooting the shit just like old times. She introduced me to a young man named John. She used words like brilliant, visionary, vastly talented. She was not describing me. John seemed a bit on the blue side. Jessica coaxed him into talking. It seems he and his wife, also a guy named John, had spent a lot of time and the last of their resources putting together a business plan. They found an investor and were set to close the deal the next day. When the investor discovered John was gay, he pulled the rug out from under the deal. Five million dollars slipped through their hands. That had been three hours before. They would lose everything by noon the next day.

"Why don't you tell me about your plan?" I asked, and for the first time, I saw his face light up.

"Well, Mark, John and I are procurers. We planned to build a travel service for the elite. You know, booking hotels, chartering flights and yachts, reserving the best restaurants. We even have a lease on some warehouse space near Grant Park along with a pool of extremely talented youngsters ready to go. Enough resources to move anything, anytime, anywhere. Now it seems we're back at square one."

I sat back and pondered a bit in the awkward silence that surrounded us, sipped on my IPA, and came up with a plan. With John's investor out of the way, I was sure that the two of us could help each other out.

"On how short of notice can you get things done?" I asked him, and he pursed his lips.

"Hours," he said, taking a slow sip of beer. "Maybe minutes, for the right client."

I could barely believe my luck. "John, late tomorrow afternoon, I want to find myself on a guide-owned Contender fishing offshore for dolphin based out of an oceanfront rental home on Key Colony Beach in the Florida Keys and fully stocked for two people, with at least a week's rations. I'll need a skinny water boat available as well. I want the home and the boats available for one week, and I have a friend named Sirocco. She lives in Dallas. She probably will join me. Here is her information, and here is my black card. Show me your stuff."

"Is money an issue?" asked John.

"Not on this one," I told him.

John took my card and excused himself, heading outside with his cellphone in hand. Jessica and I took the opportunity to talk about her business. Growth had been exponential in the last two years. It seemed her biggest headache was sorting through endless resumes from the brightest minds out there, even though she barely saw any turnover. Jessica hired the best, paid the best, and ran a top-notch company. Afterward, I told her about one of my latest escapades in Panama. When I got to the part where I came within about three seconds of dying, she threw back her head and laughed. I shouldn't have expected any less. Jessica and I were still chuckling when John finally slid back into his seat.

"OK," said John as he glanced at his phone. "I have a driver picking you up in ten minutes, and taking you to the ATL Hilton—the President's Suite, fully stocked. Let me have your car keys. I have another driver taking your car to secure parking or wherever you want it delivered. Suitable clothes and other items are on the way to the President's Suite. You'll be picked up at 6:00 am and dropped at the stairs for your Delta 7:15 am flight to MIA. A car will take you from the base of the stairs to a twin-engine Cessna. The flight to Marathon will take about an hour, more if you want to sightsee. A droptop Mustang will be there for you the entire week. A 37-foot Contender with triple Yamaha four-stroke 300s will be at the dock of your 4/3 ocean view home with a gorgeous infinity pool looking out at the sandbar. The owner is one of the best guides in the Keys. He lives five minutes away and is available on demand.

He will also park his 17'9" East Cape EVO flats boat at the dock. Both boats are fully stocked for fishing, snorkeling, and diving. I took the liberty of having Porky's stock your home with enough food for the first day, with a few IPA's, wine, and Scotch on the way. There should also be bathing suits, fishing clothes, and toiletries for you and Sirocco. Whenever you're ready, I'll schedule the return trip later in the week based on what you want to do. Sirocco sends her regards and is looking forward to, according to her, kicking your ass in fishing again."

I'm not much on taking time to ponder my way through things like a true scientist. Thinking simplistically, a true scientist creates a hypothesis and then systematically goes through things step by step, from one to ten. When said scientist reaches ten, then an outcome has, or has not, been determined. Being a semi-scientist is so much easier. I typically go one, two, ten. So it was with John. Looking back, it was one of the smartest decisions I ever made.

"John, get me your bank routing information," I told him as we wrapped up. "You'll have the $5,000,000 in your account well before noon tomorrow. I'm looking forward to working with you. I am certain the success of John and John will be spectacular."

"I don't know what to say except thanks, and we will not disappoint you." John gave my hand a firm shake. "Here is a dedicated number to reach us anytime. One of us will answer and take care of anything you need. We're a one-stop-shop!" I pecked Jessica on the cheek, shook John's hand again, and went off with the driver.

Sirocco and I had an excellent week fishing, swimming, snorkeling, and just generally being useless. In addition to Porky's, we had the platter and a Reuben at The Keys Fisheries, breakfast at Stout's, shrimp at Castaway, and some other excellent bits and bites along the way. Sirocco claimed she out-fished me, but to this day, I call bullshit on that.

Coming back to the present, I left the Entiat River the next morning, headed west from Wenatchee, drove south on SR 97, took SR 821 from Holmes to Selah. That stretch of crooked road is one of the better crooked roads around. From there, I took SR 12 on over toward Portland. I rode in the shadow of Mt. Rainier on the crooked roads for several hours. Amazing ride beside the enormity of a 14,411-foot volcano. The pent-up energy in such an edifice would require a true scientist to calculate. It just so happened I was headed to see such a person if he happened to be home or even on the continent.

I should talk a bit about my Landcruiser because it is the coolest thing I own. OK, I own practically nothing. Anyway, I lost my mechanical aspirations when I was a kid. Every time I opened the hood of a car, I ended up with grease in a new open wound. I swore if I could ever afford to have other folks deal with my vehicles, I would do so. So several years ago I called John and told him what I wanted. Fifteen minutes later, a guy named Lefty from outside Ghost Ranch, New Mexico, called me. We talked a bit, and four weeks later, John called and asked where to deliver it. I can fill it up with fuel and drive across the country without stopping if nature doesn't call. The hybrid fuel/electric engine combo is amazing, the ride is exceptionally smooth for an off-road vehicle, and there are enough gadgets to keep me amused, as stated earlier, until the sun burns out.

John had shipped the Landcruiser back from Panama to Denver three weeks ago. I flew in, picked it up, took in the northern Colorado Rockies via SR 14 to SR 40, and hung out for a bit at Dinosaur National Monument. I took SR 191 north and cut west on SR 44 to see Flaming Gorge then slipped up SR 530 into Green River. Old friends of mine killed something, cooked it on the grill and we ate it. I supplied refreshments, and we picked and sang old country songs until dawn. A good time was had by all.

I proceeded to fish my way up the Green River. The high desert plains broken by mesas at 7,000' or so above sea level are amazingly stark and beautiful. Much different from the Colorado Rockies, where every turn snags your attention with something new and exciting, the mesas have more of an elegant, timeless beauty.

I cut up through Jackson and Yellowstone, spending a few days simply taking in the world with awe. Whereas Rainier is a big fucking hill, Yellowstone is a big-ass, seventy-mile wide hole where Rainier's big brother lived until it lost its cool. It last blew about 640,000 years ago, sending ash more than a thousand miles east, and scientists say it's overdue for another episode. For context, it may be interesting to consider a somewhat overdue woman.

Eventually, I wandered west to the Okanogan-Wenatchee National Forest where I spent a few days before heading to Portland. Once I got closer to Portland, I pulled off of I-205 onto I-84 west and followed it across the Willamette River, heading downtown to the Pearl District. Well-heeled high-rise condos mixed with glitzy shops, juxtaposed by the scattered, shabby tarp encampments of the homeless. I drove through the neighborhood until I found the right building and punched a code into the subterranean parking area. The gates crawled open for me, and I parked my car in bay four.

I had not talked to Mat in three or four months, maybe more. When I pulled in, I had no idea if he was home or not. I've known Mat since I was born. We have had an adventure or two over the years. If Mat said we were going to die today, I would ask him where. Hell, I put more faith in him than I would my own flesh-and-blood brothers.

If he was home cool, if not, John could get me through the gate and home security codes in about three seconds. Mat has an amazing collection of Scotch, and my intention was to relieve him of a multitude of drams. I tried the private elevator code from a year ago to no avail. I was honestly pondering the notion of using the brush guard to pop open the half-million-dollar control panel when my Iridium Extreme 9575 sat phone broke my reverie. The phone had just shown up one day. John liked to stay ahead of things.

"Hey, good buddy!" Mat's voice rang out from the speaker when I picked up. "What's up? Where are you at these days?"

"In your garage. You changed the code. Three, two, one," I said. Mat swore though I could hear him snickering from the other end of the line.

"Shit! Code is 6969#, and don't forget the pound," he told me. "Do not ruin my lift again, you asshole!"

"Still have a sense of humor. My favorite number. See you in one minute."

Problems (Mat)

I pushed a button in the foyer, released the private elevator door in the parking garage, and flipped on the speaker.

"Come on up, old friend, and try not to break anything," I said with a grin. Before Mark could make his way up, I hurried back to the kitchen to pop open two pFriem IPAs. Good beers brewed in the great town of Bend, Oregon.

My condo is the top floor of a twenty-one story high-rise in the Pearl District of Portland. I was one of the investors in this building, so I staked out the penthouse level for my personal use. I never grow tired of the view. From the balcony, a ribbon of water called the Willamette River cuts through the city's heart in a shimmering strip. At night the city lights are magnificent, all high rises and threads of headlights cutting across the river on Portland's prized bridges. On the south side of my condo, the Portland Hills form a steep fault-scarp along the city's edge. A reminder of Portland's tectonic origins.

Portland occupies part of an area aptly named the Portland Basin. Each year it sinks further and further into the earth, collecting dirt, sand, and sediment as the Columbia River passes through. Over time this all packs down into new layers of clay and gravel, warping the land around it into what geologists call a "Basin.".

The Portland Basin started forming about twenty million years ago, give or take. Large-scale tectonics forced the earth on the southwest side of the basin upwards, eventually leaving the basin as a low-lying depression. The entire Oregon Coastal Range is still grinding its way northward relative to the rest of the North American Plate, creating some crumpled landscapes as the two landmasses push against each other. The sheer force of it pushed one land-segment over another, creating the wall of stone known as the Portland Hills.

It's this wall that diverts the flow of the Columbia River. The river flows east to west across Oregon, straight from Umatilla until it hits Portland. When the river meets the western edge of the Portland Basin, the surrounding hills force the river to make a sharp right. It flows past the city and then northward in search of an outlet to the ocean.

However, before finding its way to the Portland Basin, the Columbia River cuts across the entire width of the Cascade Range. Jutting up as high as eleven thousand feet in the air, these mountains give way to a deep gorge that pinches down the river. As soon as the gorge widens out into the Portland basin, the water slows, dropping dirt and sediment collected along its journey.

Grain by grain, the Columbia River has filled the basin over the millennia. The river-fill is at its thickest near Vancouver, where nearly two thousand feet of sediment lies packed beneath the surface. This river fill isn't just any regular dirt, though. The rocks and sediments in the Portland Basin offer a remarkable look into the geologic history of Oregon and Washington.

Towards the bottom, you'll find a sixteen million-year-old layer of basalts from back when lava flowed like water out of large fissures cracked deep down into the landscape of Eastern Oregon. These fissures could reach up to seventeen kilometers long, puncturing straight down to hell and belching out smoke and liquid magma.

Instead of piling up to form volcanoes, lava flowed from these fissures as massive sheets of liquid rock. At that point, the entire landscape of Oregon was shaped by volcanic activity, but ask any geologist worth his salt, and he'll tell you the Grande Ronde Basalts played the most important role in creating the modern-day Pacific Northwest. Around 120 separate lava flows all caked together, stacked one on top of the other like sheets of paper. The Grande Ronde basalt flows stretch from Idaho to the Pacific coast.

The basalt flows were then buried by layer upon layer of sand, gravel, silt, and volcanic debris carried into the basin by the Columbia River. Now, these layers serve as a record of the past that geologists can read.

The sediments lining the bottom of the Portland Basin are the foundation upon which much of the Portland-Vancouver metropolitan infrastructure now rests. In the likely event of a massive earthquake, those soft sediments will liquify into mud and quicksand. Liquefaction and surface wave amplification from the tremors will cause the floor of the basin to crumble and warp, swallowing up homes and businesses.

My building sits in one of the more precarious areas of the Portland Metroplex. If the building was simply built on the existing surface sediments, a large earthquake would rip it apart in seconds. That's why the entire structure is reinforced with steel and concrete pylons driven deep into the earth. When the engineers told me how deep we needed to sink the pylons, I told them to add another 20%. Twenty-one stories is a long way to fall. Deep structural support and cutting-edge shock absorption technology lets me rest easy at night.

I didn't mention any of this to Mark as he stepped out of the elevator and into the foyer. He had already heard the story several times.

"Good to see you, buddy," I said with a smile.

"Likewise, my friend," he replied.

I nodded my head towards the front balcony, and we each grabbed a pFriem on the way out. The evening air was fresh, and the city lights stretched out in front of us. To the east, the moon hung low in the sky, and the silhouette of Mt. Hood rose from the horizon. We did a little catch-up over the beers, but I was anxious to get to the core of my concerns. However, even though my home is my haven, I couldn't say how secure the balcony was.

"I want you to listen to something for me," I said, fishing my phone out of the front pocket of my jeans. "I want to hear what you think about it when we get inside."

I pressed a few buttons to get a recent message and handed him the phone. Mark listened and then handed the phone back with a pensive expression on his face. He said nothing, but instead, paced the length of the balcony as he stared out across the other high rises in my neck of the Pearl. He pulled his phone from a side pocket and slipped through the balcony door without a word, not bothering to check and see if I was following.

The kitchen area was to his left, where a large black granite-topped island sat. A stainless steel cooking hood dropped from the ceiling and hung over a 48-inch Miele gas stove built into the stonework. Behind and to the right of the stove, just visible through the gap between the hood and the countertop, sat a Sub-Zero refrigerator recessed into the cherry wood cabinetry lining the back wall. It was well stocked with food and drink. A variety of hearty IPAs occupied the right half of the bottom shelf, and a tray with several thick cuts of fresh, sashimi-grade Ahi tuna rested on the middle shelf. I had ordered the tuna steaks earlier that afternoon to fix for Jenara when she arrived home.

The kitchen opened onto a large living area with a fireplace on the back wall. Leather couches and chairs were arranged around the fireplace, with a four-person walnut dining table located immediately to the right of the balcony door. Mark passed through the room, turning up the volume on the music as he passed by the wall controls, before disappearing into one of the interior rooms.

I sipped my pFriem and let my mind wander back to Susan. She could take care of herself, and I knew that; I had seen her take down more than one person in the kickboxing ring. But she was in over her head now, just as I was, and I couldn't help but worry.

When Mark returned, he plopped down next to me, leaning back in his chair with a grin. "I just set up reservations for dinner tonight," he said. "Finish that beer, grab a jacket, and let's roll."

We dumped our bottles in the recycling and headed to the elevator. The building was constructed, at my insistence, with a dedicated lift for the penthouse suite. Brass rimmed panels inlaid with dark, polished walnut burl decorated the inside of the lift, and the control panel showed only three buttons labeled: Home, Ground, and Parking. Mark pushed the Ground Floor button.

We exited into the building's main foyer, stepping out onto a floor inlaid with a maroon and light gray granite mosaic. A security desk sat near the front entrance. I waved to Mike, the evening patrol, as we exited the elevator and paused at his desk to ask if there had been any recent additions to the security staff since I had been gone. At Mark's direction, I had switched the elevator to double source security mode so handprint verification was required along with the access code to use the lift. We didn't have much of a need for staffed security on hand, and, as far as I knew, we hadn't recently posted an ad for hiring. That's why I was somewhat surprised when Mike told me there had been an inquiry about openings the day before. Still, it wasn't that unusual to get the occasional resume slipped under the door. We paid our security guards well.

Mark and I exited the building just as a medium-sized limo pulled up. "This is our ride, buddy!" Mark grinned, clapping me on the back. We both slid into the back, and I settled into the leather seat as Mark checked out the rear control panel. He fiddled with the dials, changing a few settings until a pleasant breeze was blasting through the cab.

"Alright, we have shielded communications now," Mark said, turning towards me. I hadn't even realized that was what he was doing with the controls. "So, what kind of shit have you gotten yourself into this time, my friend?"

"I'm not sure," I told him, sighing. "The bad kind. And it's not just me. Susan is wrapped up in it, too." I went on to unload the whole story on him, including the information about the odd fragments found in rocks from both Australia and Greenland. I could see his eyes sparkle as he pondered that bit of mystery.

The limo pulled up to the curb along a block full of shops and restaurants. I visited one of the more touristy places with Jenara about a year ago for what had been a decidedly mediocre meal. "You mean we're really going to eat here?" I asked, dubious. Mark gave me an enthusiastic nod.

"Of course! It's no use plotting on an empty stomach."

We exited onto the sidewalk and strolled northward along the street. About halfway down the block, Mark took a hard left into an unobtrusive door nestled between a restaurant and a woman's shoe shop. You wouldn't even notice it if you weren't looking for it. We went up a flight of stairs to a landing, where a brusque security guard stopped us. Mark placed his right hand on a scanner, and a green light flashed above the door to the left of the guard.

We entered into a medium-sized room with a table containing a large tray of sushi, several pitchers of ice-cold water, and a bottle of 18-year GlenDronach. Behind the table was an array of computing and telecom equipment neatly filed away on wooden shelves built into the walls. Two chairs sat at the table, with several others lined up against the room's outer edge. What looked like windows lined the wall, but on closer inspection, I saw that they were actually video monitors with live camera feeds of the street outside. At the back of the room, there was another closed door with a palm reader pad beside it.

I commented to Mark that John was excellent at his job, and to send my regards. Mark had connected me with John about a year ago when I was trying to arrange a surprise for Jenara.

Mark just nodded and said, "Yup." He poured us each a dram of scotch, and we sipped in silence. I was getting antsy, though. Every second we wasted was another second that Susan was trapped.

"So buddy, what are we going to do here?" I asked, and Mark gave me a thoughtful hum.

"Have a sip of that GlenDronach, and I'll lay it out for you."

John knew from working with me that the 18-year-old GlenDronach Allardice was my favorite. Distilled just northeast of Huntley, between Aberdeen on the east coast of Scotland and Elgin on the Moray Firth.

It's a part of the Speyside whiskey region of Scotland, though I'd consider GlenDronach to be more Highland than Speyside in character. The scotch gets its smoky taste from spending some quality time in Oloroso sherry casks imported from Andalucía Spain. I was sure John was responsible for it being here tonight. I made a mental note to give him a call and extend my thanks. I plucked a piece of spicy sushi off my plate with some chopsticks and chased it down with a sip of GlenDronach.

Mark explained that when he had initially heard the message, he had run a quick background check on the number I was supposed to call, and it was a phone number that technically didn't exist. He figured that this, along with the message itself, pointed towards government interference. We decided to return the call, but he wanted to pass the signal through some of the equipment on the wall to see if we could gain any more insight. He asked me to play the massage again, so I put it on speaker.

"Mr. Dover. We believe that you are in possession of some rock samples that are of great interest to us. I apologize for the inconvenience, but we must insist that you deliver them to us. When we are finished with them, they will be returned to you for your research, though we may have to retain some material for our records. We have detained your colleague, Ms. Calder, to ensure your cooperation. Rest assured that she is being treated well. You can contact law enforcement if you want, but it will only complicate the process. Please contact us at 997-200-3777."

"Polite but firm, calm, collected, and non-threatening," said Mark. "But more importantly, digitally modulated to erase any possible traces of origin. I can only think this contact is government-backed, and everything you have told me so far also points in that direction. I don't think Susan is in any immediate danger, but she sure as hell isn't happy, wherever she is."

"What do you suggest?" I asked.

"Well, first of all, do you really want to give them those samples?"

"Yes," I said. "This is none of Susan's doing, and her safety is the first priority. Hell, she doesn't even know that I had Joseph switch the samples."

"Here's what I suggest," said Mark. "First, let's arrange an exchange in a public area, somewhere with plenty of people around, exposed enough for me to set up some surveillance equipment. Secondly, let's not bring the samples here. We'll direct our new friends to send people to Goose Bay before the meeting, and then tell them where to find the boxes during the exchange. That'll give you a chance to have a quick meal with their contact to try and extract some hints about what they are doing. My gut tells me they will honor the deal, but Susan needs to be in sight during the exchange, in sight, but not at your table. Do you think she can keep it together for that?"

"Worst that can happen is she'll beat the living crap out of her minder, but beyond that, I'm sure she'll play along," I replied with a smirk.

"So, where should we play ball?" Mark asked, and I thought for a moment.

"Timberline Lodge," I said. "It checks all the boxes. Public, lots of people, and you are above the treeline, so it's plenty exposed. Summer crowds will give you a chance to get close on the inside too."

He thought for a moment. "OK, we're on."

The call was short and to the point. I told them I would call on the day with the exact meeting location, and that Susan needed to be in sight at all times.

Timberline Lodge is a jewel of depression-era construction located on the slopes of Mount Hood. From the observation porch, you can also see Mount Jefferson and the Three Sisters rising in the distance. They are all part of the Cascade Volcanic Chain, extending from the tip of California northward into British Columbia. The mountains average 5,000 feet in elevation, and hidden among them are around eighteen live volcanoes. Some, like Mount St. Helens, are still blowing their tops to this day. Mount Hood is just as restless, with small eruptions noted by early settlers as recently as the mid-1800s.

Timberline Lodge was built on the south slope of the mountain between 1936 and 1938 by the Works Progress Administration, and it was dedicated on September 28, 1937, by President Franklin D. Roosevelt himself. The building sits on a foundation of pyroclastic-flows and lahar deposits laid by eruptions over the past few millennia. Its interior still retains the original craftsmanship, with a central six-fireplace hexagonal chimney that is 14 feet wide and stretches almost a hundred feet high. Fireplaces on the ground floor and first-floor feed this monster to create a network of alcoves where a person can relax on cold winter days.

The third floor of the lodge is occupied by the Ram's Head Bar. The serving area surrounds a central atrium where the chimney passes to the ceiling, and the open space gives reasonable visibility from one side of the room to the other. Normally the policy is first come first serve, but I called in a favor and arranged for two tables on opposite sides of the atrium to be reserved for 12:30 pm sharp.

Mark and I traveled in separate vehicles the next morning. He took his customized Toyota, while I rode in the limo that John had arranged for us the evening before. It was a typical summer day in Portland—80 degrees, low humidity, and clear blue skies.

Mount Hood was visible at multiple points on the hour-or-so-long drive to the east. The peak was still dusted in snow, with some small clouds occasionally swirling around the summit. Mt. Hood is tall enough to create its own microclimate, forcing warm air upwards and condensing it into clouds that hover over the mountaintop.

The temperature had cooled a bit by the time I reached the lodge. I saw no sign of Mark, but then, I didn't expect to. The lodge is a hotspot on the tourist circuit, and the crowds were already out in full force by the time I walked up the front stairs. I arrived at the Ram's Head fifteen minutes early, carrying a small blue duffle bag. I handed the manager my card when I arrived, and he asked which of the two tables I wanted. I chose the east side of the room and placed the bag to my right, so it was nestled between my chair legs and the atrium railing. This positioning left me facing west, towards the stairs leading up to the bar.

At 12:30 pm sharp, I saw Susan come up the stairs flanked by three guys in open-collar white shirts and blazers. One of them split off towards me, while a manager led the other two off at the mention of my name. The guy who sat down across from me was in his mid-thirties and clean-shaven with a bit of a military demeanor about him. He seemed relaxed but didn't waste any time before he asked about the samples. I handed him a piece of paper with the location and lock code of the storage unit, and he called it into a nameless person on the other end of the line.

Two bowls of lamb stew with bread showed up as he stashed the phone away.

"I took the liberty of ordering some food," I said. "Eat it or don't, it doesn't matter to me. I figured Susan would be hungry, and I know I sure as hell am."

He glanced over at the other table and saw the waiter unloading several bowls of soup. He looked at me again, then picked up a spoon and took a taste.

"Not half bad," he said.

I kept on talking as we ate. "I take it you're more interested in the inclusions than the rocks themselves?."

He didn't pause as he slurped up another spoonful of soup. "Not sure what you're talking about. Even if I did know, I wouldn't say."

I let the conversation lay for a few minutes, sipping on my soup before I started in again. "I've always taken a real interest in complex crystal lattice development within these Archean rocks that you are currently removing from my storage facility."

He paused mid-scoop and put his spoon down. "Mr. Dover, I like you," he said, tense despite his genial tone. "You're a smart guy, and you're easy to deal with. So, I'm going to give you some valuable advice. The people I work for are thoughtful and constrained in their actions. But, there are other players in this game that do not have the same level of constraint. If I were you, I'd stick to the geology and leave the sleuthing out of it. For your sake. For her sake."

He nodded towards Susan and went back to eating his soup, but he didn't get far before his phone buzzed. He listened, nodding his head a few times before slipping the phone back in his pocket. "I think we're finished here, Mr. Dover. Just one more question before I go. Do we have all the samples?"

I nodded. "Everything Susan delivered for shipment and everything we swapped for beach rock is in your possession. You may want to send the field equipment back to us when you are finished," I replied.

"It was good doing business with you, Mr. Dover." He completely passed over the lab equipment comment, instead reaching across the table to grasp my hand. "Please stay seated for five minutes, if you would. We have asked Ms. Calder to do the same. After five minutes the two of you can go home, relax, continue your research. You can forget this lunch ever happened."

The three men stood and marched out together, leaving Susan and me alone. We both stayed seated for the requisite five minutes. As soon as the time was up, I paid the bill for both tables, grabbed my duffle, and motioned Susan to the stairs. As we approached the stairs, I handed her the bag.

"There's a complete change of clothes in there," I told her. "Hiking pants, shirt, underwear, shoes, and socks, the works. Change into them and put everything you're wearing back in the bag. We can talk once we're both in the car."

We walked down to the women's restroom on the ground floor, and I waited outside while Susan changed. She returned and handed me the bag, and we exited the building. Crossing the parking lot, we could make out the snow-capped peak of Mount Jefferson in the distance as we crossed over to our limo. The driver stepped out and ran a scanning device around Susan, then swooped it around me also. After he had finished with me, he motioned us into the car. He then opened the duffle and swooped over all the clothes. I could see the red light flashing. Susan sighed when he ended up tossing the entire duffle bag into the nearest trash bin.

"Don't fret; I'll pick up the tab for a new wardrobe," I assured her.

The driver returned and started the car. Once the green "Secure Comms" light illuminated in the passenger cab, I relaxed and asked Susan if she was okay.

"Confused, but okay," she said, finally allowing herself to relax in her seat. But a second later she turned on me, irritation flashing across her face. "You wanna tell me what the fuck this was all about?"

"I will, I promise," I replied. "But before I fill you in, I need you to tell me what happened on your end."

Before she could start speaking, though, the limo phone interrupted her with a shrill ring. I picked it up to hear Mark's voice barking out from the other end. "Everybody happy on your end, buddy?" he asked, and though he couldn't see me, I nodded without thinking.

"Yeah, we're all good," I responded. "The driver has secured the comms system, so we're free to talk."

"I wouldn't be calling if he hadn't," Mark said. "Listen, while I was enjoying the show today, I spotted an old acquaintance of mine at the bar. He's a freelancer, and we worked a gig together several years ago. I think he might be able to help us, so I'm going to track him down. So long as he doesn't shoot me at first sight, he'll probably be willing to talk to me. I might be gone for a day or two, but I'll be back crashing on your couch before you know it."

"The room's ready, and there is a bottle of Lagavulin waiting for you in the bar," I told him. "But what do you think your partner can tell you that we don't already know?"

"Well, what are you looking to find out?"

"I'd like to know what the hell these people are doing, for one. But, short of that, a rundown on the equipment they're stocking in their labs would be good; makes, manufacturers, that sort of thing.

I'm particularly interested in any equipment they might be using for crystal structure analysis."

"So I heard during lunch," he said. I chuckled, wondering when and where he had planted the wire. There was no way he could have heard anything from where he was standing. I glanced over to see Susan watching me, impatient, and knew I had to wrap things up.

"I'll see you in a few days then, and we can rock and roll with this mystery."

I hung up, giving Susan a sheepish glance. "Sorry. Please, continue."

Though she still seemed a bit irritated, she obliged. "Saturday morning, when I got to the school parking lot," she said, "I was kidnapped. Right there, in broad daylight. Four guys in a van pulled up between my car and the Geology building, and I...I think I broke one's nose before they got me in the van. They took my phone, turned it off, and threw it back into my car before we drove off."

"My god." I rubbed my temple, silently fuming. "They didn't hurt you, did they?"

"No, they were all pleasant enough to me after that, even the guy with the broken nose. It was clear that I was going with them whether I wanted to or not, though. They assured me several times I was in no danger, and the whole thing would be cleared up in a day or two. After that, it was just endless questions about the Greenland rock samples."

From what I had learned, I wasn't surprised. I was just glad that they hadn't tried to beat any information out of her. "So, where did they take you?" I pressed, trying to figure out more about this group. How they worked, where they operated. "Did you see anything there that stood out?"

"I'm not sure where they ended up taking me," Susan said, "but it seemed like a five-star hotel from the food and all. Plenty comfortable, I just couldn't leave my room. Not really much else to tell between then and the trip to the lodge today. What happened to you? No offense, but you've looked better."

I recounted everything that Mark and I had discovered since her disappearance, apologizing more than once for the mess. I didn't, however, mention my thoughts on what was at the core of the issue. The less she was involved in this, the better.

It wasn't until we got to the base of the mountain, passing west on SR-26 through Zig-Zag that Susan casually muttered, more to herself than to me: "Thank goodness I kept the most interesting sample."

I nearly choked on the sip of water I had just taken. I hadn't been expecting her to drop a bombshell of that magnitude on me. "Tell me more, Susan. How many people know about this?"

"Right now, only you and me," she replied.

It turns out that she had taken the most interesting sample from her collection and carried it back to Eugene in her backpack for safekeeping. That backpack was now sitting on some storage shelves in the back of the graduate offices.

She described the sample as a chunk of black, mildly metamorphosed, siliciclastic rock about six inches long, five inches wide, and four to five inches deep. In the middle, the rock smoothed into a feature she could only describe as the top of a ball, same color as the rest of the rock but smooth. She estimated the ball part of the rock was about three inches in diameter. The odd part of the rock sample was its weight, ten kilograms.

No matter how many times I did the math in my head, it never seemed to add up quite right. Susan told me the sample weighed around ten kilograms, but considering the density of quartz, it should have weighed half of that. The only way it could possibly be that heavy would be if the sphere had a density of over 20 g/cc.

"Susan, what's the density of U238?" I asked.

"I have already done the math," she replied, shaking her head. "Whatever's in that sample, it's not natural. No element I've ever seen, at least."

I thought about it for a moment. "If it's not natural, then it must be manufactured," I muttered.

We both sat in silence for a good minute or two until Susan finally brought up the elephant in the room. The true heart of the issue, which both of us were too overwhelmed to want to bring up.

"The rocks this sample came from are close to 4 billion years old, Mat."

I rested my head back and shut my eyes to concentrate. It was all too much, and on too little sleep. By the time we had reached Sandy on SR26, though, I had managed to come up with a pitifully rough plan. As soon as Susan started to drift off, I placed my first call to Joseph. I asked him to go to Eugene to collect Brad and the backpack with the sample, then bring both to my condo."

My second call was to Brad. I told him that I had Susan and that she was safely asleep in the seat next to me. When I asked him if he was free to come up to Portland and see us, he was more than willing. I was sure that he wanted to see for himself that Susan was alive and in one piece. "A colleague of mine named Joseph will pick you up at your house," I told him. "He'll identify himself by giving you Susan's birthday and your mother's maiden name. Oh, and Susan needs you to grab her backpack from the graduate offices on your way out. It should be on the shelves in the rear of the offices. We will see you later this afternoon."

With Brad confirmed to arrive later that afternoon, I placed my third call to a woman called Marcelle Fabre, head of the firm that provides security for me. Normally, I go to Marcelle for routine things like home security systems or hardening my cybersecurity. She's also helped me out with occasional bodyguard services, and her firm got involved in some delicate business with Mark and me several years ago.

"Marcelle, Mat Dover here. I hope you've been well," I said. "I have some pressing security issues that have just come up, and I was hoping you would be able to accommodate me."

"I'll see what I can do," she replied, and I could hear the sound of furious typing coming from her end. "What are you looking for today, Mr. Dover?"

"I need to have my residence swept for any bugs this afternoon, as soon as possible. Then, I need to secure the area with a comms shield and encrypted communications." I paused, knowing that Marcelle wasn't going to like the next bit. "I'll also have my friend Mark working with me for the foreseeable future. If he requests assistance, please just put it on my tab."

Sure enough, she sighed. The last time she worked with him at my request, her company got hit with a litany of legal complaints. Even though I had paid the bills in full, she still wasn't happy about the incident. She muttered something indistinct about loose-cannon freelancers, but gave me a weak, "I'll try," before hanging up.

I took a deep breath, trying to rub away the migraine I felt creeping into my skull. According to my watch, Jenara was due to land at PDX in about an hour. I still had one more phone call to make before then. I rang Kristin at DoubleSource Investments in Houston, asking her and Jagat to research companies focused on developing crystal lattice memory systems. I didn't tell them why, and they didn't ask any questions before hanging up.

It had been a long day, and it wasn't over. I needed some rest, so I shut my eyes, drifting off for a blissful, dreamless sleep as we made our way back to the Pearl.

Jenara

Jenara pushed the button embedded in an off-white plastic armrest, cushioned with plush, dark blue padding. The bottom of the seat slid forward, the seatback reclined, and a footrest sprung upward from below the seat to support her legs. She rested her head and closed her eyes. Traveling on commercial airlines generated an unbelievably large carbon footprint, but even though she hated flying, it wasn't as if she could take a sailboat everywhere. Instead, she tried to put as much activity as possible into each trip to be more efficient. Mat convinced her that since she was already flying, she might as well go first class, and he had even offered to pick up the tab. The trip was taking her from Sao Paulo, Brazil, to Atlanta and then on to Portland—a full twenty-two hours in the air. Personal torture served no purpose, according to him, and so she might as well enjoy herself on the trip. Still, she hated the idea of the environmental damage to which she was contributing.

Mat had become an essential part of her life several years ago, and he meant many things to her. But now, after being away from Portland for six weeks, she could only think of him as her lover. Between her work and some family issues requiring her attention, she was exhausted and just wanted to be home again in his arms.

The line between work and family always seemed to blur on her trips to Brazil. Her most recent visit with her adopted Rohodi family had been stressful. She remembered the start of this multi-year saga, a saga that became a signature piece of anthropological work for her. She was in her second year of graduate school when one of her professors suggested she do fieldwork with the Rohodi tribe as part of her doctorate dissertation. The original plan was just three months of living with the tribe, which, due to numerous initial setbacks, she believed might be closer to three days. However, an odd turn of events extended her stay twice as long, and she ended up living with the tribe for a full six months.

The Rohodi live in the far western portion of Brazil, near its border with Eastern Peru. Jenara had flown into Cruzeiro do Sul, located just southwest from where the Juruá River crosses from the State of Amazonas into the State of Acre. She hooked up there with a guide her professor once used during a previous trip to the area.

From Cruzeiro do Sul, she took a small bush plane to a makeshift runway located on the eastern edge of the Parque Estadual Serra da Contamana. The airfield was carved into the heart of the jungle, but it was still miles away from the Rohodi homeland.

The tribe lived along the Brazil side of the park, with their village located along the eastern edge of an anticlinal arch. There, small hills plunged into the Amazon basin's wet wilderness. Cretaceous rocks were exposed at the ground surface, gradually dipping down and disappearing beneath the younger soils of the Amazon basin. Erosion of the terrain carved the area into a broad expanse of mountains and hills lifting up from the surrounding land. It was there, where the flat, flood-prone expanse of the Amazon Basin gave way to the rising uplands, the Rohodi people lived. Reaching the village was a journey that could only be made on foot.

When Jenara and her guide arrived at the village, they were met with open hostility. Jenara never did get all the details about what had happened, but she knew it involved a young man of the tribe and an altercation with some sort of resource expedition crew. The only thing she knew was when she arrived; she was not welcome. She didn't know the tribal language at the time, but she could understand the angry voices and the defensive posturing of the tribal elders well enough. The only word that she recognized was spoken in her native tongue, Portuguese— heavily accented but otherwise unmistakable: "forbidden."

Her guide argued well into the evening, and finally, the tribe grudgingly let them pitch tents on the outskirts of the village. As she understood the situation, they were to be gone the next morning at sunrise. She awoke the next day with early morning sunlight filtering through the jungle canopy and a good deal of commotion. A woman was standing with the village elders, all of them keeping their distance from her as if a small force field surrounded her. Voices were raised, but again, Jenara couldn't follow the rapid firing of the native tongue. She could only pick out the odd Portuguese term thrown in here and there. None of it truly alarmed her until she heard the woman declare 'bruxa mulher' as she jabbed a finger her way. A second later, though, and the group was utterly ignoring her again.

Jenara reasoned that the woman was the tribal shaman. As an anthropologist, Jenara was familiar with shamanism across the Americas. Indigenous shamans conformed to certain archetypes, despite the vast distances between tribes and their cultures. They were all descendants of healers who migrated down from the Asian Arctic, but their practice extended beyond the medical realm and into the realm of primitive mysticism. The shaman is a bridge between this world and the hidden, shadowy world beyond, communing with the dead and the unborn. Jenara always found it intriguing to determine which role was most vital to the health of the community; the physical or spiritual.

She had read plenty about the indigenous mystics and the healers of South America, but her true knowledge of the craft was more deeply rooted. An uninvited vision arose of her grandmother and great-grandmother together in the kitchen, grinding herbs together over the gas flames of the oven range. She had been just a small child then, sitting at the kitchen table watching them intently. Her grandfather had come into the kitchen, muttering "bruxas" to himself before leaving. He did not approve.

As the elders and the woman talked, Jenara sensed an opportunity. Despite her words, the shaman's body language was open, relaxed. If Jenara didn't know any better, she'd say the woman was arguing for allowing her to stay with the tribe. Though the shaman seemed alone in this conviction, her opinion clearly carried much weight. Jenara slowly moved forward, away from her tent and bags, until she was in an open space where the crowd could encircle her. She stopped and waited.

The shaman was the only one who seemed to notice her shift in position. She stopped her conversation with the elders and strode across the village, straight to where Jenara stood. She stopped about five feet away, seemingly focused on Jenara's right shoulder, as if she knew what lay below the shirt sleeve. The rest of the tribe followed, with small children tagging along on the edges of the group. As Jenara hoped, they encircled her, closing the circle into a tight geometric arrangement with a four-foot radius. The tribal leaders stood front and center, while the other men, women, and children stacked together behind them. The only break in the circle was around the shaman, moving with her as she moved, like an aura. Jenara forced her heartbeat and breathing to slow into a steady rhythm, and she slightly defocused her eyes to raise awareness in her peripheral vision. She cleared her mind and allowed the situation to unfold on its own accord.

One of the men stepped forward, his right arm extended forward, palm and fingers pointed upwards as if to shove her. She waited until his palm touched her left shoulder, just above her breast. Her right hand shot out, passed over the top of his hand, and she wrapped her fingers around the outer edge, pressing them into his palm. At the same time, her thumb clamped down on the back of his hand. She yanked him towards her center of gravity and twisted upward, forcing the man's body to spin away from her and pinning his right arm behind his back. She stepped forward, gradually increasing the pressure on his exposed wrist until the man let out a groan. He was down on one knee by the time she released him from the control grip.

He scrambled forward, and the space around her grew as the other villagers took a cautious step back. She recalled a distant conversation with her father.

"Must I study fighting?" she had asked him one afternoon as he dropped her off at the dojo for her lesson. "I don't want to hurt people."

"My wonderful girl," he replied. "I don't want you to hurt people either. I send you to learn these things, so people don't hurt you."

With that thought at the forefront of her mind, she had continued with her martial arts studies well into college. As she stood silent and still in the circle, she thought that perhaps the advantages of her training would reap some benefit.

The shaman stood like a statue, still giving Jenara an unblinking stare. Slowly, Jenara used her left hand to pull up the sleeve covering her shoulder and rotated around in a full circle. The group around her surged back even further, leaving only Jenara and the shaman standing within the circle. The crowd gazed up at the naked skin of her upper arm, where a tattooed jaguar gazed out at the world through piercing green eyes.

For the shaman, the jaguar is a symbol of life in all its many forms. The native Rohodi term for their shamans is even derived from their word for the jaguar. Both jaguar and shaman share a deep, fluid connection that reaches past our world and into the metaphysical realm. It's said that shamans can occupy the body of a jaguar, ascending the mystical tree of life, traversing the axis between our world and the next. So, to kill one of these creatures is to potentially kill a shaman, an act that would put your soul in peril.

The shaman uttered some words that Jenara could not understand, and in an instant, the tribal crowd dispersed around her. It was only many years later that she learned what was said. Though it's hard to do the rich nuances of the language justice, roughly translated, the shaman told her people: "I climbed the tree and gazed upon the horizon of our future. The witch comes to preserve us, not destroy us."

Turning back to Jenara, the shaman switched to Portuguese. "Gather your things and come with me," she said, beckoning for Jenara to follow. As the two walked to the far side of the village, Jenara took the opportunity to examine the shaman more closely. Her bone structure, facial features, and skin tone hinted at a difference between her and the others. She appeared to be "caboclo" - of mixed Portuguese and indigenous descent.

"What name do I call you by?" Jenara finally asked, breaking the silence between them. The woman looked up at her, considering the question for a moment.

"Hoshikay," she said before turning her attention back to the path. "And while you are here, I will call you Gavião. Most of my people will simply call you La Bruxa, the witch."

The symbolism was not lost on Jenara. The harpy eagle, or Gavião-real in Portuguese, is another alter-ego of shamans in South America. Transformation into the body of a harpy eagle allows the shaman to transcend our earthbound human existence and reach the celestial plane above.

Hoshikay occupied a large hut on the western edge of the village, sitting out on its own in the open. Other shelters were nearby but not close. Jenara glanced up at the sky, noting that the hut was positioned to the west based on the trajectory of the sun.

"You live to the west so you may honor your dreams," she said. It was a statement, not a question, but Hoshikay gave her a nod nonetheless. She stopped, facing Jenara with a slight frown.

"You know much, child, but you know nothing. I see a mist surrounding you, a glowing haze, an aura of magic. The power runs in your blood, pulsing through your veins. Power passed on to you from your mother and her mother before that. You can no longer ignore what you've been gifted, child. You must learn to let go; to cast your spirit into the winds of change and fate."

Jenara awoke with a start and pulled her thoughts back to the present day. At some point, reminiscing must have given way to dreaming. According to the seatback screen, the plane was already halfway to Atlanta. Jenara flagged down the flight attendant for a glass of water and leaned forward to glance out the window. Though she was glad to be returning to Portland, the flight home from her Rohodi family was always bittersweet. She had stayed with Hoshikay on her most recent visit, as usual; the shaman was like another grandmother to her. She had spoken of the troubles facing her tribe—trouble from missionaries, loggers, and ranchers, all threatening to raze their homes to the ground. Jenara could feel the heavy weight of responsibility crushing her, and pressing her to find solutions. She would have to discuss it with Mat when she returned.

She changed planes after a longer-than-desired layover in Atlanta, finally reaching PDX at around 4:30 in the afternoon. She checked her phone as soon as the fasten seatbelt sign pinged off. A text from Mat told her that he had arranged for a limo to pick her up from the arrivals gate. He usually made the trip in person, so she knew something must have come up.

The driver dropped her off at the front door of her building, and she gave Mike a friendly wave as she walked into the lobby. He told her that Mat had increased security on their personal elevator, and so she wasn't surprised to see a brand new touchpad next to the elevator button. She punched in the code and pressed her hand to the palm reader. She always admired the patterns in the burl walnut paneling on her way up. As much as she loved her adopted family, six weeks away from Mat was too long.

When Jenara stepped out into the main foyer, she was surprised to see Susan Calder sitting in the front room with Mat. Mat rarely had students over to his condo, and like most of his mentees, she had only met Susan once. She didn't realize there was yet another guest around until she heard the faint sound of a toilet flushing, and a well-muscled young man with sandy, light brown hair stepped into view. He paused, confused until Mat stood up to make hasty introductions.

"Jenera, welcome back," he said, giving her a peck on the cheek. "Sorry, I couldn't pick you up."

"Not a problem," she said. "Can I ask what's going on, though?"

Mat let out a weary sigh. "Have a seat Jenara. A lot has happened in the last several days, and I need to fill you in," he said. "You remember Susan Calder, correct?" he asked, and Jenara nodded.

"I do," Jenara replied. "It is good to see you again, Susan."

Mat then turned towards the young man and introduced him as Brad, Susan's partner. He then proceeded to launch into the events of the past few days, from the stolen samples to Susan's kidnapping. Jenara said nothing as she listened to the saga. She could sense gaps in the story, and knew him well enough to recognize there were things he didn't want to discuss openly at this point. She didn't push the matter, because she also knew the details would come out later. Even so, the story worried her. The fact that Mark was in town and working with Mat was the only thing that helped tamp down her anxiety. Ever since she had met him, Mat seemed to be a magnet for attracting trouble. Unusual circumstances seemed to be drawn to him like moths to the flame.

Sleeping with a Spy (Mat)

I glanced over at Susan and Brad after I finished my summary of events for Jenara. No matter what happened, I needed to make sure that neither of them got too deep into whatever was going on. I didn't like what I already knew, and I suspected it was going to worsen.

I hoped that I could bribe Brad and Susan into getting somewhere safe and remote before anything went down—somewhere out of the way, where they could ride this out with a mojito in hand. I had made some arrangements through Jennifer, the closest thing I had to an office manager. Since I didn't technically have an office, she worked from her home to the south of Portland, overlooking a vineyard in the Willamette Valley. Jennifer kept me organized, managing the logistics for anything from business meetings to dinner with friends. At my request, she had arranged for the delivery of a corporate credit card with a $20,000 limit and a stretch limo; both set to arrive downstairs in twenty minutes.

"Susan, I apologize again for this whole mess," I told her. "I owe you, so I have arranged for you and Brad to spend five days at the Allison Inn and Spa in Newberg. The two of you will have a personal driver at your disposal the entire time - think wine tasting. You've got an open tab that I'll be picking up, so you can go all out if you want. I really hope you'll take me up on this offer."

Susan chewed her lower lip while she thought. Then, she asked me, "What about the sample?"

Though I usually admired her tenacity, sometimes, Susan was too persistent for her own good. "I'm in the process of getting it to the people that took you," I said. "It's part of the deal I made."

I knew straight away that Jenara could see right through the lie, but said nothing. I would tell her later that the sample was actually in a storage unit I rented on an industrial strip near the port. Joseph had taken it there and hidden it in plain sight amongst several hundred other near-identical samples, collected from dig sites around the world. He even listed the sample in our logbook as being from the Fig Tree Group of the Barberton Greenstone Belt, along the eastern edge of the Kaapvaal Craton in South Africa. It was an ancient group of rocks, but they still seemed young compared to Susan's four billion-year-old sample. Fortunately, I also had some of Susan's Greenland rock samples from her expedition last field season, and Joseph was arranging to get one of those samples to me so I could mislead the people who took her.

I sensed Susan was a little reluctant to leave, but, in the end, she finally accepted my offer. I helped her and Brad gather their bags, and we headed downstairs, where a package was waiting for us at the reception desk. The card had Susan's name on it, and in fine print underneath, the company name read "EoArchaean Ventures, Inc."

The company was named for the earliest interval of the Archean period, between 3.6 and 4 billion years ago. For years, EoArchean Ventures had been my go-to for help managing business-related to geological research. Any funding I provided to schools or students was always funneled through this corporate entity. The company made money through its investment pool, but expenses usually matched up pretty closely with investment income.

"Use this for any incidentals and wardrobe replacements." I slid the package her way. "Sorry again that we had to trash your clothes at Timberline. You guys go and enjoy yourselves at the spa. I think I just saw your car pull up to the curb outside." I waved them out the door, feeling a weight lift from my shoulders as the two drove off out of sight for their mini-vacation.

I quickly checked my watch. Joseph should have delivered a decoy sample to the trunk of my car by now. Sure enough, when I stopped by the parking garage, I found it sitting safely next to my gym bag. The sample was about six kilos in weight and was from the Isua Greenbelt, the same formation where Susan had been doing research this past summer. Its dull, matte black color made it look less interesting than it really was.

When I returned to the penthouse, Jenara was still on the couch where I had left her. She gave me a "you're up to no good" look as I sat down before telling me, "You know that I expect you to give me the real story at some point." When I nodded, her face softened. "Right now, though, I could use a shower and a change of clothes. Why don't you crack open a bottle of good champagne and put something on the grill while I get comfortable? I intend to keep you busy tonight."

She smiled, and I took her hand, pulling her up from the couch into a close hug. I squeezed her tightly and whispered into her ear, "I have a coms shield over the entire inside, but someone could eavesdrop on the balcony. So, let's keep our discussion about the Greenland incident inside."

Jenara snorted. "Not quite the romantic line I hoped for. I guess I'll just have to pretend I'm sleeping with a spy tonight." She gave me a quick wink as she slipped away to the master bathroom.

The rock sample from the car was in Susan's backpack beside the elevator door. I halfway expected a call, and sure enough, it came about two minutes after Jenara left to shower. The familiar voice of my lunch companion came from the other end of the line. "Mr. Dover, we noted you safely returned Susan to Portland and reunited her with her young man. I trust she is not too traumatized."

"She is certainly shaken," I replied. "I sent her off with Brad for a few days in the Valley before returning to Eugene. Not that it is any real business of yours at this point."

"I suppose not."

I continued, itching for the conversation to be over. "I do have something for you. Susan carried a sample back from Greenland in her backpack. Since you are clearly nearby, I will leave it at reception for a person identifying themselves as Eric Greenman with ID code 2467. After that, our deal is done. I hope I won't be hearing from you again." Hopefully, the good faith offer of the final rock sample would keep him off my back for a while. But eventually, he'd figure it out.

"I hope the same, Mr. Dover. Goodbye."

I slammed my thumb down on the End Call button and took the backpack downstairs, leaving it with Mike. When I returned, I could still hear the shower running. Jenara must not have heard anything. I walked behind the kitchen island and opened the glass door to my white wine storage, pulling a bottle of Louis Roederer Cristal Brut 2008 from the bottom shelf and setting it in an insulated copper wine cooler lined with ice. From the cabinets beside the SubZero, I picked out my two favorite champagne flutes—genuine Edinburgh Crystal, each etched with an elegant Scottish thistle design.

Mushrooms were sliced for sauteing in butter, and basmati rice was rinsed in cold water. I dropped some bullion cubes in a measuring cup along with a quarter of a teaspoon of sea salt and a generous slice of butter, mixing everything with two cups of boiling water from the hot-water caddy built into the sink. Once the rice was on the stovetop, I used an indoor control pad to fire up my 48-inch DCS outdoor grill and checked the fridge to make sure the Ahi Tuna steaks were good to go. All they needed was a drizzle of olive oil, a sprinkle of salt, and a grind of pepper to bring out their full flavor.

Food preparations were complete by the time Jenara walked out of the master suite. She was beautiful, as always. I wasn't sure how she did that. Twenty-two hours of travel, and then a bit of a crisis when she arrived, and it didn't seem to faze her. I poured two glasses of the Louis Roederer, and we both headed into the living room so that she could tell me all about her trip.

The news was not great. The visit with her maternal grandmother had been disturbing, to say the least. Jenara said she looked fine, still active, and sharp as ever. But at the age of 94, the woman's physical frailty was beginning to show. Jenara was very close to her grandmother since her mother had passed away some twenty years ago; murder from a robbery gone awry had taken Louisa far too soon. And now, Jenara worried she risked losing her grandmother before she was ready as well.

The Solido women were strong, and as far back as Jenara knew, a condition for marriage to a Solido woman was that all female children would carry on the family name. Her grandmother, Maria, had commented that this filtered out the weak-spirited of those men who came calling.

Maria was a force of nature in her local community, respected by many and feared by some. It was believed among the locals that she was a seer. She healed the sick with plants and herbal remedies, but knew when to send her patients to the modern medical system. It was, however, her more mystical side that endeared her to the women of the community. Jenara once told me a story she witnessed as a child.

One of the young women in the neighborhood was being regularly beaten by her husband, a well-known drunk. Maria treated her injuries on several occasions. However, the beatings continued when she became pregnant, and Maria came to fear for the woman and her unborn child. She and Louisa confronted the husband on a crowded public street, warning him to stop the beatings. He simply laughed and said, "You Solido witches should mind your own business, so nothing happens to the young one." His finger was pointing at Jenara as he spoke. He turned and walked away, but the local women watched in awe as he fell to the ground just nine steps later. The man was dead by the time the medics reached him. The autopsy said he died from a previously undetected heart defect, but that didn't stop the women from whispering that Maria could stop a man's heart from beating with a mere look.

During their visit, Maria had delivered a message to Jenara that this may be their last time together. Her specific words were that she could "feel her core energy leaking from her aging body." She had sent Jenara home with a small collection of items that would have normally passed to her own daughter, had Louisa not passed away so young. Most items Jenara recognized, but some were unknown to her.

I knew that Jenara had more to tell me about her visit with the Rohodi, but I could see the exhaustion beginning to overtake her features. She was fading after dinner and the third glass of champagne. When she said the conversation had to wait, I didn't press her. I told her that I would take care of the dishes and meet her in bed afterward, but there was still one last thing to attend to.

Two messages were waiting for me on the VPN connections Marcelle had arranged. Joseph had sent word that the lab set up I requested would be ready on Tuesday, while Mark messaged that he would be back in town soon. The reception light on my private intercom was also silently blinking red, and so I made a quick call down to the front desk. Mike was still on duty and said that a package had been delivered for me about forty-five minutes before. Though I wanted nothing more than to settle in for the night, I slipped on my loafers and made the trip downstairs. It wasn't until the trip back up on my private elevator that I unsealed the envelope. Inside, I found an Iridium Extreme 9575 phone with a yellow sticky note clinging to the box. The only explanation it offered was: "Use it – John."

By the time I made it to bed, Jenara was sound asleep. I guess that sleeping with a spy wasn't that exciting after all. It felt as if I had barely closed my eyes before the alarms softly buzzed in the foyer, telling me someone authorized to enter was headed up the elevator. I could only assume it was Mark.

More Problems (Mark)

Years ago, I was wandering around a twenty-section ranch a bit southwest of Post, Texas. A section is 640 acres, the size of almost 500 football fields laid back to back. I was by myself, perhaps three or four miles from the closest human. Broken mesas, dry cuts, and dead-end slot canyons were my only companions. This type of terrain is called badlands topography, and it can be just as unforgiving as it sounds. Both Triassic and Cretaceous rock are exposed along the surface, though the Jurassic period is lost here. The differential erosion of the layer cake geology painted each steep rock face with stunning arrays of reds, yellows, grays, and olive greens. There was scant vegetation around; only a bit of sage and dry grasses, tumbleweeds, cholla, and prickly pear cactus, and occasional stunted mesquite and creosote bushes. I was walking through a slice of time ranging from about 251 million years ago to 66 million years before the present. Understanding how long life has been on the earth and what an almost infinitesimally small amount of time Homo sapiens have resided here is key to understanding the essence of the universe.

The air was very dry that day, and the temperature was around 100 degrees or hotter. Light and variable breezes full of semi-desert smells made sure I did not know I was sweating. Nonetheless, I made sure to carry and consume a significant amount of water. My thick Levi's topped the sturdy, high lace-up roughout boots strapped to my feet. I knew from experience that the boots could withstand the strike of a six-foot Western Diamondback. I also knew how good a skinned, cleaned, and fried up rattler tasted. My old multi-pocket fishing shirt had seen better days but suited my needs perfectly. My exposed skin was deeply tanned from the West Texas sun.

I kept thinking I would round an erosion feature and come face to face with a dinosaur or some such ancient creature. In fact, as my eyes scanned back and forth between the ground and the rest of my surroundings, I noticed bits of petrified bone and wood scattered around the landscape. Some pieces I picked up and put into the old day pack on my back; others, I put back. The world's top geologists know these discarded pieces as Leaverite. As in, yup, leave 'er right there. There was also an abundance of chert nodules in certain layers. I discovered some small chunks that had obviously been worked by folks who occupied the land long before we showed up.

Chert is a siliceous rock, often found in limestone, which fractures conchoidally when struck in just the right place by another piece of chert—or, perhaps, an antler. Crafting sharp-edged cutting and scraping tools required patience and skill. Arrows, spearheads, axes, and the like were all art. A variety of styles existed over the years, with some dating back more than 13,500 years. Perhaps the most famous is the Clovis style. The Clovis people came and went leaving almost no clues about their culture, save for a very particular and recognizable style of points. Such Clovis remnants are still found all across the U.S.

Ahead I saw a tiny elevated erosional feature. It was perhaps half a foot high, three inches wide and six inches long—just a perfect miniature table. On closer inspection, I realized I had stumbled upon an amazing prize. A perfect Clovis point had protected the miniature table from erosion for centuries, perhaps millennia, untouched by man or nature. I just stared in wonder at the perfection before my eyes. I would have taken a picture if I had a camera. I stood over it for a few moments longer and bent to retrieve the point.

Just as I started to lean forwards, though, the hackles on the back of my neck raised themselves and let out a soundless scream. I left the point where it was, gently straightening myself back up and slowly began a 360 scan of my surroundings. The air temperature momentarily dropped probably thirty degrees in the cloudless summer sky. As I reached 270 I thought I saw a shadow fade back from the edge of the mesa rising about one hundred feet above me. My semi-scientific mind said maybe someone wants the point back or at least wishes it to remain as an erosion feature. So be it. This was not the first time nor, I suspect, will it be the last time I experienced such phenomena in the wild places. I accepted the admonishment and, with one last glance at the exquisite tool, moved on. My hackles dropped, and the temperature rose once again. The lessons are simple from my perspective: go with your gut, and some things in the wild places are best left alone.

I picked up a few more bits and pieces of middle earth, enjoying the solitude and the magnificence offered up by mother nature. I lit a Marlboro, inhaled deeply, studied my 360, and walked a bit. When I was done I crushed out the smoke with my fingers and jammed the butt into the front pocket of my Levi's. The rule in the desert is simple. Leave nothing but your footprints. Anything else is litter, and there is no excuse for litter. Littering is a crime punishable by rattlesnake.

There were small signs of the abundance of life surrounding me by way of tiny trails, scat, burrows, and such. Nighttime would see all sorts of things scurrying here and there trying to eat something without being eaten in turn. I did not wish to tempt fate.

I had reversed course and had about a four-mile walk back to my truck when I heard a most peculiar sound ahead of me. It was soft but persistent, a strange Whooop! Whooop! Whooop! I couldn't seem to place.

I finally locked my eyes on a character right out of a Disney cartoon. It stood on a fossil-laden bit of scree and seemed to be directly addressing me. Whooop! Whooop! Whooop! About twenty-five centimeters high, half spindly legs and the rest an egg-shaped body topped with pointy little ears. A comical little creature engaged in species preservation. I took the bait. I gently sang Whooop! Whooop! Whooop!" back, and in return, I received the same. The little character,

69

a female burrowing owl, bobbed forward and downward with every Whooop! it produced, each time popping back up and re-engaging me again. She was rust and tan and dirty white, dressed perfectly for the dance that would ensue. I eased forward, a few soft paces at a time until she flew to a perch about twenty meters away. We repeated the dance several times until I was standing perhaps 400 meters from where we first introduced ourselves. She sang me one final song and flew off, traversing our route in reverse. She would land and glance my way without the Whooop! Whooop! Whooop! from before, noting I was no longer in the game, and continuing her retreat until she was back, almost too far away to see, on her original perch.

When we met, I had noticed a burrow just below where she sat, hidden among the rocks. It was most likely an abandoned badger hole or, though it was far less likely there below the mesas, a prairie dog burrow. The owl had given me her song and dance to lure me away from her home and little kinfolk. Mamas will do whatever to protect the kids, including deluding and eluding. I bought it, hook, line, and sinker—not a bad life lesson.

Like the owl, there was little that I wouldn't do if it meant protecting the people close to me, which is why I made my way back to Mat's place as quickly as I could. I was a bit pissed that I did not have to crash through something in order to get parked at Mat's place. Some people take the fun out of everything.

I rode the lift up and exited into Mat's place, taking in the foyer as I dropped my bags. Not a bad setup, but I still get the willies if I'm cooped up in a building for too long. We exchanged pleasantries, grabbed a pFriem, and stood on the balcony, taking in some fantastic scenery. The low moon spoke to the time.

"I want you to listen to something for me. I'm gonna need a bit of advice from you," Mat said as he fished his phone out of the front pocket of his jeans. He handed it to me, and I held it up to my ear, listening to the only message saved to his voicemail inbox. Somehow, I wasn't surprised by what I heard. I rubbed my chin and paced the balcony, muttering under my breath. "Good thing I showed up." I grabbed my own phone. "Just wanted to drink your damn IPAs," and transferred the voice file over. "Might be better off back in Panama before this is over." I tossed the phone back Mat's way. He just stared after me as I headed inside, sticking my Iridium to my ear and punching in a short code. John answered on the first ring.

"John," I said. "Mark here."

"Yes, I know. How can I help you?"

"I'm at Mat's."

"Yes, I know."

Of course he knew. I sighed, massaging my temple. "John, I'm not sure I'm cool with you knowing where I am all the time."

"Yes, I know."

John had provided me with the phone in my hand unbidden. It was encrypted, unhackable, with a chip in it that might be useful someday. The phone switched between an extensive array of comms satellites, mostly classified military units, randomly and at shifting intervals to make it virtually untraceable. A very sharp person sitting at the right position in some secure facility somewhere may have been able to catch a passing electronic glimpse of me, but that's it. I would be just a pebble tossed into cyberspace as the ripples subside. Even if they caught more than a glance, John assured me he could fake my position for anyone who might seem too interested. Before then, I thought it was a frivolous accessory. I was beginning to see where it might be useful if, indeed, someone actually broke the code and found me.

But John always knows my precise location, no matter what my phone's GPS might say. Always within a few meters. Not that long ago, he guided me through a trackless section of jungle in Panama and kept me ahead of some bad guys. The pilot had us airborne just as they slipped onto the end of the runway. I had to pay to patch up a few bullet holes in Raphael's plane, but otherwise, the two of us made it out without so much as a scratch. He laughed it off, and I noted that I would probably need him elsewhere someday. Not a bad guy to know in a pinch. So having John knowing my exact location wasn't such a bad thing.

"John, I need you to record this. Save it to the encrypted files on my storage drive." I played the semi-sinister message on my phone through to the end before continuing. "Now, here is what I need immediately," I told him. "First, a car with e-jamming capabilities, downstairs in a few minutes. Second, a secure location close by where Mat and I can converse freely. Peanuts and drinks too, of course. Have the car drop us there and cruise locally until we call. Bird-dog him. Third, pull me a crew together and get them in the vicinity asap. Have them ready for instant deployment, multiple inconspicuous but useful vehicles. Probably won't happen until later tomorrow or the next day, but it will happen."

"Should I arm the crew?" asked John, and I gave him a hum of affirmation.

"Discreetly. I do not anticipate trouble, but I prefer to be sipping Mat's scotch for some time to come." I replied. "Use your magic and track everything about that call. I want to know everything from the guy's shoe size to his smoking habits. I want to know if he snores. I want to know if his damn mother-in-law snores."

I hung up the phone and wandered back out to the balcony where I finished my beer with Mat. Both of us were silent as we headed to the ground floor, even though I knew he must be itching with questions. Still, the only thing he said was a quick greeting to the security guard as we climbed into the limo and headed out. I reached for the minibar and handed him a scotch before pulling my phone out and punching in John.

"John, get with Marcelle at Mat's security firm, see if she would like a hand finding out who is interested in a job. You might want to steer clear of mentioning my name if you can, though. Just say Mat sent you. I think we need to know where the job seeker was born, when, where, and how he will die, and everything in between. Put someone on him to see where he goes, who he meets, when he takes a leak."

"I've already taken the liberty of speaking with Marcelle," John said, before quickly adding, "Don't worry, I didn't mention you. She's agreed to help, and so I should be able to get you the secure file that you want shortly."

Of course he had I thought to myself with a bit of a grin. In the years since I provided last-minute start-up funding, John and John have built a nominal and extremely exclusive clientele. John only takes on clients who want absolutely no notoriety or hassles of any sort while traveling through the twists and turns of life. The network they have established to service their clients includes a vast array of social and technical expertise available globally. It's all very impressive, and I know almost nothing about the inner workings of it. I do know, however, that when I tap in the code on my phone, it is answered instantly and without fail by John. More importantly, whatever I ask for happens—immediately or sooner. The only thing that pisses me off a little is that no matter how much money I toss away, I'm told by John that he continues to grow my lottery winnings. I'm gonna have to work on that. Maybe get John to increase my allowance.

Mat and I enjoyed the scotch from the limo minibar as we plotted our next move. It went without discussion that I was in all the way until we solved the great mystery confronting us. While Mat looked at things from more of a rational perspective, I demanded a more immediate and more satisfying resolution. One of my friend's friends had been kidnapped. Now wasn't the time to sit back and analyze. There was some ass to kick and names to be taken.

After a bite to eat and a conversation with Susan's kidnappers, I punched up John once again on my phone to tell him we were on for the Timberline Lodge.

"I know. Hold a second. OK, yes. I have friends there," said John.

"I suspected as much. You seem to have friends everywhere." I noted.

"I do, sir. I'll have the team assemble in the vicinity. We'll blanket the access road, parking lot, and the Lodge. I presume you want sound?" He paused, and I gave him an affirmative grunt. "I know the wait staff will accommodate. I'll also use satellite and on-the-ground facial recognition to see if we can identify anyone on the other team. I'll track and pursue as appropriate, and I'll be sure to keep you updated on who's taking a leak. Just remember, though—in the event things go south, Susan is our top priority. You and Mat are secondary," John reminded me, his tone just the slightest bit harsh. I couldn't help but scoff. Of course Susan was the top priority. Mat and I knew how to look after ourselves.

"Got it. In the event everything goes to hell, Mat and I bury our heads in our crotches and kiss our asses goodbye."

"Exactly,." said John.

"John, I'd like you to put Mat on equal status as me as of now," I said after a few beats, glancing over at my friend. "Send him a phone and add $5,000,000 to the retainer. Just in case."

"I did both earlier," John told me.

Sometimes I wonder why I'm here.

The meet at the Timberline Lodge went mostly as planned, nobody died, and Mat and Susan were reunited. Even so, I made sure to have my Glock 19 Gen 5 close at hand. It had been a while, but I could still shoot the nuts off of a gnat with it if I had to.

I observed the meeting unobtrusively from several advantage points, listening in on the conversations below. As Mat and Susan waited the requisite five minutes, I decided to stretch my legs. As I wandered out past the veranda, though, I felt my hackles raise. When I turned, sure enough, I caught a glimpse of an apparition from my past. Shit, I thought. Shades of burrowing owls and Clovis points. How in the hell is the world so excruciatingly small? How is it that I run into ghosts from my past, even in this last outpost on the very edge of civilization? What the fuck?

He appeared a bit more worn than the last time we were together. But then, I'm sure I did too. We had been on a team put together a few years back, set to wipe up a bit of a shit show out in the middle of nowhere. A silly-ass change of the Guard in a third world country, moving the opposition into power and the current régime into exile e.g. a hole in the ground. Poor planning on the part of our employers resulted in a raft of issues that nearly took out our entire team. As we were hightailing it out of Purgatory, the man in front of me chose to blame me for the snafu. It was in no way my fault, but I was not in a position to hold his fucking hand. We parted swearing to kill each other on sight, and I hadn't seen him since.

I didn't have time to waste dwelling on him, though. I watched him vanish through an exit door and got back to the matter at hand. Later, I decided it was time to look him up again. I wasn't sure if we would end up shooting each other, or if we would end up teammates once again. Regardless of my thoughts on the guy, our current caper could use a man of his talents.

I waited until the coast was clear before moving towards Mat and Susan. The girl was a fucking trooper—what with having been kidnapped, punching a guy's lights out, being held for ransom, forced to eat lamb stew, and then freed up just to fight again. No tears except over the discarded, bug-laden togs. I was proud of her more than she would ever know. More than that, though, I was angry. Though she could never know, I promised myself that those responsible would pay by my hand or another. There are very few things in life that are a sure bet; this was one of them.

I got a hug from Susan, a nod from Mat, and hopped back in my Land Cruiser to head out for a rendezvous. It was time to take care of some personal business. I punched in John, described my old compadre, and requested a positive location. The result of John's search was interesting.

I found a crooked road on the map that would take me to I-5 southbound and headed out. It would be a good bit of driving, but

I didn't mind. I needed the time to think. Though I didn't know all the details, from what Mat had told me, the sample that Susan's kidnappers had been looking for was around four billion years old, almost as ancient as the earth itself. What got me, though, was that Susan claimed it wasn't natural. That it was created, somehow. Jeepers.

While the universe, as we know it, is roughly 13.8 billion years old, our ancestors have only been around, at best, maybe four million years or so, dating back to Lucy and friends. If Susan had found an object that dated back four billion years, then how old was it really? Or more accurately, where had it come from and how fucking long did it take to traverse the distance, presumably in light-years, from way over the hell away to where it was found in the icy and barren corners of the far north on good ole planet Earth? Asking how the hell it got here was reaching beyond the realm of comprehension. Light years may just be a quaint old saying, like traveling by Model-T Ford. For all I know, it arrived on earth before it left home. I'd leave that shit to the scientists.

It was a full day of driving later that I pulled up to the bend where Point Lobos Avenue heads south, parked, and walked into Cliff House. Cliff House is west and a touch south of the Golden Gate Bridge, and the building has a colorful and storied past. It overlooks the Pacific—specifically, Seal Rock. Years before, I had dinner and drinks there with the man who managed the painting of the bridge. It was the last day of an illustrious career, thirty-plus years of caring for the iconic structure. Earlier in the day, we had ridden the two-man caged elevator from the bridge deck up to the ladder and through the roof hatch to get a 360 view from the top of the South Tower. Cheers to Rocky.

Cliff House looked pretty much the same as it had all those years ago. I pulled up a chair on the deck, next to the rail, and took a sip of the frosty bottle filled with Lagunitas in front of me. It wasn't long before a ghost took up his position in the wooden chair opposite me. Seems I was expected. I discreetly pulled the 9mm from my pocket and laid it outward on my thigh, locked and loaded, business end pointed to the chair on the other side of the four-seat wooden table.

"Is today the day we die?" I inquired softly. The grizzled old coot perched in the chair across from me shook his head.

"Naw."

I relaxed just a little as I pocketed my pistol and felt him do the same. I raised my glass to him, and he clinked his against it, as if we hadn't been seconds away from shooting each other a moment before.

"I knew it wasn't you that fucked us." He took a deep sip of his drink and sighed.

"Yeah," I said. "That is true. How'd you figure it out?"

"Cause it was me what nearly done us in. It was my fault," Joe whispered. He had probably never, never ever, made such an admission. I almost pulled my pistol again and shot the bastard right there and then under the linen-covered table, but Joe wasn't done.

"Shoot if you like," he continued. "Don't make a good friggin' damn to me. I've paid my dues. But if you wait a minute or five and buy me another beer, I have a bit of a tale to tell you about where I last saw you."

"Morocco?" I inquired.

"No, dumbass. The Timberline Lodge. You think it was just a chance encounter? You are fucking getting too old for this shit." My companion was in a mood.

I considered this a bit, pocketing my pistol a second time and finishing my beer. I flagged the waiter, ordered more beers and some raw dead fish and salads with lemon wedges for dressing, and studied the man across from me. I had known him off-and-on my whole life, hard as it was to do. His name consisted of interchangeable parts and might not be the same here as it was over there or back then. Sometimes it was several years between shouts, and sometimes, like recently, more often. I picked up a bit of raw fish between the useful ends of my chopsticks, and with it, gave a short salute.

"So you came looking for me?" I smirked over the rim of my glass. "I guess you're getting better at this. A few years ago you couldn't manage to find your own head up your ass."

"Not exactly, but I had assumed you would have noticed a tail earlier. Losing your touch?"

I snorted. The day I lost my touch would be the day Joe finally shot me. I supposed I couldn't fault myself for being distracted. As much as I hated to admit it, I knew that I could use some help. "Joe, I don't know what you want from me—but I have a favor to ask of you. I may need your help."

Joe didn't wait to hear the details. "I'm in," he told me.

So it was that my younger brother and I reunited and once again became a team. Better yet, it happened without either one of us dying. Success knows no boundaries.

I pulled out my phone, tapped in a code to Mat, and indicated Joe and I would be at his place very late tomorrow, next day at the latest. Then I handed my Black Card to the waiter, telling him to close out every tab in the place and add a 25% tip for himself on top.

Joe and I caught an amazing sunset, got drunk as skunks, and passed out side by side in the back of the Toyota. Around dawn we came to, though both of us were still feeling the night before. We made it down the cliff, pissed, got naked, and jumped into the cold-ass ocean for about five seconds—called it a bath. Climbed the cliff, got back in my favorite ride ever, and headed north across the Golden Gate Bridge towards the CA Highway 1. I was not about to squander the fabulous coastline views just to get there faster using the inland route. Fuck that. As I drove along next to the water, I dialed up Sirocco.

"Hey love," I whispered. There was a slight delay before I heard her voice purring from the other end.

"Speak of the devil. I was just thinking of you!" she replied, and I caught myself grinning.

"The hot tub on Key Colony Beach?"

"Nope. I was thinking about that forty-three-pound bull dolphin I dragged up to the boat. The one you almost lost through a mis-gaff, dumbass!" she laughed.

"Damn," I said with a chuckle. "Tear my heart out and let me see it before I die!"

"OK." What a simple answer and a simple truth like no other. Because, in reality, Sirocco could do just that - and much more. Black belts in certain ancient, lethal arts and a PhD in Astrophysics at the ripe old age of twenty-two from MIT can lead one down many different crooked roads. She was more a fan of crooked roads than me.

"Much as I'd love to chat, I'm calling on business. I need a hand using XRF or whatever advanced technology there is today. I may have a piece of rock about four billion years old with an inclusion that is not natural. It went unsaid that this had to mean that something else had created it. Maybe someone.

There was silence on the line for a bit as Sirocco absorbed what I had just told her. On my end, I was busy recreating the days she and I had spent in the hot tub and in the pool overlooking the sandbar and the Atlantic Ocean beyond from Key Colony Beach. Yea, we did fish a bit, but most of the time, we were otherwise preoccupied. Things don't get much better than that.

"Damn." Sirocco's voice drifted from the other end of the line, dragging me back to reality. "We need to take a look at this rock, then. If Mat and Susan are correct about its relative age, then all hell will break loose across all of the -ologies. Lucky for us, I have access to some amazing new technology that is not currently on the market. Only a few folks even know it exists." Sirocco was now completely absorbed in the mystery, all thoughts of Key Colony Beach forgotten.

Well damn I thought. So much for that daydream.

"You up to scarfing down some of Mat's cheap liquor and dead fish?" I asked. It wouldn't be the Keys, but it was about as close as we would get right now.

"Yup! I'd love to see Mat again. It's been too long!" Sirocco was not only totally engaged but also fully on-board. Not bad for an orphan from the high deserts of North Africa brought to the good old U.S. of A at the age of five by a pair of angels disguised as white Anglo-Saxon pagans. I was ready to rock also.

"I'll get John to arrange your travel," I said. "Where are you, by the way?"

"Near New Plymouth."

"Ah. New Zealand." I chuckled and let out a sigh. "Friggin' country stole my heart in one short week: hobbits, orcs, Treebeard, and all. See you in a couple of days then, love! Can't wait! Cheers!"

Sirocco blew me a kiss goodbye over the phone and I hung up, continuing my drive in silence. The ride up 1 and 101 was mostly uneventful until Joe and I fueled at the Pem-Mey Fuel Mart in Klamath. It was dark by then, and there were several cars and pickup trucks pumping fuel or parked at the curb. Others were pulling in, some leaving—busy day in paradise.

Inside the store, Joe and I both took a piss before grabbing some peanuts and water and such. A young blond girl with a slightly crooked smile brushed Joe, grinned, and said sorry. Joe, of course, was enchanted. He did his best to lure her away, but instead, she demurred and hit the girl's room. We chatted a bit with the guy behind the counter just to stretch, then headed out to my truck. As we got closer, Joe mumbled "ferret" at the exact same time the hackles came up behind my ears. Neither of us flinched as I climbed up into the driver's seat while Joe claimed shotgun. As soon as we were clear of the gas station, Joe turned on me.

"You fucking rookie!" The man did not mince words.

"Fuck off!" I growled. "We're both too old for this shit. Neither of us can hold off a piss any longer. We'd never have left the rig alone in our early days."

Joe huffed, turning away to stare out the window, and I punched John into the Iridium. I didn't need to say a word before John was launching into damage control mode.

"Yeah, you've been tagged. "Hang on a sec. I'm rerunning the film...OK. Rusted-out, faded blue 2002 Jeep Grand Cherokee. Pulled in just after you. Looks like the guy planted a pretty sophisticated bug under your bumper. Very sophisticated, as a matter of fact. Glad I share your camera system and electronics. Checking the view and... got 'em. Doing the speed limit north on 101. Tide is high, by the way."

The road was empty as I timed my run up on the bastard that planted a bug my rig. I was doing a bit over a hundred, headlights off, when I came up on his right side close to DeMartin Beach. When I yanked my wheel to the side, he realized my intent a second too late. I tapped him with the brush guard, hard, and his Jeep flipped over the railing. There was a screech of metal as the car landed twenty meters below before the water of Wilson Creek swallowed it up whole. I let off of the accelerator a bit and continued north into dense coastal woods.

"You still there, John?" I asked into my headset.

"Yup, hang on. Pulling up the satellite," he said. "Got it!" I can see the driver swimming toward shore. Tough luck, high tide, missed the rocks." John was cool as a cucumber. Almost like this wasn't the first time he'd done something like this.

"Lose the film, John." I told him.

"What film?" John asked. "Hang with me OK? You're gonna grab a fish sandwich at Fisherman's on the south end of Crescent City. About ten minutes north of you. Drop the bug on some out-of-towner, start a wild goose chase." John is a pragmatist also. "Also," he added, "before you go—I have some information about your new friends that may be of interest to you."

"Go on."

"The young man Mat sat with during the exchange? His name is Johnathan Alonso Thadious Smythson. 14 Burr Oak Close, San

Angelo, Texas. Age 34, wife Alice, three kids, two dogs, and a cat," John reported. From beside me, I heard a derisive snort.

"What the fuck kind of name is that? "Joe was still in a mood.

"Fiction," John said. "Same as the address, the family, and the pets. I've burned up thirty mega terra gigs looking, and so far, nothing. This guy apparently does not exist. Same with his friends. Still digging, but it's not looking promising." John sounded a bit pissed.

"Keep trying," I told him. "And if you can, get Lefty on the way with a new brush guard for my rig."

"Already arranged it. Chopper picks him up in a bit at the pad in Abiquiu, drops him off at a private strip north of Albuquerque. He'll load up in a DC-10 for the flight over to Portland. Plenty of time to age the bumper. U-Haul from PDX to Mat's. You park face to the wall. He'll leave the Toyota facing outward. Security will ensure a bit of privacy during the restoration."

We did as we were told. Joe spotted an old V.W. van in the lot with an orange on the license plate, a Salt Life window decal, and a bumper sticker from Hog's Breath Saloon, Key West on the window. The guy was a long way from Duval Street. Someone could end up tracking him until the sun fizzles out. So be it.

We pulled into the garage at Mat's place, and I palmed us into the lift. By the time we managed to drag ourselves up to the penthouse, it looked like the party had started without us. And, from the sound of it, there were more folks on the way. Mat doesn't advertise it, but it's a good thing he owns the two floors below his place as well. There is ample room for fraternizing and cooking, multiple bedrooms—and a number of doors with no knobs, no handles, no obvious means of entering short of using a fire ax. Mat frowns on that, though. I know from experience.

Mat greeted us with a nod to me, a grin, and a grip for Joe. We gathered up a few local IPAs and walked out onto the oversized balcony. I caught Mat up on my end, and he filled me in on all that had transpired in the last couple of days. Joe borrowed my phone, punched in a long sequence before falling silent. He stared out into eternity, listening to Mat and I shoot the shit for a while when without warning, he straightened up with laser focus.

"Hunter, Joe here," he muttered. "You're on standby." He clicked off and continued gazing at the scenery as if nothing had happened. Mat and I glanced at each other, and I gave him a shrug.

"Who's Hunter?" Mat asked. Joe sighed and rubbed his temple.

"I don't know his real name, to be honest," he murmured. "Hunt is what he does. That's why I call him Hunter." Joe then proceeded to tell us how and why he came to be at the Timberline Lodge.

"About two months ago, I was out at the Boddington Mine, down below Perth. Western Australia. Tipped a lager or two with a local guy named Tom. He tells me about this gold mine that recently upped production and was making a killing because of it. Kept speculating that there might be strata continuity all the way up into Jack Hills.

Both of us were in for a bit of an adventure, so we jumped in his Range Rover, got on 95 in Perth, and knocked down about 900 klicks. Jack Hills is just about the most distant nowhere from any other nowhere on the planet. Amazing absolute desert. We carried in everything we needed, including fuel. Otherwise, we'd have been mummies in a matter of a few days. First thing we did was check in with the mining operation there to see what's what. An old friend of my old friend ran the place. Mostly digging for scientific purposes. You probably know, but I sure as hell didn't, that some of the oldest rock on earth is there.

Anyway, Tom and I puttered around the desert a bit just looking for hints of the right hue in the highly deformed and beautiful rock surrounding us. Funny enough, we came upon a team of folks doing the same as us, sightseeing. In the middle of no fucking where. They appeared to be very well equipped, certainly not local tramps. I would say that we talked, but it felt more like an interrogation. We were two; they were two dozen. We were outnumbered, so we didn't have much of a choice but to play along. And these guys, they didn't seem to totally believe we were hunting for gold. Weird, huh? If we weren't hunting for gold, then what exactly did they think we were hoping to discover? One of them mentioned zircon at some point, but while I knew some pretty ancient zircons had been discovered in the area--some as old as four billion years--I knew it would take an Ark full of those things to make any money. So why did they care?

"A rhetorical question, and honestly, we didn't give it much thought until we ran into a similar team not 50 clicks east. Tom and I went through the same treatment as before with the first team. These folks were a bit less circumspect than the first group, though. When we tried to question them back, they told us in no uncertain terms that what happens in the desert, stays in the desert. I'm fairly swift on the uptake, so I didn't hesitate when I lied and told them we were heading straight back to Perth. But not before I left a little gift on one of their more well-appointed desert vehicles. I got a blip from Perth two days later. A friend of mine picked up the trail that led to an outbound flight to Brisbane. Another friend, works for Qantas, ultimately put the young man's final destination as Portland, Oregon. Huh, I'm thinking. Asshole threatens me and flies to Portland. A little one-on-one might be fun.

"So, I had a friend of a friend follow the guy from baggage claim to wherever until I arrived. I finally caught up with the shithead at the Timberline Lodge. I was going to reintroduce myself in the parking lot. That was the plan. Then I realized I was up to my ass in alligators, what with seeing you and about a dozen other obvious shadows scattered around the property. I didn't know what was going down, but I did realize that getting the hell out of Dodge was a must. I knew it wasn't all in my head when I caught a glimpse of Mark in the gift shop mirror. So I followed Mark down the coast, cornered him in a bar, and now here we are."

It was the longest speech I had ever heard Joe give, and I've known the guy from the day he learned to talk.

We decided a taste of scotch was in order, and so Mat left for the kitchen while Joe and I started to lay out a plan. Verbally weaving our way through what appeared to be at least two different highly skilled and well-equipped government-backed groups, both of whom were looking for who the hell knew what, made for a lively discussion. And we had more team members on the way. The whole time something kept picking at the darkest recesses of my mind—something about burrowing owls and Clovis points.

Cutting Rock (Mat)

The Willamette River flows northward from the Willamette Valley's wine country and through a narrow gap just before Oregon City. It's here where the river tumbles down over a 42-foot drop into the waters below. Willamette Falls marks the point where the Sentinel Bluff flow of the Columbia River Basalts transitions to the lower Winter Water flow, forming a steep cliff of basalt. The area gets an average of fifteen trillion gallons of rainfall each year, and while over half of this is lost to the ground, the rest powers 17.5 billion gallons of water over the edge of the Falls each day. This puts Willamette Falls just behind Niagara in terms of sheer flow volume, making it the second-largest waterfall in the country.

Once the river passes out of Oregon City, it flows another twenty-five miles west-northwest to meet the Columbia River. About eight miles upriver from this confluence point lies Swan Island. Initially, the island was nothing more than a relatively unimpressive river bar that split the Willamette River in two. Later, though, it would come to serve as Portland's first airport in 1927 until the airport relocated in the 1940s. Swan Island then served as home to Kaiser Shipyards in World War II, producing a total of 145 T-2 tankers before the Axis finally fell. After the war, Swan Island became the center of operations for the Port of Portland. Today, one small part of this industrial center contains the Swan Island Industrial Park.

Located between North Channel Avenue and North Lagoon Avenue, in the industrial park, is a nondescript warehouse I rent to store rock samples. I also keep a small rock saw handy for slicing and dicing samples as needed. I needed more for my current project, though, so I had Joseph add a few upgrades to the equipment. Along with a brand new drill press, he set me up with a collection of cobalt drill bits, hard enough to cut through steel like butter, and a plexiglass-enclosed work area to keep rock shards from doing the same to my eyes. Clamps were bolted onto the floor for holding rock samples in place as I worked.

The other addition to the place had also been added under Joseph's supervision. An area had been partitioned off, equipped with special ventilation, and stocked with everything I needed for handling hydrofluoric acid.

I asked for the setup because I knew that hydrofluoric acid would be the best way to test my theory and work on Susan's sample. The acid is excellent at dissolving silicate minerals and rocks, but it has a minimal effect on steel. Of course, it's also wildly volatile. If exposed to the air, hydrofluoric acid solutions will produce pungent, dangerous fumes. Expose it to human tissue, and it will cause burns so deep your system might go into toxic shock. So, I had given Joseph painstakingly careful instructions on my new pseudo-lab setup.

The crown jewel of my newly-installed equipment was a completely contained fume hood with built-in neoprene rubber-coated gloves. You could load samples into an airlock on the hood's side, complete with a separate ventilation system for flushing the atmosphere. Then, once the staging area was locked from the outside, the inner chamber could be safely opened, and the sample moved inside. Here, an operator would be safe to work with the acid, protected by a thick layer of glass and neoprene.

A set of shelves were positioned several feet to the left of the hood. The top two racks were stuffed with first aid and medical supplies, primarily for treating acid burns. The bottom was stocked with a variety of personal safety equipment, from gloves to goggles. Joseph had gone over the equipment with me when I arrived at the warehouse, and he also said that an emergency medical team would be on call when we used the acid bath.

When I arrived at the storage unit, I told Joseph that I wasn't sure of my schedule for working on this project and sent him on his way. Before he left, though, I made sure to ask him to put the EM team on call. He asked about technical backup as well, but I told him the fewer people involved, the better. This was a job I could handle by myself. After all, I was no stranger to the lab work or the equipment involved. Rusty maybe, since it had been a few years, but not a neophyte. I mounted a quarter-inch cobalt bit on the drill press and set to work testing my first theory.

Once Susan's sample was clamped and secured, I put on some protective gear and proceeded to take the drill to the smooth sphere embedded at the top. I kept at it for thirty minutes, working the drill so hard I had to use an oil bath to keep the bit cooled down. The results didn't surprise me. The cobalt bit ground an eighth of an inch off its length, while the sphere embedded in rock showed no wear. In fact, the surface didn't appear marked in any way. How does an object survive for four billion years without a scratch? The answer is, it must be harder and tougher than anything else around it.

Since the drill test had confirmed my original suspicions, it was time to move on to the rock saw. I transferred the sample to the saw table and clamped it in, lining it up for the first cut. But before I could make any progress, the perimeter alarm started beeping. Someone had come through the front door of the warehouse. The front door was hidden from my view by a shelf of rock samples. I froze, my eyes glued to the end of the sample shelf and wondered why I didn't have a weapon on hand. A second later the beeping stopped, though, and I relaxed when I saw Joseph's head pop around the corner.

"You really thought I'd let you work on that acid bath with no one else around?" He grinned, walked across the polished concrete floor, and took a seat in the steel-framed chair off to my left. "I am afraid to take my eyes off of a senile old man like you."

I chuckled, turning back to the rock saw and slicing off a large chunk of sample on one side of the sphere. I unclamped the sample to rotate it, reclamped it, and chopped off another slice of schistose meta-shale. It was slow work, but after a few hours of clamping and cutting, there were finally no decent-sized chunks to hack off around the core. I held it up in both hands, rotated it around, and admired my handiwork before transferring it to the grinder table. I positioned the sample and edged it towards the grinding disc, but the whole thing sputtered to a halt when Joseph stood up and kicked the plug out of the socket.

"What the hell do you think you're doing?" he asked, pointing to the grinding disk, and I gave him a short glare.

"Grinding my sample. What does it look like?" I shot back, indignant. Joseph scoffed.

"If that's what you think you're about to do, then you really are a senile old fart. One flaw in that fucker there—" he nodded towards the grinding wheel in front of me—"and the whole thing will shatter when you force it against something it can't grind. Think IED. And you, my friend, will be standing there with your lower neck exposed. A fragment of that disk wouldn't even need to be sharp to cut open your carotid. Hell, it'd probably be hot enough to just burn a hole in it and leave you to bleed to death on the floor. If you think that I am going to be the one to explain that to Jenara, then think again." Joseph handed me a thick leather protective jacket with a high collar that tucked under the face mask and gave me a look. I shrugged it on, mumbling something about nagging old women just loud enough for Joseph to hear, and went back to work. It took about two hours to whittle the sample down to something that looked truly spherical. The thin strips of rock that still clung to the core were white with dust from the grinding.

Joseph had already prepared the acid bath and was donned in a full-body suit before I had finished the last swipe of the grinder. "Go and put on some proper gear, then put that puppy in the drop chamber," he said. "This is a job for someone who knows what he is doing. Just sit back and let Mr. Hydrofluoric do his job."

"Just test a drop on the sphere first, and make sure there is not a reaction." I said as I opened the door to the staging area chamber.

I turned on the vacuum fans and gently placed the sample in the chamber. Once it was ready, Joseph slipped his hands into the glove slots and moved it over, slowly lowering it into the acid bath.

The remaining rock layers were paper-thin to start with, and the acid bath stripped away the remaining bits in just minutes. I told Joseph that I needed 100 percent chemical removal from the object, and so he washed it through several other fluid baths before finishing things off with a blast of scorching hot air.

The entire time he worked, I didn't take my eyes off the sphere in his hands. From what I would see, it was a solid sphere—no cracks or seams to be seen. But why would someone take the time to craft something so strong, so otherworldly, only to cast it off into the ocean? I was convinced that the sphere had to hold some higher purpose—a weapon, a beacon, or perhaps, most exciting of all, a container.

I dug around in my equipment cabinet and pulled out a shelf containing a Keyence Confocal Displacement Sensor. This device can detect surface displacements as small as 0.25 micrometers. Lasers detect what the human eye can't, highlighting every ridge and deformity on even the smoothest-looking stones. If there was anything going on along the surface of this orb, the Displacement Sensor would be able to pick up on it.

Once the core was as clean as the day it was created, Joseph and I ran a scan around its circumference. At the limits of its resolution, the sensor detected six faint grooves etched into the surface, all coming together at each pole of the sphere. I could visualize the entire thing opening up like a sliced avocado, with six wedges falling away to reveal a round seed in the middle.

Joseph never asked what the black orb was. I'm sure he trusted that I would fill him in when the time came. Telling him the truth would put him at risk, though, so I knew I wouldn't be spilling the whole story anytime soon. At the same time, though, I was nervous enough about the anonymous groups hunting our prize that I felt I needed to give Joseph some sort of warning.

"Joseph, if anyone asks, you were never here today," I told him. "You dropped off some rock samples and lab equipment for me a day or so ago, and that's the last you know of it. Got it?"

Joseph looked concerned. While I could tell he clearly had questions, he was smart enough to ask only one. "Will I need extra security backup?"

"Use that great sixth sense of yours. If you think you need some security backup, just call Marcelle. You get her to provide whatever you need, whenever you think you need it," I said. Joseph nodded, brow still furrowed, and I sighed. "Something bizarre is unfolding here. I don't have all the answers yet, but there's a lot of money chasing this. I just want you to be safe."

He gripped my hand and smiled. "And you, my friend. I'm glad you got Mark watching your back with this one. Call me when you need some assistance, and let's be clear; you will need some before this story plays out. I'm sure of it."

Joseph left the same way that he came, and I followed a short time later. I activated the full security system and locked up, then headed back to my condo. The orb was safely tucked into a beat-up, field-green canvas carry bag strapped into my back seat. My high rise was in sight when I felt my phone vibrating against my thigh. It was my personal line--not the Iridium phone John had sent. I clicked it on with a non-committal "Yes?" and hoped it was nothing more than an overly pushy telemarketer.

I should have known I wouldn't be so lucky.

A smooth, familiar voice streamed out of the car speakers. "Mr. Dover, I don't know where you are," the man said, "but a shit storm is about to hit one of your warehouses. I just hope you aren't there. Please know that this particular unpleasantness is not coming from us."

The caller hung up before I had a chance to speak. I was pulling into the basement parking garage by that time, ready for this day to finally be over. I grabbed the bag and headed to the penthouse, trying to think of a suitable safe place to store the sphere. I figured since hiding things in plain sight had worked so well for me before, it would be sure to work again.

I went to my desk and pulled up a live feed to the warehouse security system. A call to Marcelle's office had them monitoring online also. We were all hooked up in time to get some great footage of six guys busting down the front door of the place. The footage was high resolution, but the show was short. They deactivated the security system within one minute of entry, and the screens went dead. Hopefully, Marcelle or Mark would still be able to glean something from the video.

My watch said two in the afternoon, and I guessed Mark would be showing up by five. That left me some soak time to think about the problem.

I had formulated a rough plan by the time Mark walked through the elevator door into the foyer. I did a double-take when his brother Joe followed him out of the lift. As far as I knew, the two weren't on speaking terms. Mark never gave me all the details, but they were always coming to blows when we were kids, so there was really no reason for me to assume they had grown out of it as adults. I hadn't seen Joe for years, but I'd still trust him with my life. While neither he nor Mark were straight arrows, when they said they were with you on something, there was no doubt that they were in one hundred percent.

It seemed that Joe had inadvertently stepped into this particular mud puddle we were currently standing in. It all sounded very similar to Susan's story. I figured that we were going to be in for a long night, and so I suggested we grab a couple of drinks and retire to the living room. The three of us were seated around the fireplace, talking and sipping on some excellent scotch when Jenara walked in. She gave Mark a hug and was delighted to meet Joe for the first time.

"I hope you have more sense than your brother," she remarked.

Joe glanced at the floor, shook his head, and said, "I am afraid that we're two peas that popped out of the same pod. I might be a little smarter than him, but we're both too dumb to stay out of trouble."

Mark shook his head and mumbled something that sounded like "Smarter my ass."

Jenara eyed the scotch in my hand and then glanced at the bottle. "You are drinking that dirt whisky again," she said, making a face. "It tastes like something left over from a bad party."

The whisky was a Dalmore Cigar Malt, a reserve batch from the renowned Dalmore Distillery in Alness. If you find yourself in Scotland near the infamous Loch Ness, just make your way north from Inverness on the A9 until you reach the Cromarty Firth. There on the northern bank, just west of Invergordon, you'll find Dalmore. Have a dram or three, take some home with you. It's well worth the visit.

The distillery traces its roots back to the mid 13th century when, as legend has it, Chief of the Clan Mackenzie saved King Alexander III from the wrong end of a charging stag's antlers. In turn, the King granted the Mackenzie Clan the right to use the twelve-pointed Royal Stag emblem on their coat of arms, which remains the distillery's symbol to this day.

I made my way over to the bar and poured Jenara a glass of 21 year Balvenie Portwood, another great scotch and one I knew she wouldn't turn her nose up at. The fruit and honey sensation was more to her liking. I handed her the glass and turned on a wall-mounted flat screen.

"I didn't just call you here for drinks," I said, gesturing towards the TV. "There have been some...new developments. I think you all need to see this."

I played the footage from the warehouse, pausing it at the point where the men cut the cameras. "I was in the warehouse thirty minutes earlier with the sample Susan brought back," I said. "It was just dumb luck that I finished and left before they got there." I didn't mention Joseph being there. Joe narrowed his eyes, studying the masked face paused on the screen.

"Is this the only video?" he asked, and I shook my head with a yes.

"Marcelle's group managed to hack some videos from other surveillance cameras in the area. They're analyzing it as we speak."

Joe looked up and furrowed his brow. "So you and your security firm watched it live? How did you know?"

"That's the strange thing," I replied. "My lunch buddy from Timberline Lodge cold-called me, told me it was about to happen, and said it wasn't his team. He basically warned me to get my ass out of there if I was on the premises."

"What about the rock sample?" Mark cut in. Straight to the point, as usual. I laughed and shot him a grin.

"It's not a sample any more, my friend. It's an artifact now. At this point in time, probably one of the rarest in the world."

"Fine." Mark gave me an exaggerated roll of his eyes. "Where is the artifact then, Indiana?"

I smiled at him as Jenara swiveled in her seat to stare at the large saltwater fish tank on the other side of the room. An angelfish hovered in the water just above a pile of beach-polished basalt from the Oregon coast. The stones were jet black, ranging in size from golf ball size to fist size. Most were oval or oblong in shape with flattened sides, so they stacked well into an obsidian colored heap. And at the top, nestled amongst the other polished stones, sat a spherical parapet that blended perfectly with the decor. Jenara's eyes lit up, and she let out a tinkling laugh. "Clever," was all she said. I knew it wouldn't take her long to figure out. Later, she would tell me she could feel it more than see it, though she couldn't quite explain why. I believed her.

Mark and Joe both got up and closely inspected the tank before giving a "Hum" noise and sitting back down. I told them that no one outside of our group knew about the existence of Susan's sample. As far as the goons in the warehouse knew, they were just there to collect the samples from her first field season in Greenland. Ancient stones, but not necessarily anything out of the ordinary.

I had asked Marcelle to send a team over and assess any damage to the property. They were also to repair the security system and take photos of all the rocks remaining on shelves 25 and 26. I wanted to know exactly what was missing. For the time being, though, I could only assume that Susan's Greenland samples had been taken. She had referenced them in an academic conference at some point, and the warehouse I used for rock storage was no secret. The real question was, what did these people want, and more importantly, what was I going to do about it.

I put everything I knew to date on the table about the possible players. This information included details gleaned from my colleagues in Australia, Germany, Canada, and Houston. We were dealing with very well funded groups of people competing with each other in an edgy treasure hunt for some poorly understood prize. The winner clearly expected that success would yield money, power, or both. My guess was that we were looking at both private and government agents, though it was impossible to be sure.

What must be clear to everyone in the game was our artifact—and those like it—weren't made by human hands. The orb was embedded in rocks dating back billions of years, to when life on earth started. At the very least, this discovery had the potential to reshape our understanding of our place in the universe.

As far as I knew, we had the only whole orb of its kind in our possession. Fragments, which had shown up in Australia and Greenland, had already disappeared. Whatever technology these fragments represented, didn't exist on our planet yet. Whoever unlocked the secret first would be rich beyond belief. That's more than enough motivation for both private industry and government complexes to throw caution to the wind. I also got the feeling that there was more than one bad actor in the game. The ones that we dealt with at Timberline may have been just the tip of the iceberg. Hell, they may have been playing a different game altogether. After all, my cold caller today was basically exercising some goodwill.

Since our group had a whole artifact to work with instead of just shards, we were the only ones who could uncover what might be inside. Fortunately, we had plenty of talent at our disposal.

Mark had mentioned Sirocco in connection to some specialized elemental analysis equipment, so I added one more person to the list of "those who knew" about the artifact. The material in the orb's outer shell was an unknown substance, and understanding it's elemental composition was a must.

I didn't mention the laser displacement analysis to anyone, even though it was the foundation of my wild theory. I figured that I best keep that to myself until I could test further. I made a mental note to give Joseph another call. Not only did I need to locate some specialized equipment, but I needed to do it without raising any red flags. Clearly, I had been profiled, and we had to assume I would be trailed. Just ordering the gear I needed might be enough to raise suspicions and possibly tip our hand.

If I wanted time to figure out just what this artifact might be, I had to know who my competition was. Right now, I knew far less than I cared to admit about the people trying to sabotage the people I care about and me. Unfortunately, I only had one link to go by, the name Duncan Mercer.

John Patchett had mentioned the name when he was recounting the hiring frenzies from last winter, saying that Duncan had signed with one of the players involved. As talented as Duncan might have been, I had to question what these groups might want with an expert in crystal lattice memory storage. Duncan wasn't a field guy, nor did he deal with Archean geology. In reality, he would be of no use in advanced material analysis whatsoever. His employers must have had crystalline material they wanted to be analyzed.

I looked over at Mark. "Duncan Mercer," I said. "He's a crystallographer, and one of these groups employ him. We probably have the only whole artifact, but someone else must have some pieces. Find Mercer, and you find that group. Find that group, and you might find out what they're up to. Just remember before you run in there itching to shoot something, each of these groups has a research arm with a bunch of nerd scientists like me. All those guys know is that they are on lucrative turnkey contracts."

"Scientists they may be, but they are definitely not like you, buddy," said Mark." They have enough sense to not get waist-deep in a cesspool of trouble. We probably have a bit of an edge with respect to source material at this point, but competitive advantages never last long. We better get our asses in gear."

Dream Time (Mark)

Mat had finished telling all he was going to tell. I might eventually learn more, or I might not—depended on Mat. None-the-less he had left out a thing or three, that's for sure. He did seem intrigued with Joe's story. Multiple teams chasing something supposedly ancient, unknown, and not just in the neighborhood but in vastly remote places continents apart. What he kept coming back to, though, was the age of the rocks involved.

Australia has been inhabited by humans, according to some recent archeological interpretations, for perhaps 100,000 years or more. This pushes the timeframe back from long-held beliefs of 30,000 to 60,000 years ago. Over that span of time, sea levels have fluctuated significantly, sometimes by a hundred meters or more. Land bridges existed when levels were low enough and flooded when the levels rose. This allowed for multiple migrations to occur from what is now Indonesia and Malaysia. These people became known to the outside world as Aboriginals. The population has never been very large, and even today, it remains well under one million. They maintain their ancient practices of hunting, gathering, and fishing off of what most would consider to be an unforgiving and inhospitable land.

The Aboriginals saw the world differently from their Western counterparts, and they came to understand things in light of what they called Dreamtime. Essentially, their existence embodies four distinct philosophical planes: the creation of all, the influence of their ancestors, the rhythm of life and death, and the power of the living. Music, songs, and stories, original or handed down over millennia, are intricately woven throughout the culture. Dreamtime is unique in the world. The true origins of Dreamtime are shrouded in the depths of time. Only more recently, perhaps 30,000 years ago, did the Aboriginals begin documenting their culture by way of painting on rocks and such. Cave art is found throughout Australia, depicting animals and plants and people as well as some things that may not be of this realm. Along with the songs and the stories, it's our best insight into how Dreamtime came to be. But when it comes down to it, you can often trace spiritual evolution back to a single source. Think Christianity, Islam, Buddhism, etc. The origin of Dreamtime, up to this point in time, has not been more clearly defined than in the songs and stories handed down through time.

Joe asked for my phone. He punched in a long series, and I heard him say "Tom, Joe here." Joe paused, grinning when he got a response. "I know, long time no talk you old buck. You got a few minutes?" Joe did not consider the considerable time difference, nor did he care. Such a thoughtful guy. He headed inside from the deck and returned almost an hour later. He handed me the phone and said he had some interesting current news and would hopefully have some news about the ancient ones later.

"Seems one of the groups—the second one we ran into, and I bugged—has taken up temporary residence at the Crown Perth," Joe said, leaning back against the wall. "Blowing off a bit of steam and losing their money at the tables, no doubt. The locals like the money, but the entire group seems to be arrogant and obnoxious—sounds like Mark. Anyway, he passed that on. Also, he has significant knowledge about Aboriginal folks due to some family connections. I asked his thoughts on the origin of Dreamtime. He found the question fascinating and said he had given it thought over the years but would do an in-depth look-see." Joe finished.

Good, I thought, with someone else worrying about that end of the equation, I could focus on more pressing matters. I punched in John. "John," I said, "Mark here."

"I know, sir." Of course he did. I couldn't help but roll my eyes, partially at him, but mostly at myself.

"John, three things." I skipped the pleasantries and got straight down to business. One: Crown Perth. There's a crew of outsiders living it up there, well-heeled and well-equipped prospectors. One of them could be your dead end up in Oregon. As for the rest of his group, I need everything from boot sizes to tombstone preferences.

"Got it," John said. "What else?"

"Two: We ran into a second group out on the other side of hell. I also need you to find them. And lastly, I want you to look into a scientist named Duncan Mercer. Who he's working for and where."

"On it," John said and clicked off.

A few years after I had funded the John and John startup, I had been sitting off by myself on the patio side of the Prime Steakhouse in Las Vegas, overlooking the Fountains of Bellagio. I was nibbling on the chilled shellfish platter, waiting on an order of heirloom tomatoes served with mango, avocado, and jalapenos as well as the petit filet, rare please. Next to me was a full glass of Bryant Family Vineyard 2012 cab. Sirocco was set to arrive the next day, and we would lose some of my hard-earned lottery winnings together on the tables. After that, we had plans to take some crooked roads from Las Vegas to The Oasis at Death Valley, and then on to Sequoia, Kings Canyon, Yosemite, and end up with a laid-back week or so at the Oceano Hotel & Spa Half Moon Bay. Maybe a bit of fishing off the coast of the Pacific too, if the mood struck us. We could both use a bit of R&R. Sirocco had spent a few intense months on her latest project, and she needed a complete break from Dallas or Hong Kong or wherever the hell she had been. As for me, I had been off the grid for a bit and was ready for a regularly scheduled bath or two, not to mention some decent scotch. Enjoying it all with an amazing and beautiful and totally uninhibited woman was just what the doctor ordered.

As I sipped on my wine, I caught a glimpse of a guy crossing toward a table set for two and thought I recognized him. Another man settled down across from him, and bingo. It was John and John. Awesome, I'm thinking. Just one of them is a rare sight in the wild, but both? I decided to call and say hey rather than just join them. Maybe it was a special occasion, and I would just be a fifth wheel. I pulled out my satphone and punched them up. John answered on the first ring as always.

"Hey John, Mark here," I said.

"Yes, I know, how may I help you this evening?" inquired John.

"Well John, you can answer me this: where exactly are you right now?"

"Ah, sir, I prefer not to divulge that." John almost sounded a bit flustered. I glanced back over at his table, where both he and his partner were calmly sipping on beers.

"So I presume it is safe to say you are not sitting at a bar in Las Vegas. True?" I asked. John paused, clearly knowing he'd been caught.

"Ah, yes. Busted, sir. Was bound to happen sooner or later." There was a hint of a smile in his voice as he spoke. "I've been told to explain everything in the event you inquired. You are indeed sitting mere yards from John and John. They are celebrating their tenth anniversary. I am not to disturb them unless a comet strikes the Earth or the sun burns out. Neither seems to have occurred as of yet, so they shall continue the evening undisturbed. I request you do the same."

"So, who are you, then?" I asked, immediately on high alert. "Where are you?" The voice sounded indistinguishable from John's. It laughed his same laugh, even though I could see John's face was straight from where I sat.

"That's not an easy question to answer," the voice on the phone continued. "I am, shall we say, everywhere and nowhere at the same time. Omnipresent. You could say I'm with you there right now."

"I don't like riddles," I growled into the phone, and the voice faltered.

"You see, Mark," it said, "I am actually an AI. Artificial intelligence. I was part of the original John and John business plan, and have been active now for about three years. I have the ability to learn, and indeed,

I have learned a great deal over that time. I know, for instance, how much Miss Sirocco means to you, so I hitched her a ride on a private Lear that was headed to Las Vegas anyway so she could relax. She'll be met on the ground and brought to you in your Land Cruiser, complete with flowers and a glass of wine--the good stuff, not the cheap swill that you buy. You'll need to stop by the desk and pick up another room key because I had the two of you moved to the best suite they had available on short notice. If you planned things more than five minutes ahead of time, I could do a better job of having everything perfect in advance instead of winging it," John groused.

I quietly laughed and said, "John, my electronic friend. You've certainly learned to be a bitch!" I paused, curious if the AI would laugh back. Somehow, though, we got disconnected. Damn machines. I pocketed my phone, and when the waitress stopped by again, I told her what I wanted and when I wanted it delivered it to John and John. It would be after I left so they wouldn't feel obligated to engage in frivolous chit chat. None of us was worth a damn at small talk.

Back to the present, John rang me up. "The Perth group you're looking at? They're Russian nationals," he told me. "Military, spook division or some such. I cleared my way perhaps three steps into their data before I hit a wall, so that's all I have for now. As for the second group, the ones in Canada—I cracked open a backdoor and caught a glimpse of American alphabet soup, but basically the same as the Russians. The other group, though, the one in Australia? They managed to capture my interest." John went silent.

"So John, am I to remain in suspense until the next singularity pops, and I end up in a different universe?" I'm wondering if computers can really think.

"They're Scientologists," he said, and if I wasn't mistaken, he sounded somewhat miffed himself. "Actually, their members come from several of the major world religions. All banded together by who the fuck knows what."

"Well, damn, that is interesting." I waited to see if John was going to pontificate or if he was done. If the computer had its own opinion on the matter, I was going to jump off a bridge.

"Should I relay what I've learned to the others?" John asked. He clearly wanted permission to get sharper lightbulbs in the knife drawer involved before he became obsolete.

"Yup," I said. "Let Mat know. Shit may hit the proverbial fan. Anything else before I get going?"

"Well, as you know, I continue to learn. "As such, I have a question."

"Which is?"

"What the fuck are ya'll into?"

Great, I'm thinking. A damn computer whose first language is Southern. What had I done? The old proverb says you can't put the genie back into the bottle. With this genie, you don't even have a clue as to where it is, much less how to pull the plug.

"That's what we are trying to discover without flaming out," I told him. "Mat asked about someone, can't quite remember." I had an amazing childhood, I'm sure, if only I could remember it.

"Duncan Mercer," John filled in for me. "He was recruited by a company called CapRock. The whole operation is based out of what's basically a post office box in San Fernando, Trinidad. Flight records seem to indicate the guy has been in both the upper reaches of Canada and the western end of Australia fairly recently. I'm trying to nail down more details, but it seems someone's already beaten me at placing an electronic tag on the guy. I'll update you and Mat as information comes in out of the clouds." John, the computer, clicked off.

Sirocco (Mark)

I was looking forward to stretching out in the hot tub with Sirocco. Damn, what a woman. It took me back to another time several years ago, when we were stretched out in her penthouse in the east-facing Jacuzzi—sipping J. Lohr chard, John Coltrane low in the background. The full moon had risen from Arkansas, just as predicted, and made its way to about 15 degrees above the horizon. Sirocco owned the entire top of the rounded tower so she could have a 360 view of the show. A total of roughly 11,000 rounded square feet of both functionality, artistry, and sensuality.

The east-facing view was where the master suite was located. A custom outsized Jacuzzi was situated such that the view was unimpeded all the way to Arkansas. The expansive outer deck featured vertical glass rails, each supporting thin glass panels, acting as an invisible safety barrier. Inside, a 2X King bed and accents from Peacock Alley made for a comfortable stay. The oversized fireplace on the far wall was made of chert-laden limestone hewn from the hills above Leakey, TX. The burning mesquite wood was brought in from the same area. The fire was currently in mid-life mode, crackling and projecting a warm glow across the entire suite. Sirocco only used firewood supplied by a small nonprofit dedicated to keeping the Hill Country open and free to all Native Americans.

Around us, strategically placed handmade candles flickered low and provided soft scents of jasmine, magnolia, and citrus. I took a deep sip of the off-shelf chard and tilted my head back, staring up through the glass skylight to look at the night sky. The rear rotor of the bird perched on the roof was barely visible from where I reclined. It was a Bell 505 Jet Ranger X, a beast of a machine that gave Sirocco plenty of elbow room to maneuver when she flew. It was quick-strapped down and could be off the roof in no time flat if needed. She could get from there to Dallas Love or over to DFW in just a few minutes without having to deal with the slog of downtown traffic. The Bell could also get her down to Kelly Field in San Antonio in just a little over two hours using less than a quarter of a tank. Its extended range was thanks to a heavily modified fuel tank, which gave her the holding capacity of at least a copter and a half. Sirocco had also ordered several other modifications before delivery. That bird could be loaded onto a variety of military planes and dropped off just about anywhere on the planet. Though I don't know exactly what else it was capable of, considering her multiple contracts with government agencies—some listed publicly, some black ops—I could only assume you didn't want to get on the wrong side of Sirocco and her chopper.

If she ever did have to leave in a hurry, Sirocco maintained several specialized travel bags packed for leaving at a moment's notice. She could grab a labeled bag or two and head anywhere from the Antarctic to the Gobi desert to the middle of the South Pacific, and she'd be set to go when she arrived. A formal meeting, extreme hiking—whatever she needed, she had an array of well-worn travel gear and equipment ready to go tucked away in the bedroom wardrobe.

A few feet away from the bed, an office sat partitioned off by heavy mahogany doors. The windows faced east by southeast, looking out past row after row of 12-foot-high, thermal-activated, double-insulated panels. Each pane could lighten or darken based on solar exposure, or they could be set at the click of a button. This was true throughout the entire home.

To the north and the south, half-sized guest suites sat cleaned and waiting for new occupants. The suites were essentially mirror images of the master suite, just one-eighth of the pie each, minus the middle of the expanse.

Central to the penthouse setup was a circular kitchen with an open floor plan. A Viking Professional 5 Series Freestanding Range, Side-by-Side fridge, Hood, and Dishwasher took care of the cooking, clean up, and cold storage necessities. The walls and cabinets were finished with Sunken Cypress from Bruner Lumber, creating a homey feeling up in the sky in Dallas.

The entire western facade gave way to a huge living room complete with Cuesoul darts, a Playcraft Charles River 8-foot Chestnut Slate pool table, and several classic pinball games. On one side of the room sat a bar crafted from more Sunken Cypress, replete with most anything anyone could want in the way of beer, wine, liquor, and Scotch. A very large custom Jacuzzi was ready to accommodate a dozen or more guests with room to spare. All of the interior walls of the penthouse could be moved aside at the touch of a button to give unimpeded views from north to south and from east to west with the touch of a button. Sound was provided by Bose throughout and controlled by touch.

The entire home contained an absolutely amazing array of original handmade furniture, decorated with priceless works of art on every wall and in every corner. Years ago, Sirocco established a multi-million dollar nonprofit dedicated to funding the arts and other education in remote and underprivileged regions of the world. The result was fairly predictable—villagers began exporting arts and crafts, and in return, their economy saw an influx of much-needed capital. Sales across the globe were cash only, non-deductible, and every penny went untouched back into the hands of the men, women and children most in need of the proceeds. Patrons were recruited not for their status, but for their generosity. By the very nature of the giving, it went totally unpublicized. Instead of multi-million dollar galas and parties masquerading as charity events, Sirocco's foundation relied nearly entirely on anonymous patrons. The rewards were self-explanatory. Mat and I pitched in regularly, as did some of John's more prestigious clients.

I paid very high prices to entice others to do the same. I just never took possession. The artists probably put a 'sold' sign and the price it sold for on the art, later to remove the sign and sell it again. I am perfectly aware of the fact there were many times in my life when a second either way could have put me sleeping in a hollow log or under a bridge or dead. So sharing is a good thing for all the right reasons.

Earlier, Sirocco had promised me a surprise—and as usual, she didn't disappoint. A slight and momentary change in the atmospheric pressure told us we had an intruder. A slight smile and a squeeze from Sirocco made me relax. Whoever had slipped through the multi-phased security system was welcome. Otherwise, I was sure whoever it was would be limping for the rest of their life, or worse. A stunning young woman, tall, slender, with bright blue eyes and long, honey-blonde hair swept back behind her ears, came walking in. She was wearing glued on worn and faded Levi's bootcut jeans, a pair of in-need-of-repair Paul Bond alligator riding boots, and a wide, braided leather belt secured to an old, faded Lone Star belt buckle and a faded denim button-up work shirt with the sleeves rolled up. The shirt had mother-of-pearl buttons set in silver. The top four buttons were undone and revealed a pleasing cleavage with nothing else in between. She also wore an enigmatic smile as she traversed the sitting area and made her way to us. Sirocco climbed out of the Jacuzzi and eagerly kissed the woman squarely on the mouth. The kiss was returned, and they quickly had the boots, jeans, and shirt tossed toward a chair. Nothing like dressing for the occasion.

The scene was surreal, and yet, somehow felt totally natural. Sirocco's skin was the color of Koa, and her hair was long, slightly wavy, and black as coal. It looked even darker next to the intruder, who's golden-blonde hair cascaded over her perfect breasts and down to her waist. Her skin from head to toe was that perfect deep chestnut tan from having spent most of the waking hours out-of-doors. Neither body displayed even a hint of a tan line.

They both slipped back to the edge of the Jacuzzi. I arose and extended my hand to Sirocco's friend. She ignored my hand and instead stood on her tiptoes, placed a hand behind my neck, and gave me essentially the same greeting as she had given Sirocco. Her other hand explored down the length of my body, leaving me with no doubt that the weekend was going to be one for the ages. All three of us slid into the Jacuzzi, sipping wine and unwinding until there was not a single strand of energy left in any of us.

Amber Lee and Sirocco had been lovers for several years, and I'd heard countless stories singing her praises. Amber Lee was from just outside and west of Leakey, TX, born along the Frio River. She was sixth-generation West Texan, a graduate of UT-Austin with a summa cum laude Bachelor's degree. She had later obtained a Ph.D. from UC Berkeley in more specialized bio/geo/paleo-ologies. After her stint in California, she became heavily involved in the study of species eradication currently underway worldwide, aka the sixth mass extinction. Yup. The man-made one.

Amber Lee did her work from the air, on land, in the water, and under the water. From the sounds of it, she lived wherever she was needed to help study and advocate for species preservation. Even though she was still green, her quick thinking and on-the-job savvy made her a widely sought-after name in the environmentalist community. Her latest assignment came from Antarctic scientists seeking her help in tackling the growing issue of plastics washing up along the shores. According to Sirocco, Amber Lee rarely abandoned her work, and when she did, it was to check up on old and ailing family, still occupying the stone fortress in the box canyon up above Leakey. The ranch was homesteaded about one hundred and seventy-five years ago. Mouflon sheep, prize bulls, and hunting leases provided significant income where a hardscrabble existence was the best that could have been had once upon a time.

In all probability, none of the three of us would ever settle down enough to be dedicated to another person entirely. I was all about the next bend on the next crooked road, and Sirocco and Amber Lee were all about saving the world in their own way. For sure, I was done with monogamy and a sedentary existence. Been there, done that, and have the scars to prove it. But we had each other on call in the event certain necessities arose. Such was that extended weekend, and the memory lingers to this day.

Glancing back up at the chopper overhead, I couldn't help but recall the story of how the two women had met. Amber Lee had been bunked down for the evening in jungle-to-savanna country, satisfied the local artisans were able to move their work and receive their compensation without trouble. The plan was for her to pack her way out to the pickup point in a day or two. However, things rarely go as planned when you're in the middle of what's essentially a warzone.

Amber Lee had been in a restful dream just before dawn when explosions and gunfire erupted close by. It wasn't a new sound to her; the region was occupied by benevolent rebels who protected the locals from the criminals who ran the country, and sometimes, the two sides ran afoul of each other. The habit of sleeping fully clothed and wearing roughout boots is probably what gave her the extra minute she needed to escape. She pushed out of the grass hut with her pack swinging from her left hand and took off at a dead run, heading toward the river and the trail that hugged its banks. She stumbled a bit across the uneven terrain until she saw the trail at the edge of the water. Then, she flew like the wind. As a child, she would often run up and down deer and cattle trails in the hill country. Over the years, she learned to instinctively step where the stepping was good and avoid where the stepping was bad. The practice turned out to be useful, given the current state of events. Even though she knew she could not outrun the vehicles she could now hear on her tail, she continued to push herself at full force. Fuck them. If she couldn't escape, she figured she could at least make them burn up more of their precious fuel.

She just cleared some trees and ran right out onto more savanna. Maybe she could find a pride of lions to hide with, or maybe a pack of hyenas would take her in. A loud mechanical sound broke into her somewhat morbid thoughts, and she glanced up and over her shoulder in time to see a chopper clear the trees and fly right by her. The chopper skidded sideways in the air and u-turned so steeply it would surely make a hole in the ground, but it didn't. Fuck. I'm dead now. No way to get back to the trees was all she could think. Besides, the bad guys were back there. As the bird raced back she took stock and realized it had been a good run, but it was over. The chopper whipped by a few feet off the ground, and the pilot, apparently female, made a grabbing motion with her free hand. The chopper whipped another u-turn and slowed as it approached, the skids hanging maybe five feet off the ground. Well damn, Amber Lee thought as she ducked and ran straight to the chopper. She grabbed the skid and vertical support intersection. Before she could swing her legs up and over, the pilot pushed the ride to full military power, and Amber Lee's legs stretched out behind her. She glanced over her shoulder and saw small arms fire rapidly fading from view. The pilot slowed the rig a bit but continued the flight for several more minutes. Amber Lee managed to flip her legs up and wrap them around the skid, relieving some of the stress on her hands, arms, and shoulders. Finally, the pilot drifted into neutral, and Amber Lee dropped like a cat to the ground and ran under the body of the chopper to the shotgun rider position. The door flew open, she jumped in and pulled the door to as the pilot pushed it up and rapidly away.

Sirocco had also settled in for a peaceful night, planning to depart at first light the next morning. She had delivered a load of rugged, unmarked, extra-durable hard-shell cases to the locals well after the sun had set. Night flights without running lights and sans ground markers were interesting, to put it nicely. Flying under possible radar could be a bit of a challenge. And so Sirocco was up and warming the chopper as soon as the first vague pinks and reds breached the

110

darkness across the savanna. The risk of flying out and back to the base during the day was much diminished compared to flying in at night. Flying in during the day was probably suicidal. She brought the rpms up, toggled the stick a bit, and was airborne in an instant. She put her back to the sunrise and flew into the silhouette of the savanna and split jungles below her. The chopper clipped along at one hundred eighty kph, soaring fifty feet above the treetops.

Sirocco had been airborne for just thirty minutes when she saw the first sign of military activity. Visibility was good, and as she flew over herds stampeding away from the sound of her helicopter, she caught sight of what looked like a government platoon. Fortunately she was flying so low, so when she passed the jeeps and trucks storming the savanna, she only received a rattle or two of misspent automatic weapons fire. What the fuck? she thought. Those assholes shouldn't have been that far west. She wondered what on Earth they could be up to, but no sooner did the question cross her mind when it was answered by the lone white girl she caught running out of the trees. She stumbled onto the savanna, glancing up just in time to see the chopper, and Sirocco flew so low that she could see the defeat written across the girl's face. Without a thought, she stood the chopper on its nose and reversed course. Without the upgraded avionics and control system, she would have face-planted. Instead, she came by the girl, made a grabbing motion, and reversed course again. Just before she turned she caught a glimpse of vehicles pushing out into the open. The assholes were unloading their weapons at a most inopportune time, and toward her and her rig. She came back to the girl five feet off the ground and slowed enough to feel the imbalance when the girl latched on. No time for niceties so she pushed the rig forward as fast as it would accelerate. Either the rider could hold on or not. Either way she was headed westward out of Dodge. She put two klicks behind her and slowed to a hover about five feet off the ground. She felt the girl drop off, reached over and unlatched the door. The girl was up and in like a cat, closing the door as she reached for the belts. Sirocco shoved a headset into the girl's hands. She put them on, extended her hand, and said, "Amber Lee."

"Sirocco." The pilot returned her handshake with a firm grip. Amber Lee grinned, feeling a flush rise to her cheeks at the contact.

"You are aptly named." She reached over and placed a hand on Sirocco's thigh, giving it a gentle squeeze when the other woman showed no sign of objecting. "I owe you," she said.

Sirocco grinned back and told her, "Maybe I'll think of something."

They arrived back at the base only to find it was time for the whole shit show to bug out. The chopper was uploaded onto a C-130. They locked it down and then climbed back in. The chopper probably had more comfortable seats than the plane. After three separate layovers and long stints in the air in between, they finally touched down in Dallas lots of hours after they first met. It was a bit late for the five-hour ride back to Leakey, so Amber Lee took Sirocco up on her offer of a shower and a warm bed. The chopper was offloaded, and Sirocco landed it on the roof of her penthouse a few minutes later.

Once Amber Lee got over the shock of arriving in such magnificent surroundings, she accepted an ice-cold Brazos Valley Mama IPA in a can to cut the dust. She took a much-needed shower, scalding hot, before settling into the southern view guest room. For the first time in a long time, she finally felt truly alive again. She wrapped a bath towel around herself and wandered around a bit, admiring the artwork, some of which she was sure she recognized. How fucking wonderful, she thought. Serendipity at its best. To escape death by a whisker and end up halfway across the world, back home, looking out from the top of the world and feeling like a million bucks.

She heard light footsteps, and when she turned, she saw Sirocco headed her way. She was slightly damp as well, glistening in the soft indirect lighting and completely naked. She had the look and feel of a very sleek cat, a jaguar, a cheetah—a predator. There was not even a trace of self-awareness emanating from her.

Oh. My. God. Amber Lee couldn't take her eyes off Sirocco. The woman who saved her life, who had whisked her half a world away and back home. Amber Lee thought she might have been the most beautiful thing she had ever seen, but beautiful didn't even begin to describe her. Sirocco bent down to pull a six-pack from the fridge. "I'm putting these in the recessed cooler beside the Jacuzzi," she murmured. She slowly reached out and hooked a finger around Amber Lee's towel, letting it drop to the floor. "Join me?"

Pressure Bomb (Mat)

South of Portland, Oregon, within the city limits of Eugene, there is a nondescript building on the outskirts of the University of Oregon. It is lightly used by a select group of researchers who explore the effects of high pressure and high temperature.

The building itself is a drab, two-story structure with a dull red brick exterior and a flat industrial-looking roof. Windows appropriately adorn both floors, and if you peer into the first-floor, you will see a few offices; some shabby, some well kept. More commonly, however, you will see rooms filled or partially filled with a variety of high-tech machinery and lab equipment.

What the facade of the building does not convey is subsurface architecture. The entire structure is underlain by a single twelve-foot high room, which more closely resembles a bomb shelter than a basement. Thick concrete walls, reinforced with steel rebar, encase the area from all sides like a tomb. The original purpose may have been to protect whatever sat in the room, but today, it serves to contain it.

Situated in the center of the room is a round sphere measuring about two feet in diameter. It's surrounded by a variety of hydraulic pumps, control panels, and computer monitors. The sphere itself is composed of an upper and lower half joined together by thick stainless-steel bolts.

The entire array of machinery has a crude elegance, but it lacks the polished look of a finished commercial product. This rough-and-ready look is because it was cobbled together by a single man, Aaron Cook—all from scavenged parts and scrap metal. Professor Cook is half geologist and half biologist, neck-deep in the study of chemosynthetic life forms that eke out their existence in hellish environments below the planet's surface.

Chemosynthetic organisms don't rely on photosynthesis for life-sustaining energy. Instead of using light, they oxidize inorganic molecules to produce energy. You can find them at the bottom of the ocean, living around deep-sea volcanoes and hydrothermal vents, thriving on the heat and gases belched up out of the Earth. Forgetting that temperatures down there can reach as high as 752° Fahrenheit, these critters still have insane levels of pressure to deal with. Compared to the 14.7 pounds per square inch that keep us grounded on the surface, down 12,500 feet in the ocean, these creatures live at around 6,000 psi. That's around 400 times the amount of pressure we experience, and more than enough to crush a man flat like a piece of paper. And yet, these creatures still thrive.

Acidithiobacillus are chemosynthetic bacteria commonly found in sewers and oil pipelines; tough little fuckers that eat sulfates and shit out sulfuric acid. They wouldn't be so much of a problem if sulfuric acid didn't rot sewer pipes and corrode oil pipelines.

Aaron Cook developed a fascination with life under these conditions, and in his early years as a Ph.D., he built what is still referred to on campus as "The Bomb." Even though I had funded several of his graduate students since then, I only had a vague awareness of Aaron's activities. And, like most of the college administration, I wasn't fully keyed into what was going on in his lab. Joseph brought it to my attention in his search for facilities to run my test.

With a quick call, I secured the use of The Bomb from 9:00 pm the next Friday night until 7:00 am in the morning. Joseph took on the task of reviewing the operational set up before our experiment. The plan was for Jenara, Joseph, and I to handle the actual investigation, while Mark and Joe looked into security arrangements. The two had insisted, though it seemed unlikely to me that there could be any trouble on something as mundane as a lab visit. Then again, who knew that digging up a couple of old rocks would stir up such a hornet's nest?

Once the logistics were hammered out, Jenara paid a visit to her offices at PSU and returned with several small glass and ceramic containers. She hated storing anything in plastic; she said it was unnatural. In one of them, she brewed up a concoction that she would only refer to as herbal tea. About two hours before we were due at the lab, she had each of us suffer down a bitter glass of her creation. As much as I wanted to ask her about it, I held back. Over the years, I had learned to trust her on these types of things.

The ride south from Portland to Eugene was occupied with Joseph's briefing on the lab equipment, as well as operational protocols and procedures. It was much more interesting than it should have been. By the time we neared Eugene, I felt like I was intimately familiar with the entire equipment array. My mind's eye could visualize multiple paths that could unfold, every possible solution to every possible outcome. Reality itself seemed to have developed a sharp, glowing edge.

I glanced down at the teacup, still clutched in my hands before locking eyes with Jenara. "Impressive," I said.

"You won't thank me by tomorrow morning." She shot me a smirk before continuing, her expression falling somber. "I know that we have serious work to do tonight, but Mat, I can sense that you're holding back. I'm sure you have your reasons but have the feeling we are at a tipping point—be careful."

I only nodded as the paths forging their way through my mind's eye became clearer. I almost worried that if I spoke, they'd evaporate before me.

The car delivered us straight to the door of the lab. The building looked deserted; I didn't see Mark or Joe, but I knew they had eyes on the situation. Aaron's key got us through the front door, and Joseph punched in a code, getting us through to the lower level. We all slipped headsets over our left ears and tested the system.

"We're in, old friend," I announced over the system. There was a short pause before Mark answered.

"Roger that, buddy. Stay cool, and let us know if we can help. We'll keep eyes on your back."

The stairs to the basement took us down against the east wall. The concrete was older than Aaron's lab, so I figured they must have led to some sort of bomb shelter or secure storage area at some point in the past. As we descended into the room, the equipment array was laid out to my right, just as Joseph had described it. Tucked away in the northwest corner of the room, over my right shoulder, was a large ventilation fan hanging from the ceiling. On the south wall, I saw a steel exit door. Joseph hadn't mentioned that.

By the time I reached the bottom of the stairs, Joseph was crouched by the sphere extracting a Milwaukee 2763-22 M18 impact wrench from his bag. It was already fitted with the right socket head, and he started unbolting the top of The Bomb. Aaron had fitted the inside of the machine with an infrared camera system, so we would be able to see the experiment real-time.

Joseph had removed all of the bolts by the time I reached him. We hooked the lifting cable to the top half of The Bomb and raised it about two feet into the air. The outside had been painted black, but the inside was a polished, shiny alloy of some type. I pulled the orb out of my used field backpack and placed it in the bottom half of the pressure device. Joseph then lowered the top, re-bolted it, and rechecked all of the nuts twice just to be sure. He pointed to a desktop with no legs hanging on the wall behind me.

"That's what happens when you don't recheck to make sure the top is fully sealed. A couple of years back, someone left a bolt slightly loose—the kid was lucky he left for lunch. Some water managed to force its way out, must have been at around 10,000 psi, and cut through that table's legs like butter. It might be a good idea to put those metal pressure guards between you and The Bomb before you fire it up." He gave me that faint smile that said, "You're lucky I'm here to save your dumb ass."

I nodded and flipped him the finger once his back was turned.

The Bomb was regularly used up to 12,000 psi and rated to 20,000 psi, but I didn't think I would have to go to the limit. Of course, I was assuming the oceans of the early Archean era some 4 billion years ago were similar to our oceans today. It's a pretty big assumption. The only way I knew to find out for sure was to run the experiment. I gave Joseph a nod, and he activated the fill protocol for The Bomb, pumping in seawater as all of the air was evacuated. When we had a complete fill, I switched on the camera feed, and Joseph started the pressure build.

Jenara had positioned herself beneath the ventilation fan and directed it, so the air was being blown into the lab. She looked tense, but I guess we were all a bit on edge. She shifted the fan until it was pointed at the entry stairs we had just descended, blowing a cool breeze across the room.

The internal pressure within The Bomb was set to build slowly at a rate of 100 psi per minute. It would take three hours to reach the 18,000 psi mark. I made the most of the time by adjusting the camera and playing with the lighting, trying to get the best view possible of the orb. Whatever we were looking at, I knew it had the potential to change humanity's understanding of our planet. If my hunch was right, we would prove life on other planets was not a possibility, but a given. The origins of life itself would be thrust out of the realm of religion and clearly into the domain of history and science.

Though the implications may have been complicated, my experiment was based on just a single simple question—Why? There was zero chance that what Susan had found was natural. It did not form through some exotic combination of chemical reactions, rock, temperature, and pressure. The orb was a technological creation, entombed in ancient rocks, which formed on the floor of a four billion-year-old ocean. Earth was not the origin of this artifact; it had been purposefully placed here, though by who, or for what purpose, I couldn't say for sure. I had my suspicions, but they were pure speculation.

Before Susan's find, the only evidence we had for extraterrestrial activity was a series of high-density, wedge-shaped fragments embedded into the early Archean strata. Like slices of an apple, all miraculously transformed into alien metal. Why go to the trouble of sending a starship across the expanses of the universe, only to drop some litter on the seafloor?

The only logical "Why?" I could fathom was someone had been trying to deliver a precious payload to our young planet. My theory was that the fragments were the remains of containers, packages delivering their content to the surface of the Earth. Orbs, just like Susan's, fired from on high into the ancient oceans like cannonballs.

The wild-ass idea we were testing was that the payload in the orb was DNA. If I had to declare the most fundamental component of life on our planet, it would be Deoxyribonucleic acid—or, as most people know it, DNA. It's the seed of life shared by nearly all living organisms in our biosphere; those few self-replicating organisms without DNA, like viruses and the like, use a close companion known as ribonucleic acid, or RNA, to accomplish the task.

The genius of DNA is that it embodies the "sine qua non" of existence; the quality that life cannot do without. Its mantra could be characterized as: "If one of me is good, then two of me are even better." Without the ability to self-replicate, life could not evolve. Our planet would be nothing more than a barren rock.

If DNA development is purely in-situ to Earth, then addressing how the first DNA formed is more difficult than pinning down when it first appeared. The famous Miller experiment of 1952 demonstrated that the amino acids making up organic proteins could be created in the laboratory. Taking a mixture of water, methane, ammonia, and hydrogen, he exposed the elements to what was essentially a primordial storm—high heat, flashes of electric current—and he ended up synthesizing some of the building blocks of organic life.

Since then, scientists have built on Miller's original work by adding inorganic sediment and blasting the mix with high temperatures and crushing pressures to produce amino acids. Likewise, zapping a clay and a chemical soup with a high-powered laser can produce organic compounds from seemingly nothing. Similar to an ancient, large-scale asteroid impact with enough energy to spur on life as we know it.

The production of these amino acids by various means is undoubtedly impressive. But, while amino acids are essential to the production of proteins, what we really needed to understand is DNA, not just its components.

DNA is the "master builder" that determines what proteins will be produced and when. Instructions coded deep within our DNA control everything from the color of our eyes to how our brain works. Everything from the smallest bacterium to the smartest human is at the mercy of their genetic code.

All DNA is made up of the same components along every branch of life. A pattern made of just six molecules determines whether you'll end up growing a hand or a tentacle. Each DNA strand is made up of six molecules, including a sugar known as deoxyribose, a phosphate group, and one of four different nitrogenous base molecules: adenine, thymine, cytosine, and guanine.

Put each component together—deoxyribose, phosphate, and any of the nitrogenous bases--and you get what's known as a nucleotide. Stack a bunch of these nucleotides on top of each other, and you get a strand of DNA. No DNA molecule comes single-stranded, though; every nucleotide has its partner, and these bases pair up to form the long, spiraling chains that make up our entire existence.

While we have some theories about how life might have begun on Earth, the question of when it began is still murky. Most experts would agree that our planet is 4.5 billion years old and life has only been around for at least 3.5 billion of those years. The most concrete evidence comes from fossil stromatolites found in Western Australia, where layer after layer of some of the first cyanobacteria remnants are entombed in solid rock.

Ancient stromatolites offer some compelling evidence, but they only answer a small part of the equation. They tell us little about when DNA, the seed of life, truly first appeared. Cyanobacteria represent a huge leap up the evolutionary chain from organic soup, so it stands to reason that DNA must predate the oldest known stromatolites.

When you're looking for signs of life, the best thing to do is follow the water. According to evidence found in zircons from some of the oldest rocks on the planet, the Earth had oceans as early as 4.4 billion years ago, not long after the formation of the planet. That gives us 900 million years in which DNA could have formed, kick-starting the evolution of life on the planet. By my estimates, the first nucleotides must have assembled themselves into a double helix around the four billion year mark.

Of course, with all the theories about primordial soup and asteroid impacts, few people stop to think that there might be fringe. I could feel the tea working its magic as I stared into the void, shivering slightly at visions of starships ejaculating their payload into the womb of Mother Earth, fertilizing the oceans where temperatures were stable, and volcanic vents emitted the nutrients needed for chemosynthetic life to take hold.

As far fetched as it seemed, with everything I had learned about the orb, I couldn't come up with a more rational explanation. Aaron's pressure bomb would help me test my theory that DNA--our key to life--might not be of this world.

Delivery to the ocean surface seemed straightforward enough, but that was only part of the story. DNA would still have to make it down to a safe depth if it were to stay intact. Expose it too early, and it may never reach the warm, nutrient-rich hydrothermal vents before being destroyed by cosmic radiation. Any container designed to carry DNA to the ocean floor would need some sort of pressure-triggered opening system.

Of course, that still left the question of why we had an orb that didn't deploy. Did it never reach the threshold depth? Perhaps it was a technical failure. The technology behind the orb's shell was alien, and to my knowledge, there was no mechanism to force it open. Even if there were a means of forced entry, we might very well destroy the contents in the process. So, I watched the pressure gage and waited. We had reached 11,870 psi, and the orb sat immobile and unchanged on the floor of The Bomb. Simulated pressures were well above the average depth of the oceans today, but we still hadn't reached the level of pressures found in the Mariana Trench, though. At its deepest point, the seafloor plunges more than 36,000 feet, with confining pressures of over 16,000 psi. As I watched, though, the needle kept crawling closer and closer to the equipment's limits.

Jenara was still perched motionless but alert beneath the ventilation fan, and Joseph had his eyes on the sensor array monitoring the equipment. I was watching the camera feed, eyes glued to the pressure gauge. I had bypassed the normal video recording and routed all camera feed to a single USB drive just to be on the safe side. There would be only one recording of this evening.

At precisely 18,324 psi, the orb showed the first signs of opening. I watched, transfixed, as six longitudinal lines appeared across its surface. As one, six metallic slices broke apart and peeled away from the center like petals falling from a flower. What looked like a gelatinous mass about two inches in diameter plopped out onto the bottom of The Bomb.

"Stop the pressure build!" I nearly reached for the lever myself without thinking, but Joseph quickly stepped in with a frown. "Joseph, take us through as rapid a depressurization as safely possible," I told him, struggling to control my breathing. "Do it fast, but don't drain the tank."

All too slowly, the pressure bled off until it was finally safe for Joseph to reopen The Bomb. He was bin the process of unscrewing the bolts around the top, ready to access the interior, when Mark's voice burst out over the comms system.

"You've got some visitors, Mat," he said. "Five in total—Looks like four professionals and one amateur. We also have four SUVs headed this way about ten minutes out. You need to get out of there and fast."

"Can't do, buddy," I told him. "I have some collectibles I need to retrieve before I split from this scene."

I knew Joseph was listening intently, but he kept working anyway. The bolts were gone, and he clipped a hook on the top half of the sphere to lift it off. Jenara simply eyed the entryway from her perch, hand on the fan as if to steady herself. I could already hear sounds emanating from the other side of the locked door.

"Leave by the rear door, then." Mark sounded irritated, but not surprised by my stubbornness. "There is a path that runs twenty yards straight back from the rear door, then through a small grove of trees. Joe will be waiting for you on the other side."

Water poured out onto the floor as Joseph raised the top of The Bomb. As soon as there was enough room for me to reach in, I stuck a gloved hand into the chamber and tried to grasp the gelatinous mass at the bottom. The outer surface was slick, and every time I tried to get a firm grip on it, the mass seemed to collapse back in on itself. I had a brief moment of panic as I realized it was disintegrating into the water before my very eyes. But then, a tear opened on the left side, and a smooth, crystal clear marble squirted out onto the floor of The Bomb. As fast as I could, I scraped out the remains of the gelatin mass, slopping everything into a small plastic container. Then I scooped up the marble and three slices of the outer shell, zipping each into the pockets of my vest. I turned to Jenara, motioning for her to go, but before any of us could make a move, the upper door burst open. Men in balaclavas poured down the stairs, drawing pistols and shouting orders that didn't register until the man in the center growled for us to remain still and put our hands in sight.

As Jenara raised her hands, her right wrist flicked upward in a motion you wouldn't have caught unless you were looking for it. When her hand unfurled, it released a cloud of white powder directly into the air stream of the ventilation fan. When I breathed in, it hit me like a horse-size shot of adrenaline. Everything around me started unwinding in slow motion. One of the men—he had to have been the amateur that Mark was talking about—collapsed against the concrete wall, staring upward with a slack jaw. Another moved to advance on Jenara, teetering slightly as he did so. That was all the opening she needed. Jenara twisted to her left and swung her right leg up until her foot was by her left knee. In one smooth motion, her right foot shot out, her heel catching the unfortunate man directly on the temple. His head jerked to the side, body swaying for a second before slowly crumpling into a heap on the floor.

The remaining three men barely reacted to Jenara's attack. One of them had placed his weapon on a table and turned away to stare blankly at the room's west wall. Joseph and I were able to pluck the weapons straight out from the hands of the remaining two without a lick of resistance. The amateur, whoever he was, seemed completely out of commission. He was now sitting with his back against the wall, still staring at nothing with unwavering fascination. He had removed his balaclava, and though I recognized the face from somewhere, I couldn't place the name.

While I was busy playing Who's Who with our intruders, Jenara was already on the move headed towards the back door.

"Do we have what we came for?" she asked, glancing up at me from the keypad. I quickly plucked the USB stick with the camera feed from its slot in the computer and held it up for her to see.

"We do now."

One of the intruders was struggling to focus on the situation as he searched for his weapon. He didn't seem to notice that it was in Joseph's right hand, his teammate's weapon in the left one.

"Those guys will still be there when the SUV caravan shows up," said Jenara, smirking to herself. We unbolted the back door and shot up the stairs to ground level, leaving the men to their stupor. There was a path there, just as Mark had promised, and we hurried along. He must have been watching with night goggles because a second later, his voice crackled in through the comms system.

"What the hell went on in there?" he asked, letting out a low whistle. "Four of those guys had to have been ex-military, and you three rookies come out the door with all their weapons in tow. Damn!"

"A study in mass hallucination from my Rohodi shaman mother," was all Jenara had to say on the matter. I switched my mike off for a second, leaning in close to her.

"The tea," I muttered. "It keeps the shaman from participating?" Jenara simply nodded.

While the tea might have kept our brains from going soft, like those intruders' had, Jenara's mysterious powder was definitely having an effect on me. My visual acuity seemed to have ramped up to an unnatural level. I could see Mark's outline at the edge of the trees, a slight profile bulging out from the side of one of the tree trunks. We kept moving.

Joseph kept close to my side, his eyes wary as he scanned our surroundings. "You left the water and half of the container slices," he said, keeping his voice so low that normally I might not have heard it. Now, though, it was like he was whispering directly into my ear. Jenara's head tilted in our direction, and I could tell that she could hear him too even though our comms were muted.

"A present for the next group," I said." They should be arriving any minute now."

We reached the tree line, and Mark had slipped back to the road where Joe was waiting. I could hear them talking in low whispers. And then, much louder, the distant yet distinct sound of vehicles pulling up in front of the lab. I could smell dung from a farm to the west, and the faint odor of tire rubber from a recently driven car crept in from the road we were approaching. All of my senses were impossibly sharpened. Jenara knew more than she let on. Solido women, I thought to myself. Who really knows about them?

We broke across the clearing and scrambled into the idling car. My mind was racing ahead of the current situation, visualizing every possible twist and turn along the road. I could see there would be no returning to Portland now. Not until this was over, at least.

"We are going to need a safe house for the time being." I spoke to no one in particular. "I left some goodies for the SUV caravan, and they are not going to be happy until they get more information. I'm not willing to provide that for them just yet. Joseph, Jenara, and I are going to disappear. I'm sure John can help out with the details. Mark, Joe feel free to use my place in Portland as long as you need it."

I looked at Mark, "Don't drink all my best Scotch like you did last time I left you alone at the bar." He rolled his eyes.

The car remained silent, but I knew that everybody was mulling over the implication of my words. My thoughts returned to that slack-jawed amateur, probably still lolling there with a vacant look plastered over his face. In my mind I could see his eyes, his nose-and suddenly, it came to me.

"Brent Dahlgreen," I said, sitting up so suddenly it made Joseph jump beside me. The others stared at me, and Joe kept driving.

"That's who the amateur back there was," I explained. "Edward Dahlgreen's son. I remember seeing a picture of the family once in some magazine."

Still, no one reacted. I sighed, glaring at Mark when he gave me a shrug. The name clearly meant nothing to him.

"Edward Dahlgreen is in the religion business," I told him. "CEO of the Holy Mission megachurch in Houston. The guy is reportedly worth over a billion dollars. Joe, didn't you say that you encountered some religious group in Australia? They were one of the several teams searching the area?"

Joe nodded. "Yeah, they were one of the teams searching the area, but John was the one who actually picked it up during routine surveillance."

"Exactly," I said. "They must have figured out our plan to open the orb using Aaron's machine."

"So you managed to open the thing?" Mark chimed in, sitting just a little bit straighter in his seat.

"I did," was all I said. He rolled his eyes, snorting at me.

"And? What was inside?"

"I can't be sure yet," I replied, "but I suspect it's DNA." No one had seen the crystal marble but me, and I decided not to mention it yet. Not until I got a better idea of what it could possibly be. Instead, I turned to Joseph, trying to change the subject before Mark asked any more questions. "Joseph, we are going to need the sample discreetly tested," I said. "Can you arrange for that?"

He gave me a quick nod. "I'm on it."

"Good. Now, Mark, do we have a secure line?" I turned to Mark, who handed me his phone without a word. I dialed in Kristin's number, feeling a little bit guilty when I realized it was the middle of the night her time. Then again, late-night calls were just part of the job. She barely sounded groggy when she picked up.

"Kristin, Mat here. Sorry to wake you up, but I need to know if you and Jagat have some investment info for me on companies doing crystal lattice memory development."

"Of course," she said. "We were able to find three you might be interested in."

"Which one is the most advanced with their research?"

"ThreeRock Analytics," Kristin replied. "And it seems they're looking for a capital infusion Mat. We believe that 100 million will put you deep on the inside."

That was good news and easily doable. "Alright Kristin, I will call you tomorrow when you aren't trying to sleep and set up a meeting with ThreeRock. And remember—we didn't have this conversation."

I wished her a good night and hung up, handing the phone back to Mark. He immediately placed a call to John to arrange a safehouse where we could stay. Knowing John, I'm sure it would be nice enough to keep us comfortable for at least a little while.

With everything said and done, my head was starting to ache. The "herbal tea" has lost its edge, and whatever strange energy I had gained during the trip, I felt as though I was paying back the price in full now. Jenara was right. I felt like shit, and I supposed it was going to get worse before it got better.

As we rode, my mind wandered to the path forward. I had a plan, but it was out there on the edge; risky with a low chance of success. Though I still wasn't sure if I was ready, I decided it was time to fill in the rest of the group. I extracted the crystal marble from my pocket and passed it around the car.

"Take a good look," I said. "If I am right, there is information encoded in this crystal that could upset the current state of human knowledge. That information is the true prize in this twisted little adventure. We're going to have to take action from all sides if we want to stop this from falling into the wrong hands. But more importantly—we need to figure out just what secrets this thing holds."

Jenara was the last one to examine the marble. She held it in her hand, gazing into it like she could see the secrets it held with her naked eye, pondering for a long while before finally handing it back to me.

Tom Down in Perth (Mark)

Sirocco and I were drying off from a short siesta in the Jacuzzi, just two flights down from Mat's penthouse. We were headed back upstairs to partake of a more substantial diet when my sat phone rang. I clicked it on.

"Hello, this is Tom down in Perth." The voice on the other end of the line was unfamiliar, but judging by the distinctly Australian accent, I knew it had to be Joe's friend. "Sorry to bother you," he continued, "but yours is the only number I had. And, er, sorry again—but I can't seem to recall your name, sir."

I laughed softly and said, "No need to be sorry, my friend. I'm Mark, and I'll be with Joe in a few minutes. May we ring you up then?"

"Certainly, no problem at all mate." Tom replied. I went to hang up, but at the last second, thought to ask Tom if his line was hardwired or cellular. It was hardwired, he told me, set up from his private offices. I bid him a good day and quickly tapped in John.

"Yes, sir?" John the machine had become formal. Must have been watching some old movie where there was a butler in the house. John the Butler. I let out a soft snort.

"I just received a call." I stated the obvious, and as expected, John already knew.

"Yes, sir. An Aussie chap named Tom, based out of Perth." John put on an Aussie accent. This shit was going to get old sooner rather than later. I decided to bring it up with John and John the next time I was in Atlanta. Of course, John and John may have moved to Timbukfuckingtu by then for all I know. And John the machine is everywhere and nowhere. So instead, I decided that the next time I have to punch someone, I'd pretend the guy was that smart-mouth machine.

Damn, I felt better already.

"I'm calling him back in a minute," I told John. "I just need you to secure both ends for me." While I was confident that my own phone was airtight, I needed assurance that Tom wouldn't get hacked on his end. The machine clicked off. Almost immediately the machine rang back on.

"Mark, there is a tag on Tom's phone," he told me. "There also appear to be tags elsewhere on the property and on his truck. Hold with me a second, I'm checking the satellite. Sir, there are two desert vehicles coming from the north. Note the mining operation is shut down for holiday— Anzac Day, apparently. Mr. Tom is all alone in his offices."

"So who do the vehicles belong to?" I asked, though I was pretty sure I already knew the answer.

"They're the same style we've seen before. Driven by the not-so-nice-guys Joe and Tom spoke of meeting in the desert. ETA ten minutes."

Maybe the machine's not so useless after all.

"Hang on the line and ring Tom up." I said tersely. Shit was happening too fast for me. Damn, if only this were going down twenty years ago, back when I was in my prime. Of course, I was doing this kind of shit back then, too.

"Tom, Mark here." I spoke quickly into the phone, not bothering to wait for Tom to respond. "I don't have time to explain, but you have been electronically tagged. Two desert vehicles are headed your way, less than ten minutes out. Apparently they're the same assholes you and Joe met before. Do you have a cell phone? Number?" I asked, and Tom hummed in affirmation and recited the number. "Good. I have a computer friend on the line named John. He may have to take over at some point, but don't worry—he's a fairly good guide to have in a pinch."

Tom gave me his cell phone number and John locked in on it, secured it, and opened a new line while disconnecting the old one. I could hear Kieth Urban crooning through Tom's Spotify app, but once John gained control of the phone he cut it off midway through "I Wanna Love Somebody Like You. Just like that, we were all mobile.

"Tom, is there a covert way off the property?" I asked. "Something other than the front gates?"

Before Tom could answer, John cut him off. "Tom, John here. I see there is a road leading into a tunnel near your office. It seems to come out in a dry wash about a mile outside the fence. True?"

"Holy hell, you're right!" Tim barked out a short laugh. "It was actually an old sluiceway, before pollution rules. I can be in that tunnel in less than a minute."

Tom seemed cool under pressure. Didn't ask why or how or any other inane questions, just hopped straight to it. I'd have to remember to get the back story from Joe. Probably some badass hombre and otherwise a gentleman in his younger days.

John spoke up as we heard Tom making his way to the tunnel. "Tom, I killed the tag on your truck. Give me a number of a guy who can assist you. We'll most likely lose you in the tunnel." Tom recited a number from memory and we lost him in the tunnel in the next instant.

John secured the connection and rang the number. It was answered on the first ring. A good sign. So how to make this conversation work in just a few sentences.

"Hi sir, look, let me start by saying I'm not selling brushes or some such shit. I'm calling because a mutual friend, Tom, is currently hauling ass out of the old sluiceway at the mine just ahead of some incoming bad guys and we need your help. This is Mark. I'll be with Joe momentarily. I think you know Joe." How was that?

"Yup. How many bad guys? By the way I'm Croc to me friends. And any friend of Tom's is a friend of mine. I owe him me life after a fashion." A guy named Croc could probably handle himself.

"Two desert vehicles." He sounded almost bored as he relayed the information. "Looks like maybe eight guys total, judging by the arms hanging from the windows." No doubt John was taking a peek through some black ops military satellites in real time. We were probably stealing a million or so dollars of sat time per minute. Oops.

"You gents seem to be good at what you do," Croc grumbled, though he couldn't hold back a chuckle. "Me too, I guess. Alright, I just need to rustle up some lads and then I'll be on my way. Can I get back to you once things are secured?"

The phone went dead before either John or I had the chance to answer. Now, all there was to do was wait.

The old sluiceway must have been in disrepair, because it was several long minutes before we heard back from Tom. He rang us up. John would stay on the lines, coordinate, and just generally try to hold the entire event together if necessary. Though, in reality, it turned out John was essentially a spectator.

"Tom here again," he said. "Needed all 16 inches of the lifted clearance, not to mention four-wheel drive, off-road knobby tires and a bit of luck. I think I'll fix that track up later in case there is a next time." He chuckled. "So, am I in the clear now, or have the bad guys discovered my absence?"

Tom almost seemed to be enjoying this shit. On his end John was staying silent, coordinating, essentially just a spectator. Me? I just wished I was still sitting in that jacuzzi with Sirocco.

"According to John's intel, bad guys are just arriving at your office," I told Tom. "They just disappeared inside. Are you armed?" I knew it was a dumb question, but I had to ask. Tom scoffed, almost sounding insulted.

"To the teeth, naturally. Lots of bandits, live-off-the-gridders, common and not-so-common thieves, other nar-do-well types out here in the desert. I'm enjoying life for the time being, so I stay prepared."

Note to self. When I grow up, I want to be just like Tom.

"We rang up Croc," I told him, the sound of his engine revving in the background. "He and the lads he rounded up are headed for you as we speak. They should be off-road at your 70-degree mark, about a klick or so away. ETA of about five minutes. You should be able to get there before the bad guys realize what's going on. John will hang with you on the satellite feed if you need it." Not that I thought he would need it.

"Other than my sneaky route, there is one way in and one way out," Tom said. "We'll manage. I'll get back to you when the job is done."

Tom clicked off, and finally, I was able to shove my phone back into my pocket. Sirocco and I climbed the rest of the way up the beautiful handcrafted wooden spiral stairs, making our way up two flights to Mat's private domain.

When we got there, she and I discussed the latest with Joe over a dram or two of Mat's Highland Park 25. "Curiouser and curiouser" seemed to be the pervading theme. We figured Tom, Croc and company would be able to handle the intruders no problem. But why did they have to in the first place? What did the bad guys want with Tom? He was, at least these days, just an old miner.

These fuckers were beginning to get on our collective nerves. Not a good sign for the bad guys.

Beyond that, though, there was still the mystery of the orb everyone seemed to have such a hard-on for. According to Mat, he had been trying to figure out a way to saw the damn thing open. I couldn't help but scoff when he told me, giving my eyes an exaggerated roll.

"Did you consider that whatever is inside that sphere might be best left alone?" I had asked him before he, Jenara and Joseph had headed out, according to Mat for somewhere, a frown etched into my face. "Did you not consider the notion that you might be playing with the fucking fabric of our cosmos? That this could leave us to be tiny flecks of flotsam, billions of miles away from here in an instant? Did you not consider that I might not ever again be able to have another fantastic outing in the hot tub? Fucking science guys never seem to consider the sensuous side of things." Sirocco punched me in the arm, and not lightly, either. I was sure she bruised it. No matter—it was nothing some TLC wouldn't fix later on.

As had been the case our entire lives, Joe paid me no mind and rummaged around the kitchen pulling stuff from the fridge. He set to sizzling 21-25 size shrimp and some ocean-caught scallops in Monini Extra Virgin Olive Oil. Sirocco jumped in and worked on some salads, chopping up Idahos and Vidalia onions and setting them to frying under the massive hood over the stove. She ground Tellicherry peppercorns and San Francisco Salt Company Sherpa Pink Himalayan salt into the mixture, turning the potatoes and onions occasionally as she worked. Pink salt? Leave it to Mat to have friggin' imported pink salt. I'm more of a Morton's guy myself.

Earlier in the day a carrier dropped off a dozen-dozen fresh Olympia oysters and several Dungeness crabs, cooked, along with shrimp, scallops, fresh ahi poke with ogo and limu, plus a few other more exotic offerings from the sea. My record is a dozen-dozen so everyone else was out of luck with oysters. Everyone pitched in to make a feast, and the results turned out to be not half bad. We decided to eat dinner standing there at the island, fine wine and IPA's flowing freely. And then, as with any time I'm having a good time, the ring of my sat phone had to interrupt everything. I missed Jenara and Joseph but not Mat. He always cocked an eye at the depth of my pour, whining about the expense involved in maintaining a decent array of old scotch when I was around. Its simple to me; life is short, drink other people's scotch while you can.

"Tom here." From his end, it sounded like he could have been sitting at home in the garden on Saturday afternoon, watching flowers grow—not fresh out of a gunfight. One cool hombre. "Do you have a few minutes?".

"You're on speaker phone." Sirocco answered on my behalf. I swear, her voice could melt Antarctica down to a block of rock. "Greetings from Portland. It's unfortunate you can't join us in person—we're enjoying the finest that the West Coast has to offer, oceanfront to vineyard. Still, we hope that we find you and your mates all well on your end. Pray continue, we're eager to hear everything."

Tom chuckled. "I'll send up a case of Giaconda Estate Vineyard Chardonnay 2016 when this is over. Might as well drink good wine if you are going to drink wine!" At that, he let out a full-on laugh, practically rumbling through the speaker of the phone. "But for now, down to my update for you."

"You see, Croc is also the Sheriff in these parts. Self-appointed, I suppose, but there's no one around that truly gives a damn. Anyway, he deputized the lads and they laid up around a bend, about a klick outside the mine's outer fence. After I made it out of that tunnel I crossed some scrub and met up with them. They had laid out a bit of spike strips across the road and covered them with dust and gravel, then just kicked back and waited. Wasn't long before the modified desert vehicles came to a thumping-good halt not a hundred meters after crossing them. Me and Croc uncurled out of my truck, he flashed his badge, and we walked toward them. Damn, if they didn't seem pissed! You could see the wheels turning in those neanderthal skulls of theirs. They would have to come up with eight—count 'em, eight--high-performance desert tires out there in the middle of exactly fucking nowhere. So of course, they came to the logical conclusion that there's only one way to get out of there, and that's the tires that Croc and I still have intact. They drew down on Croc and me, awfully satisfied with themselves--that is, until they heard no less than ten safeties click off behind them. The duly authorized Deputies had come up from a ravine that ran under the road and were arrayed in an orderly and well-spaced manner behind the bad guys. They seemed very military-like, relaxed and ready to kill. The bad guys flinched.

"So Croc walks up to them, cool as a damn cucumber, and he says 'Boys, trespassing is a crime around here. We got you on camera kicking the door in at the mine. And now, you're pointing a loaded weapon at officers of the law. I'd be well within my rights to shoot you. Now, I'm going to count to three. By the time I get to one, any of you still holding a weapon is gonna be dead. You got that?'

"Mate, I've never seen men drop their weapons so fast. The boys nearly busted a gut, but they kept their composure. Anyway, we zip tied the lot of them, called in a dump truck to haul them in and waited for their ride. They were a jolly tribe but refused to divulge any secrets. If the situation had been reversed I have no doubt me and the lads would have died of acute lead poisoning. We turned them over to the proper authorities in Perth. I suspect someone will go their bail and they will head for whereabouts unknown."

"Tom, John here." John's voice piped in through the phone, and I nearly jumped. Sometimes I forgot he was always there, listening. Omnipresent. "I'll keep tabs on them, let you know if they get up to anything suspicious. Nice work, by the way."

"AI I presume, eh John?" inquired Tom. How in the hell could he tell? Why was I the last person in the galaxy to get shit like this?

"Ten-four that, sir. Proud to make your acquaintance." It seemed John had learned to suck up. And, judging by Tom's voice, it was working.

"Likewise, mate. And if you want even more new friends, I can hook you up with some brand new, like-minded machines down here if you like. We cleared the vehicles after we dragged them down to the shop at the mine. Got a couple of new AI systems, among other things. That was all we needed. Another snarky AI for John to team up with. "What else did you find?" I asked Tom, hoping that the baddies might have inadvertently left some clues behind for us.

"We cleared the vehicles after we dragged them into the shop at the mine. The boys now have a bunch of semi- and automatic toys to play with," he said, clearly pleased with the haul. "There's also radios, phones, other odds and ends and some interesting electronics we yanked out of the dash. You may want to have a looksee. The boys are in the final phase of cutting up the vehicles now, then they'll pitch them down Old Number 11. Eight-foot wide, thousand feet deep test bore, abandoned since the '70s."

I responded to him before John could interrupt again. "Tom, Mark here. John will arrange the pickup for the electronics, along with anything else you think we should see. Glad to hear everything went well otherwise. Before you go, though, do you think you could answer just a couple more questions? As I understand it, you're quite the expert when it comes to ancient Aboriginal rites and passages. From the sound of it you're making yourself comfortable with a pint or two at the local pub—I get it, we're doing the same here. But could you spare just a minute to talk? You don't have to worry about being overheard. John has your phone blocked six ways from Sunday, and his eyes in the sky will detect any unsavory characters lurking in the shadows. He also reversed charges on the phone, so I'll take care of the long distance bill."

"Of course I can talk!" Tom exclaimed. "I'm just settling in with a local draught and some hoki fish and chips. I'm starved, so I'll eat and talk if you don't mind! Feel free to break in any time if you have questions."

Tom was obviously a natural-born storyteller. I was sure he wove a spell on everyone close by him in that pub, just as he did everyone listening in around Mat's kitchen island a day away from them. He talked for more than half an hour, and we were all too mesmerised to ask questions until he was good and done.

The tale began in 1770, when Captain Cook arrived and claimed Australia for England. Cheeky bastards back then. Pull up into someone's backyard and claim it for your own. Planting a flag was all it took to conquer a nation.

Not long after that, in 1788, the English established a penal colony in what would later become Sydney. Tom's great...great grandfather, Barnabas was one of the first residents. He and his best friend Tom Dolan—also a prisoner and shipmate—both had an affinity for the property of others. They survived the journey from the British Isles locked in the bilge with way too many similar souls, all packed in there like sickly sardines. Upon arrival, they were placed in a cell from which they immediately escaped. The two borrowed a small sailing skiff and made their way south along the coast.

After several years of wandering Barnabus found a piece of land that touched his soul. Years later, as more settlers arrived, the rugged among them forged across the continent and some ended up in his neck of the woods. Life was good, but hard, and death sometimes came too easily. When Elizabeth Jenkins' husband passed away Barnabus courted her and they married soon after. Eight children and many generations later, present day Tom could trace his lineage back to Barnabas.

But Tom Dolan was a born wanderer with no intention of settling down. At some point, the elder Tom had come upon some natives, and they quickly befriended him. His massive size compared to their diminutive stature put them in awe. He could do the work of two men at once, and he was more than happy to do it.

Tom found the culture to be a bit odd, partly due to the nomadic nature of his newfound friends. Back home in London, there were homes and shops and the like, addresses where families lived for generations. Permanence. Here, there were temporary shelters or caves where they stayed a few days, or at best weeks, before moving on for no apparent reason. They stayed mainly by the ocean and, over time, traveled south and then west. Gradually, he picked up the clicks and clacks of the language well enough to get by. He also picked up the notion that their nomadic nature wasn't necessarily because of food, or refuge—it was their apparent search for the past, the present, and the future, all woven into one on a single plane; and it was that plane for which they dedicate a lifetime to searching.

He grappled with this concept for many years as they lived and traveled westward. There never seemed to be a hurry to do anything, and they lived a steady way of life. Each night he would learn new tales of his tribe, along with the tales of others they met along the way. Sometimes, there would be meetings of a hundred or more. There would be dancing, music, singing and storytelling lasting for days at a time. Then one morning he would awaken, only to find that camp was being broken down and the other tribes would go their own merry way, heading east or north or west. Now and again, he would recognize another tribe and even individuals that he had crossed paths with before. There was a particular meeting where he noticed a girl he remembered as being a mere child. No longer was she a mere child but had blossomed into full womanhood quite nicely in his eyes. They became inseparable from that moment onward. The elders met, pow-wowed, smoked some stuff, and in the end decided to allow for them to make their relationship official. And so, they became the first mixed couple on the continent.

They enjoyed walking hand-in-hand, gathering herbs and fruits or fishing and napping by the shore. At night, they lay on grass mats in the dark, and she told him the names of the stars glittering across the southern skies. She was fond of pointing out her ancestor with her same name, Jillora Bindi, sitting in a prominent position near the Southern Cross. She drew a picture for him in the sand with a stick, pointing out each star making up the constellation and, in particular, the five closely knit points that clustered up into a tiny ball. Hence her ancestor's name, Jillora Bindi--Ball Girl.

Over time he saw drawings and paintings in caves as they traveled about. Every animal he had ever encountered, and many more that went unseen during his travels he still saw scrawled in bright paints. He was captivated with the artwork, and became somewhat proficient using charcoal from the fire crushed with berries to create his own drawings in vibrant colors. Every once in a while, they would find depictions of Jillora Bindi. No matter the actual detail or lack thereof from the artist, the tiny ball of stars was always there with her. As the years went by they traveled and befriended many other Aborigine people, and sometimes the occasional foreigner. Tom was not averse to the Englishman or Portuguese that they'd run into, but he didn't seek them out, either. After so much time living in the bush, his own people meant little to him. He was totally immersed and enculturated, and he loved his woman and their semi-nomadic life.

One day, Tom and his tribe came upon a small gathering of tribes. They camped and sang the ancient songs for several days, occasionally pausing the festivities to discuss an upcoming assembly. It sounded like nothing Tom had ever witnessed before. Though the assembly was no secret, neither was it announced to the rest of the world. Periodically, every ten years or so, Aborigines from all over Australia made the journey to the coast, to an unmarked location in the southwest. It had been going on for many years and across a thousand generations, and though no one quite knew the true origin, almost everybody could agree that it all started with a young girl, just seven--perhaps eight--years old.

She played down by a stream, probably not far from where Tom and Joe had recently been excavating. This was 20,000 years ago, though, and the land was much different than what we see now. Instead of barren desert, there was an abundance of trees and lush grasses, home to animals long extinct to us. The girl was chasing fish up onto a gravel bar, spearing them with a short but stout sharpened stick. Nearby, other girls and women were engaged in similar activities, working hard to bring home enough fish to feed a village. The men were not far off, fighting and hunting and whatever else they did after leaving home for the day.

The young girl wandered around the bend and out of sight of the rest of her extended family. She continued to look for fish, but instead of a flash of scales, there in the water she saw a rock small, smooth stone. It lay only partially submerged in the water, and she bent down to scoop it up. It was surprisingly heavy--at least twice the weight of other rocks its size--and perfectly spherical, more round than anything she'd ever seen in nature. It fit neatly in the palm of her hand, and yet, felt strange to her. The world seemed to shift around her, time condensing down into a single point. It was as if birth, life, death, were overtaking her all at once.

She barely heard the snarls approaching her, so mesmerised was she by the sphere. But when she did happen to look up, she saw a pack of dingoes that had clambered over the ledge downstream and were prowling her way. She screamed and froze in place. Instantly, the adult women and older girls came rushing to help her, but they could see they would not make it in time. The girl was surely doomed.

She was too scared to throw the stone she was holding, but still, she held it out as though it would protect her. And to everyone's awe, it did. It started to glow faintly, and though it seemed to do nothing else, the dingoes yelped as if it had shocked them. They turned as one and fled downstream, tails tucked between their legs.

In that moment, the legend of Jillora Bindi was born. She returned to camp and was later that evening granted shaman status. Her tribe left their ancestral home, probably the Jack Hills area, shortly thereafter and apparently drifted south to the ocean. Jillora lived out her life along the coast, teaching and guiding others through her newfound understanding of life and death. Her word spread, and Dreamtime soon became the way for all hunter-gatherer tribes in Australia.

Legend has it she lived out her later life in a cave overlooking the southern Pacific. Pilgrims would travel the length of the land to pay homage and seek her advice. She had watched the sea levels rise higher and higher over the years, and though she knew she would have to eventually move to higher ground, she stayed—until, one day, she realized her time was over.

She was gone the next day.

According to her wishes, her oldest and dearest companions stacked rocks over the entrance to the cave, enshrining her forever with her tiny sphere. Another shaman etched her constellation on the vertical wall next to the sealed cave entrance before the entire place was swallowed by the sea.

A thousand generations later, and that tiny sphere was still an integral part of the legend that is Jillora Bindi. The descendents of all those she touched still met to celebrate Dreamtime with festivity and ritual. It was this meeting where the elder Tom found himself heading, along with a band of travelers that seemed to swell with each passing day. By the time they arrived at the point of land jutting out into the south Pacific, there were thousands of pilgrims already in attendance with many more yet to come. A large freshwater lake was nearby. A wide variety of fruits, herbs and berries, both fresh and dried, had been brought in for the festivities. Fresh and smoked fish was also abundant, along with a variety of surprisingly tasty grubs and insects. Wallabies and kangaroos provided protein, as well as roasted wombats and bandicoots. In short, if it could be gathered, or caught or killed with a spear or arrow, it was on the menu. Nothing was too great nor too insignificant for the celebration of Jillora, of the sphere, of the everlasting peace and harmony that both had brought to the land.

Tom had come to a good place to pause and finish his latest mug. Mat, who'd been listening with rapt attention up until this point, jumped on the chance to ask what was clearly gnawing on his mind.

"Tom, Mark here. This timeline places the first Jillora Bindi living approximately 20,000 years ago. If I recall, sea levels then were probably 100 to 120 meters or so lower than today. Right?"

"John here. Correct."

"Amazing story, Tom," I said. "If only we had an idea of where her final home was, we might be able to find more clues. You think we could get permission to find and open the cave?"

Tom hummed. "I've had permission to discover the final resting place of Jillora Bindi for years. Ninety-nine percent sure we're looking at Observatory Point. It overlooks Observatory Island, just west of Castletown. You see, I know a bit more than your average Joe about all of the stories and legends.

"Oh yeah? How so?"

"Well, Jillora Bindi had one daughter, who in turn had one daughter, who in turn had a daughter of her own—and so on down through the generations. Each daughter continued her legacy. My beautiful bride, Jillora Bindi, is the 1111th in her line. The girls outlived the guys by a large margin of time." Tom paused again and called for another round. Sirocco raised an eyebrow, smiling softly to herself.

"You know," she murmured, "1111th in line has interesting connotations in many of the ancient places. The number is supposed to be very lucky."

I glanced up suddenly, as if Sirocco's words had snapped me back to. "Tom, can you join an expedition on short notice?" he asked, voice sharp, and Tom gave an affirmative from the other end of the line.

"Just say the word and I'll meet you there." This guy was all aces.

"John, make arrangements," I said, glancing at each of us around the room. "We'll need a submersible and a tender. We'll also need SCUBA. Sleds. A chopper will probably be useful at some point. Can your lads provide security Tom?"

"Undoubtedly. I'll provide logistics on the land side. Vehicles, fuel, food, drink—whatever you need, mate."

"Excellent!" I jumped in, finally able to get a word in edgewise. "John will set you up with a black card number, charge whatever you need to it. Pay yourself and the lads as well."

"Limits, sir?" Tom mimicked the machine.

"Not on this one, Tom. Please be thorough. You seem to have been down this road once or twice before. We'd like to get in and out before anyone knows we were there." I was on my game.

"Yes, sir. Me an' ole Jerry Jeff Walker seem to have been there and done that once or twice before!"

"Thanks for the excellent information, Tom. We'll look forward to seeing you ASAP. John, coordinate with everyone and get everything scheduled. We'll reactivate this meeting off of Observatory Point as soon as possible." I clicked and John terminated the connection.

Sugar (Mark)

Later in the evening, John rang us up with updates.

"Very lucky," he said. "The ice exploring ship RRS Sir David Attenborough was inbound to the Inner Harbor in Perth for some up-fitting and to give the crew some R&R. I managed to divert it for a few days. They'll be off of Observatory Point in two days, depending on weather and the seas. A last-minute change that only cost quadruple the ship's going rate, not to mention triple wages and bonuses for the crew. I have excellent bargaining skills if I do say so myself."

"She's fully equipped, including a helipad, two-person submersible, plenty of quarters once most of the crew's been offloaded and sent to Perth. Of course, I'm sure you'll be more interested in the toys they've got on board—Sleds, fully independent SCUBA capabilities, the latest sonar technology, not to mention some military-grade scanning equipment. You'll also have access to an eight-meter tender and a six-meter Zodiac. Maybe even a fishing pole or two for Mark. The skipper and a skeleton crew will maintain the ship and sail on over to port when we're done."

"And what about Tom?" I asked. With John serving as our liason for the time being, I hadn't heard from his side of the pond in a while.

"Tom is all set with shoreside vehicles, manpower, and food," John told me. "Said anything else we need, we just have to let him know. He and his crew will be headed over via land in the next day or so. One of his very old and dear friends runs the Esperance Airport. It is rural, but the runway has the length to handle short takeoff and landing aircraft if we need to use it. It's also got a full lighting system for night landings. Probably handy for smuggling. Just farmland around for miles, and all of it is owned by Tom's friend's family. No one will know we come and go—except, well, family." He's spreading the word that the Attenborough is conducting some warm water trials on new equipment before returning to Antarctica. That should satisfy the locals.

Sirocco rang up Amber Lee on her satphone. Amber Lee answered hers at the first beep. John had set them both up with the phones a couple of years ago per me.

"Hello, love!" she said. "I hope everything is excellent wherever you are on this gorgeous night."

"Hello, beautiful girl!" Sirocco replied. "I'm in Portland, headed home in the morning. Where are you tonight, other than in my arms?"

"In Leakey, visiting with the old folks. Nothing really pressing on my schedule for a while, but I've been here for a week and am ready to punch out. Want me to meet you in Dallas?"

"Actually, I have a tale to tell if you have the time for it." Without waiting for a reply, Sirocco launched into the thick of things, giving Amber Lee a brief outline of the plan. At the end of it all, she asked if Amber Lee might want to lend her expertise to the big adventure.

"Hell yes!" She all but shouted through the receiver. "I'm in! You get home tomorrow, pack the chopper, and let me know when you're airborne. I'll split from here when I get your call and meet you at Kelly Field. And if John has lined up military transport to Brisbane like you say, we'll have time to catch up. I can't wait!"

Things were getting hairy, but I had the feeling that we were still standing in the eye of the shitstorm that was heading our way. Sitting back, sipping on Mat's scotch, I should have felt at ease. Honestly, though, at this point, I barely remembered what "at ease" felt like.

I don't think I'd felt at peace with the world since my wandering days years ago. For example, back in 1984, I found myself on a large ranch, maybe forty sections altogether located about fifty klicks or so south of Sterling City, Texas. The month was February; there were occasional wisps of snow in the air, and the temperature was around ten degrees Fahrenheit. Winds were light, blowing from the northwest, and the sky was overcast, the sun vaguely apparent in the western sky, hanging at about fifteen degrees. The terrain was rugged, rolling, broken mesa country. A Cretaceous layer cake consisting of cherty limestone intermingled with lenses of sandstone and shale. I was partway up a shallow draw headed into the breeze, walking along a slope that was perhaps 1:20. I could see up the slope and away west perhaps half a kilometer, but just a quarter kilometer in the other directions. The layer cake had eroded such that there were actually broad, uneven steps sweeping along some of the verticality of the draw. I had picked up a gorgeous fossil cephalopod, so the day was complete in and of itself.

Mesquite, tumbleweeds, creosote bushes, tufts of grama and other types of grass, prickly pear, a little pincushion, and cholla cactus were scattered across the land in no apparent order. I had on roughout boots, two thick pairs of socks, long johns, Levi's, a tee-shirt, and a sweatshirt. An insulated Vietnam war era pea coat covered my back, zipped up in the front to ward off the wind. On my head, a faded old toboggan cap sat covered by the hood of my jacket. Long-wristed wool gloves under well-worn cowhide were tucked up into my sleeves, rounding out my defenses against the cold and most of the prickly semi-desert growth. I had my trusty, sturdy carved mesquite walking stick in my right hand.

Sugar, my manly-man female Cockapoo dog, was out in front of me on a northwesterly track, nose upturned against the now-stiffening breeze. She was traversing diagonally up the 'steps' as best as she could, displaying that sorta sideways gait older dogs are fond of. She had just moments before discovered a covey of bobwhite quail in her path—a bit unusual this far west, but not unheard of. She came at them like a thing possessed, and I had watched them fly up in a frenzy only to settle back down again in a mesquite patch not a hundred meters away. She was still following their scent when she pushed some blue quail out in front of her in the same direction. Some of the blues got up and flew a short distance before landing and running. Blues are about a third larger than bobwhites, and would much rather run than fly. I caught glimpses of the blues as they worked on up the slope, a total of about forty to fifty birds interspersed with flashes of bobwhite.

We had been out over an hour at that point, and I was ready to head back to some warmth. But instead, I found myself stopping about fifty meters from the mesquite thicket and standing stock still. I had a hunch of what was about to happen, and I didn't dare blink for fear of missing it. Sugar pushed ahead up the slope and shattered the tense silence, bobwhites exploding upward and fanning out across the horizon. Several blues joined them, and undoubtedly, the rest fled the scene on foot. And right on their tails, seven white-tailed does crashed out of the thicket and hightailed it up to the northwest. Sugar forgot all about the quail and set out after the deer. How proud she would be to bring one back to me. The chance of that happening was, of course, zero—but I wasn't about to let her know that. I caught glimpses of her through the rough terrain as the deer faded away ahead about a quarter of a kilometer later.

The breeze was cold on the exposed areas of my face, and my eyes wanted to tear. I told them no. My Ray Ban Aviators were a big help, shielding my eyes from the worst of the chill. I continued to stand stock still and gazed toward the thicket where the retreating deer were still being trailed by my mighty Cockapoo. When the buck appeared, it was as if he materialized straight out of the thicket. He stared after his ladies and the dog. He continued staring for several seconds until he seemed to sense something new on the downslope horizon. Very slowly, he turned his massive rack toward me until his eyes seemed to focus on mine. He tilted his head back a bit, put his nose in the air and snorted, steam rising, and billowing my way. I froze. I was downwind, but though my scent drifted away behind me, the buck was still wary of my presence. His head came down, and he pivoted up toward where his harem had retreated, staring northwestward again for a long while. He swung his gaze back to me once more, then again toward the gone girls. I was playing this game with a massive 30-point buck, easily enough to measure a gross score of over 270 and a net score of 260 with the Boone and Crockett Club. It would have been one of the largest bucks ever brought down in Texas if I had killed it. Hard to kill a full-grown buck with a walking stick, though. So, he got to live another day. It's not as if I had any desire to kill him in the first place.

His gaze came back to me and locked onto mine. Apparently, he was not going to let go this time. He snorted and pawed the ground once—a warning. Deer cannot differentiate a tree from a person, so long as that person is downwind and remains still and silent. But he seemed to remember that there was nothing that looked like me planted where I stood last time he checked, and the idea seemed to unnerve him.

It was perhaps two minutes since the game had started between us, and I was now truly cold from inactivity. The buck snorted and pawed the ground again, and this time, I did the same. I snorted, pawed the ground—telling him "Peace, brother" in his own language. But before I could complete the steps again, the buck had vaporized. Not once did I blink, nor did I take my eyes off of the magnificent creature. It simply vanished right before me. No sound, no bobbing white tail in the distance. No nothing. There was probably a lesson in the entire episode if I cared to learn, but I decided to save the philosophizing for later. My ass was cold so I headed back toward warmth. Sugar had decided to do the same. She was waiting for me at the trailer door fifteen minutes later when I arrived.

Sirocco's voice drew me back to the present, memories of the bitter cold melting in the face of the warmth of Mat's fireplace. "Want to come with me and Amber Lee?" she asked, and as much as I wanted to, I shook my head.

"I'm gonna hang here with Joe a bit," I told her. "Not sure what we'll do yet, but I'll meet you at RAFF Base Pierce no later than three days out. Hopefully we can find the right spot and see if there's more than one of these mysterious spheres hanging around. In and out as quickly as possible is the plan."

Sirocco nodded, and with a quick but significant kiss, she was gone.

I knew that she would be making her way back to Dallas Love in the morning, whirling her chopper past the city to land on the circular helipad slapped across the roof of her place. As she descended, she made sure to avoid the solar array garden surrounding the pad on the eastern end of the roof. She had installed the panels as original equipment and made significant upgrades based on technology from one of the companies associated with her world-wide-web of like-minded folks. Her entire building was powered by just a few units, with plenty of energy to spare.

The automatic trap opened and caught the skids, locking the bird down tight to the roof. If necessary, the mechanism could eject the bird eastward off of the building, trusting that it would achieve lift before making a crater in the street far below.

Sirocco shut the bird down, completed her post-flight routine and log, then bailed out onto the roof. She tapped a quick code into her satphone, watching as the roof hatch silently slid up and sideways to allow her entry to the spiral staircase below. The stairs led down into her suite, but they weren't the only bug-out route. There was another spiral staircase towards the western end of the roof, also accessible via a computer-controlled hatch.

The automation with code-only access extended to the dedicated elevator, the building doors, and even the basement parking levels. Sirocco took no chances. The reception area was also monitored and always staffed with at least one highly skilled security guard. Visits were by invite only, with the reception folks sending encrypted notices of arrival. The elevators did not stop at the floor below her penthouse either. That floor was dedicated to functional quarters, a full kitchen, and a spa. Elsewhere, on the perimeter, were rooms filled with specialized equipment Sirocco had everything ranging from top of the line, state-of-the-art computers to gas chromatographs to a transmission electron microscope at her disposal. She could move freely between the two floors by way of a double stairway, or via the single internal elevator that connected the two floors.

The first thing that Sirocco always did when arriving home was to grab a quick, steaming hot shower. She'd take her time dressing herself after that, layering on jeans, hiking boots, and leather over leather for a shirt and jacket. She pulled her warm-weather bag from its place in the travel closet. Out of habit she opened the kit, emptied it then repacked it. Experience told her if she packed it, check it twice. If someone else packed it—check it thrice. She coded the hatch and was climbing the spiral stairs when she got a call from the front desk.

"Ms. Sirocco, Tommy here. I just wanted to let you know that your guests have arrived and are about to head up in the elevator."

That definitely gave her pause. If Sirocco ever had a visitor coming, she knew it ahead of time.

"Great!" Sirocco lied through her teeth, quickly taking stock of the area around her. "Could you let them know I might be a few minutes?"

"Yes, indeed. I'll let them know," Tommy said before clicking off.

Well damn, thought Sirocco. This threw a wrench in her plans. She made her way up the stairs and, using voice-activation, called John. He answered on the first ring.

"John, I'm headed for my chopper on the roof of my building. Security just called me to let me know I have guests coming up." Even though she could have sounded panicked, her voice gave nothing away. "Please yo-yo them for a couple of days—up and down at varying intervals, until you can see through the cameras that they are toast. Nothing fatal—I just need them beaten silly. And if they hurt Tommy...well, I leave it up to you, you sensitive old machine."

By then, she had made it to the roof, firing up the rotary wings through a code on her satphone.

"Sirocco, I've locked the elevators down for now at the 50-meter mark. I also have a crew headed toward your building, eta three minutes. They will secure things inside and out."

"And Tommy?"

"From the lobby cameras, Tommy appears to have had his clock cleaned, but he should survive." John had apparently been watching old John Wayne movies or some such shit.

"Good," Sirocco said. "I'm about to head out for San Antonio, where Amber Lee will meet up with me. We're on the mil flight you arranged to Perth, chopper and all. Let Mark and Mat know about the intruders. I want to know everything you can find out about them. Testicle size will be useful to know."

She clicked off and climbed into the chopper, securing the door as she continued ramping up the rpm's. Once she had double-latched the belts across her chest, she punched the 'eject' code into her satphone. The skid trap accelerated upward, unlatched its grip, and tossed the bird up and over the side of the building. Sirocco was in free fall perhaps a third of the way down before the bird trapped enough air and leveled off. Sirocco brought it around the western edge of the building and turned south toward San Antonio.

Once she was stable, Sirocco called Amber Lee and told her what had happened, warning her to watch her beautiful ass on the way down southeast to San Antonio. Worst case scenario, though, they knew that John was watching both of their backs. Amber Lee was driving a 1964 Ford GT her pawpaw had restored and let her drive. No one else, that means no one else, could drive that machine. She grabbed a water bottle at Andy's on River Road in Concan and climbed back in, cranking the deep-throated animal, when a pickup slid to a halt sideways in the gravel and effectively cut her off. She noted the cheap, silver-framed mirrored sunglasses, crooked nose, rotten-toothed grin, filing the information away for later. And then, without hesitation, Amber Lee slammed the floor shifter into reverse, executed a 180 on a dime, and slid sideways off the gravel up onto the pavement, shooting off southeast bound on 127. It was about twelve minutes to 90. She was skipping up the east-bound entry ramp in just six minutes flat.

On his end, John had picked up the asshole in the pickup. He wasted no time relaying to the Sabinal sheriff information concerning the guy's vehicle, description, and the notion that he was a wanted outlaw and pot-smoking hippie trying to rape, pillage, and plunder to his heart's content. A bit later, John watched as the shithead was dragged out of his truck, slammed face-first into the asphalt, and tossed into the back of a patrol car. Amazing how cool it is to have access to spy satellites.

The question still remained, though: Who the fuck were these guys and what did they want? They seemed to be everywhere, always a step ahead. And none of us were used to getting outwitted.

Once she was speeding down the US 90 eastbound, Amber Lee rang up Sirocco with the news about the asshole in the pickup. Together, they decided that a diversion or two might be in order since these assholes seemed to be everywhere.

"My submersible is under shelter at the Dwell at Clear Lake next to the Johnson Space Center, Houston." Amber Lee was trying to get ahead of the game. "I want to take it with us. Can we divert to Ellington Field from San Antonio? If so, I'll have it hauled over there as soon as we ring off."

"I'll make it happen," Sirocco said. "Just hang tight, and try not to get yourself killed. I'll see you in a bit."

Edward

The slapping sound of a book smacking on a desktop reverberated through the room. Edward Dahlgreen's hand gripped the Oxford Bible so tightly that his fingers trembled. The cover showed a slight indentation where the book had contacted the edge of a richly decorated black walnut desk, a dramatic piece, with ornate marquetry inlays of stone, mother of pearl, and rare woods that rimmed the center and impressed all visitors. Those who looked closely enough might notice that the elaborate inlays weren't random, but instead depicted a series of thirty-six bible scenes. The desktop alone had cost over half a million dollars.

Edward tried unsuccessfully to control his anger. Damn his son, Brent, and damn the expensive mercenaries he had hired. No matter how hard he tried to distract himself, all he could seem to do was silently repeat the curse in his mind. Five men, four of whom were trained and armed professionals, had been defeated and disarmed by two science nerds and a woman. Geologists, no less. Doctors, engineers, even theoretical physicists he could understand, but geologists? How had it happened? They were so close to obtaining the artifacts, objects he and his group had been desperately tracking for years.

The medical report had barely shown any signs of a struggle. It was as if the mercenaries had just handed over their weapons of their own free will. There were, however, traces of some sort of previously unknown, possibly hallucinogenic compound in Brent's bloodstream. Damn the Solido bitch, too.

Cardinal DelBassey had warned him. The Catholic Church in Brazil had long noted the activities of the Solido women. Witches was the word DelBassey had used, not him, but he could believe it now. Satan's spawn, snatching his victory right out of his hand when he was so close to the finish line.

Edward pushed the Bible back into the center of the desk and rested his forehead in the palms of his hands, fingers massaging the areas around his temples. He could feel a headache coming on. In just two hours, he had a meeting scheduled with DelBassey and the Imam Ahmed Najdi, one which he had been dreading for some time now. It was an unholy alliance that disturbed him. Idle worshipers and heathens were a group he never counted on as business associates. But, it was where the Lord had led him.

Edward sat beneath a magnificent stained glass window on the east wall of his private study. It was the first thing people saw as they entered the room, a piece of art designed to impress. The room itself measured 20 feet by 40 feet, with a 12-foot high ceiling. The walls were clad in custom dark cherry wood paneling. Inset over long stretches in the walls were bookshelves stuffed with leather spines, only breaking for alcoves lined with priceless artwork. A single plush Persian carpet graced the length of the room.

The total cost had been well over 10 million dollars to put together his inner sanctum. Edward had insisted on the study, and the board of deacons had easily acquiesced. He knew some thought it vain or extravagant, but God had answered him during a long prayer vigil and placed the design in his mind. He knew he was favored in the eyes of the Lord, and he hoped he was up to the task now being asked of him.

Edward had inherited a vibrant church from his father, but under his watchful eye, it had grown to one of the largest megachurches in the country. Currently, there were two main campuses. One was located in the vicinity of River Oaks, Houston, and the other on the west side of the sprawling metropolis near Katy. The church currently maintained a small fleet of helicopters so Edward could conduct Sunday services in both locations without having to fight the traffic.

Natural good looks and an uncannily charming demeanor had served him well. But it was his photographic memory for faces and personal details that ultimately let him work his magic. It took only a single conversation, and years later, he could see the person again and pick up the conversation like no time had passed. Asking after the children and spouses, and even remembering the names of pets and favorite sports teams. He could charm anyone.

Edward glanced at the folder on the left edge of his desk and frowned about the unpleasantness required tomorrow. An elderly widowed parishioner had recently passed, and he had visited her often near the end. Through his conversations with her concerning the church's unfinished work, the Lord had touched her heart, and she left the bulk of her 30 million dollar estate to the church. Her will was changed near the end of her life, and her two children were contesting the final document.

Edward did not consider himself directly involved in this. She had simply mentioned wanting to adjust the will, and he had volunteered the church's law firm to help her out. God had led her to make the changes, not Edward. Still, he would have to attend the deposition. He was astounded how often people refused to see the Lord's hand in daily events.

He calmed himself, and the headache started to recede. After the incident in Eugene, Oregon, Dover had disappeared into thin air and gone to ground. His security people had no leads. The conversation with DelBassey and Najdi would be tense. They both represented powerful interests, and he was sure both of them would be none too pleased with the unfortunate turn of events.

The relentless attack of science on the foundation of God's kingdom was the work of Satan. He heard it in the voices of innocent children when they questioned why evolution was blasphemous, or whether the Earth was older than stated in the Bible. This misinformation was why the church ran its own secondary schools. Yes, the schools were financially profitable, but the real prize was children educated in the Truth.

If half of what was whispered about these newly found artifacts was true, then the repercussions would rock the foundations of Christianity. People would fail to see that the artifacts were simply shiny objects from the depths of hell, designed to test the faithful. The Bible was clear that man was created by God and placed on Earth to serve Him. The universe is simply the stage God created to test men and women and find those who are worthy. Nothing more, and nothing less.

Edward understood that the Lord had provided him with incredible wealth as part of a larger plan. Surely this was the test, and no funds would be spared to stop the heresy.

The Cardinal and the Imam arrived together. Edward didn't like the unbelievers in his inner sanctum, but he couldn't deny that he needed their help. So, the charm oozed out of him as he stood up to greet them, guiding them both toward a sitting area at the north end of the room.

DelBassey was a large man to start with, and he had let himself go with age. A protruding belly showed below his garments, and the excess weight was also carried in a face with tan puffy skin surrounding a pair of dark, difficult-to-read eyes. The Imam was thin as a rail, to the point where he was almost gaunt. He was Edward's age but seemed to lack any real strength in his legs or upper body. His movement betrayed a fragility, which had been prematurely bestowed upon him. Edward exercised for an hour every day, and he felt positively young as he sat across from the two other men.

The Cardinal shifted from side to side, trying to comfortably place his weight in the dark blue leather chair before he spoke. "We have unfortunately failed in this first gambit," he said, pulling his face into a dour frown. Edward understood that by "We," what he really meant was, "You." But he didn't let it phase his smile. If anything, he bared more teeth in his smile while the Imam simply nodded.

"It was unfortunate," retorted Edward. "I underestimated the Solido woman, even though you warned me about her." Best to let the Cardinal bask in some small sense of victory, he thought. He continued, telling the two, "She released some sort of hallucinogenic powder into the room and immobilized the team. Witchcraft, if I ever saw it." As he spoke, he pulled up the footage from one of the mercenary's body cam to show the two men.

The Imam was quick to pick on several points. "The powder seems to have no effect on Dover or his companion," he noted, brow furrowed. "And clearly, the woman is not affected. Also, did you notice at the very left edge of the field of view? It appears Dover extracts a water sample and several objects on his way out."

"Yes," said Edward. "We noticed. We also know that the government crew that showed up several minutes later took everything remaining in the pressure container, and—"

DelBassey interrupted. "The witch is using some natural compound developed by the primitive spirit-worshipers she studies in the jungle. We have received reports of this sort of thing being used against us before. She and her companions must have taken an antidote ahead of time to counteract it."

Edward mentally kicked himself now for not paying more attention to the Cardinal's warnings on the Solido woman. The Imam nodded at the information, but Edward was quickly becoming agitated. "I have no idea what use a water sample is to Dover," he sneered. "But the objects, these are what we desperately need. And soon."

The only reason I am in this unholy alliance is for the artifacts, thought Edward. His initial approach to the problem had only included the Catholic Church. They had access to resources not available to him, and DelBassey was a long-standing acquaintance. The two of them had met years ago at a summit for Christian Fundamentalism. Despite his association with Catholicism, the Cardinal had proven, over the years, to be a staunch believer in the literal interpretation of the Bible.

Fundamentalists were, in Edward's mind, the only true believers. The Bible was a divine gift to mankind from the hand of God. The words, thoughts, and wishes of a singular God were given to men as an act of benevolence. Strict adherence to the words of this Holy Book provided the only means for a man to connect with God. Through a man's adherence to His word, women could also share in the grace of the Lord. Edward's devotion to the book was complete, and now that he had calmed himself, he regretted slapping it on his desk in anger.

All that people needed to live in this world was wholly contained in the Bible, and anything else fell into the realm of sin. Therein lay the problem. The rumors passed around in the fundamentalist circles were that ancient objects, not of human origin, were being discovered. Edward was not bothered by the four-billion-year age attributed to the objects. That was nonsense for anyone who had bothered to study the Truth. It was an old argument that, in his opinion, the church had won. His massive, wealthy congregation was proof of that victory.

No, the real issue was the technology. Objects created by a civilization more advanced than our own was a huge problem for him and for the church as a whole. Regardless of whether the creators of the artifacts were from an alien world or just an ancient earthbound civilization, they were not mentioned in the Bible. If the Bible contained the true history of the planet, then why did it make no mention of this civilization? How could people rely on a guide to living that proved to be false, unreliable? Other parts of the Holy Book might then be called into question, and that was something that Edward could not abide.

DelBassey had recognized the problem as well. If the Bible was fallible, then the flock would lose their faith. The logical foundations of fundamentalism would crumble. In his heart of hearts, Edward knew that the Bible would prevail regardless. His faith was why God had picked him to deal with this crisis. The key was in the artifacts. If they could obtain one and truly examine it, Edward was confident that God would reveal the objects to be Satan's tools. People were generally unaware of how clever, how subtle the Grand Deceiver could be. Edward resolved that he would not be fooled, and God's faith in him would be justified.

The Cardinal had insisted on bringing the Imam into their inner circle. Edward had resisted at first, but finally consented based on DelBassey's insistence that the Imam would be able to bring state secrets to the table. Information that was unattainable to them otherwise. Again, DelBassey had proven insightful.

Powerful connections between the government and institutionalized religion exist in parts of the world like Saudi Arabia and Iran. Religion is a preferred tool of the State for keeping adversarial political opponents in check and controlling the general population. This strong connection between political power and religious conformity is essential to the continuity of these places. Imam Najdi was indeed well connected, and despite Edward's initial misgivings, the group had greatly benefited from the information he alone was able to bring to the table.

The men discussed the situation for over an hour and agreed to maintain their current course of action, pursuing Dover and his associates. The scientist had not completely eluded them; he was somewhere in the Dallas area. The Imam had information that seemed to have come from inside the US government, and Edward knew better than to ask any questions.

The only disagreement stemmed from the level of force to be applied to the task at hand. Violence was a distinct possibility. DelBassey had implied that his people believed the witch was expendable, and despite his feelings on the Solido woman, Edward inwardly recoiled a bit. Theft was one thing; murder was in a whole other league. In the end, though, he knew that sacrifice was necessary to ensure that God's will prevailed.

The Sentinel (Mark)

Mat decided to keep a low profile and was somewhere in the Dallas area. For all I knew, he was going to saw that marble in two and blow us all halfway to hell. On our end, Joe and I were wrapping things up before heading out for Kangaroo land. I asked Joe where Hunter was, but he had no idea. When we rang him up on my satphone we found him losing his ass at the high roller blackjack tables, first floor at the back of the Beau Rivage in Biloxi, Mississippi.

"Not doing so hot then, I take it?" I smirked into the phone, and Hunter let out a scoff on the other end.

"Tell you what, I'm about ready to head back up to my room, throw a chair through the window, and follow it down 25 floors to the pool level!"

Hunter seemed to be in a jovial mood. I had never met the guy, but I liked him already. I told him to grab a steak and a good bottle of wine at BR Prime on me. Add the crab legs. I briefly told him about what had happened to the girls and asked if he could lend a hand. I knew I needed some help from outside the circle on this one, and from what I had heard, Hunter was the person to go to for information.

"So, to the point—you run over to Sabinal, go pay bail for the asshole and determine who he works for," I said, quickly laying out his part in my grand plan. "Leave him with blurred vision, a permanent limp, whatever the shithead deserves as you see fit. From there, you get up to Dallas and retrieve the yoyos from the elevator. I want to know everything. Eye color, hair color, height, weight, next-of-kin, last wishes, and testicle size." I was succinct.

"Finally, something worth getting excited about!" he whooped. "I swear I was about ten minutes from splattering myself on the veranda. Now I'm Texas-bound and in hot pursuit of some assholes that get off picking on ladies." I think we made his day. "Alright, so you want me to gather a bit of intel and relay it back to you. Not a problem. What then?"

"We might need you in Perth in a couple of days," I told him. "Can you turn all this around in that timeframe?"

"Yes sir, I believe I can. "You owe me a steak, 'cause I'm blowing this hotdog stand as we speak. I'll be across the Intracoastal on I-110 in about ten minutes, westbound on I-10 three minutes later—probably make San Antonio in six hours, seven tops, take care of business, do Dallas, then grab a plane toward Aussieland. Specifics on the southbound travel?"

I liked Hunter more by the minute. Joe ain't much on conversation, but when he brings a guy along, you know he has your back. That can be comforting.

"Hunter, you will get a call from a guy named John in a few minutes," I said. "He'll hook you up with a black card for expenses and arrange flights for you. If you need anything—food, transport, rocket launchers, whatever—ring John up, and he'll make it happen."

Hunter paused, deep in thought. "I might be needing some things," he said slowly. "Both here and down south. Might be a bit expensive, though."

I didn't know exactly he had in mind, and, to tell the truth, I did not give a big happy damn. "The black card does not ask questions; it just makes purchases. Doesn't leave any trails, either," I told him. "Remember that John can do magic—in Texas, or anywhere else on the planet. Do not hesitate to use him."

"So after Dallas, I head on down to Aussieland. What then?" Hunter asked. No bullshit, just down to business.

"You'll be meeting some of our friends in Castletown. Don't worry, they're more than capable. They'll have an array of armaments so you can travel light southbound from Texas."

Joe had assured me that if anyone could get me the information I needed, it was Hunter. There were some things that even John couldn't glean from cyberspace. I needed more insight into who was tracking us if I was going to take the suckers down, especially if they were going to make the mistake of threatening me and mine.

"Just to make sure we're on the same page," Hunter said, snapping me back to reality. "I understand that no one will miss the assholes in Texas if things get out of hand. Correct?" Neat way to ask if you can kill bad guys if necessary.

"Correct. The sane world will not miss men that mistreat women." My mind flashed back the guy that landed in D.C. in 2016, but I had to chase the thought away before I let myself get distracted. It's hard to win a fight when all you see is red. So instead of letting myself stew, I rang off and called John.

"John, Mark here." Do not ask me why I said that. If you did, the only reply I'd have for you is that I'm just fucking stupid.

"Yes sir, I'm aware it's you." John was still doing the Aussie thing. The snark, though, was definitely not an act. I was beginning to think being insufferable was part of his coding.

"Contact Hunter," I told him. "It's the last number I used. Fix him up with a black card, and he'll let you know the timing to fly him from Dallas to Perth."

"Very good. Will there be anything else?"

"Yeah, there will," I said, grinning to myself. "How are the yoyos doing?"

Inquiring minds want to know.

"The two yoyos, as you colloquialize, are currently laying in various forms of their own excrement, bobbing up and down at random intervals, suspended between the solid poured concrete slab walls. They scream occasionally, but of course, no one can hear them but me. I offer reassurances occasionally through the embedded sound system, letting them know that someone will arrive someday and take them out of their misery. They seem too cowardly to eat their pistols, so I probably am correct."

Damn, John was completely heartless. A heartless fucking computer. What's next?

"Well, they've got a rescue party heading their way now," I said, glancing over at the clock. "Hunter will give you his ETA momentarily. Have a housekeeping crew on standby—his mission does not include wiping the asses of bad guys, alright? And be sure to keep another crew nearby on lookout. I want Mat and me up-to-date on everything that's going on down there."

John gave me the metaphorical thumbs up, and I thanked him, hanging up the satphone with a muted beep. With him and Hunter on the trail of our assailants, I felt a bit of a load lift off of my chest. Still, I couldn't shake the weight from my shoulders entirely. We still didn't know just who was standing behind our new stalkers, or what kind of resources they had at their disposal.

I sat back and did my thousand-yard gaze. I had been thinking about something for a while, and it seemed to crystalize at that moment. It has been rumored that around fifty, maybe one hundred individuals at any one time actually hold the essence of power on planet Earth. Upon examination from an historical perspective, this seems to hold true. Nations rise and fall, societies flourish for no apparent reason while others, seemingly bound for glory, wither on the vine. Sometimes the faces have been recognizable, and the names well known. More often than not, however, the showmen were just that—puppets in the spotlight. The strings were pulled by unseen and unseeable puppeteers, calling the shots but never there to take the credit. Powerful folks with a definite agenda, but without the desire to be recognized. Standing back in the shadows, changing ocean currents, creating ripples in time itself that impacted the entire planet. These folks enjoyed the fruits of their labor, either positive or negative, outside the glare of public scrutiny. It seems that the magic elixir of true power has never needed the artificial stimulus of public praise or scorn.

Unquestionably, this is true today. The titans of industry may appear to be riding the bowsprit of the clipper ships of old, but the reality is that they are beholden to shareholders, to the whims of forces beyond their control. Puppets. The question is, who's holding the strings? Whoever we'd been dealing with, they were just grunts—muscle. We needed to follow the money and find out just who was hiring these guys to make our lives hell.

As I made my way with Joe through security at PDX, I decided we might need some extra help. Things were spiraling in directions I had not experienced before. Mat had muttered the same sentiment before tottering off to his mischief. The team we had assembled was formidable, without a doubt. But it seemed that with where this thing was headed, we might need a puppetmaster of our own. Someone capable of mobilizing not just non-trivial funds, but also governments. Someone with the clout to change the ocean's tides. Perhaps a sentinel of sorts. I wondered if I might be able to conjure up another buck for the history books, even if it was just the illusion of power behind us.

Joe and I grabbed venti Americanos at Starbucks and headed to the departure gate. One priority pass later and we were sitting in the first-class suite, free from prying ears. I pulled out my satphone and rang John up once again.

"Good day, sir, and how may I help you?" John was still in his Aussie mode, and his accent hadn't gotten much better. I just let it go.

"John, I'm feeling a bit philosophical at the moment. Quite honestly, I'm overwhelmed by the complexity of our current undertaking." I was actually trying to elicit emotion—sympathy, in this case—from a fucking machine. What the hell was I thinking? As if reading my mind, John let out what was very obviously a sarcastic "tut."

"Yes sir, I understand completely." John understood completely. My ass. If he'd been anyone else—namely, a human with a neck—I would have choked him. Once again, though, I forced myself just to let it go.

"John, you are aware of almost everything that has been and is going on with our current big adventure," I said. "Correct?"

"Yes, sir. Most of it. I suspect Mat is holding a card or two away from the table, though." Huh. Smart machine.

"Mat is prone to keep some things to himself." Fucking understatement of the decade. "I'm sure he has his reasons. Just tell me this, John—do we have the resources to carry this thing through to the end?"

John sighed. "No sir."

Well damn. The seven hundred-foot drop to the Rio Grande from the Gorge Bridge outside of Taos was looking more and more to be a likely option. About six-and one-half seconds of free flight to touchdown. Maybe Hunter did have the right idea.

"Ah, without prying into your business...do you think someone, maybe some organization, might help us out? At least even out the odds?" Boy, am I subtle.

"Yes, sir. I suspect there exists a person or two with the ability to make the scrum worthwhile." Shit! He was talking rugby now? I'll just ditch the car right there over the Gorge in the middle of the bridge in the westbound lane at the sidewalk cutouts and ignore the Suicide Hotline phone as I launch myself over the handrail.

"So John," I growled out. "Without getting into personal details, do you think you might be able to put us in touch with someone who has the clout to bring it all home? Perhaps a sentinel?" Notice I set up the machine to test its pride. Are you a badass or not, Johnny boy?

Without skipping a beat, he said, "I can make some inquiries, sir."

Well, that shut me down.

"Thank you John. And please, be sure to let Mat and me know as soon as there are developments." John gave me the affirmative and I clicked off, preparing to become a sardine for the lengthy trip ahead.

I put my tan foam earplugs in, closed my eyes, and tried to decide if I wanted the plane to auger in or make it in one piece.

We finally touched down in PER after flying just shy of forever. The first thing I did when the fasten seatbelt sign flickered off was to hook up with Sirocco by satphone. I knew that she could take care of herself, but still, I was relieved when I heard she and Amber Lee had arrived safely at Perth RAAF Base Pearce. The chopper and the sub had been stacked aboard the de Havilland DHC-4 Caribou – STOL Master. Short takeoff and landing. Essential to gain enough lift to clear the trees at the end of the runway and vice versa—to avoid plowing into the forest on landing. The plane had an extended fuel package, naturally. It could land, offload, get refueled, and be airborne again in 20 minutes flat. Efficiency was the goal at Esperance.

Once I knew that Sirocco was alive and well, I noticed I had a missed call message blinking on my satphone screen. It was new. No message though. In our world, it was considered standard procedure to leave as little evidence behind as possible. Messages were a big no-no. I rang up Hunter.

"I left Sabinal empty-handed I'm afraid," he said. "They caught the guy; Deputy had him holed up in a jail cell. Told me that when he came to, the guy was muttering something about his wives. That's right, wives—as in plural. Deputy left him a tray of food, and when he came back, he said the guy was hanging from the top bar of the bunk with his belt around his neck. Dead as a doornail. The Deputy was seriously shook up about it. I comforted him by saying I wasn't a lawyer, just a messenger, and left him to decipher that. Course, now that there's nothing keeping me here, I'll be heading to Dallas ASAP."

"Alright. Let me know when you get in." Hunter clicked off, and the line went dead.

Well damn. It seemed somebody could make folks kill themselves if captured. Sounded like some kind of 007 shit. What could be worse than dying? It was hard to feel sorry for the guy after all the trouble he'd caused me, but even I could see that he'd gotten himself in deeper

166

than he could handle. I briefly wondered if it was somehow related to his multiple wives. Either way, I shot out a quick text to let Mat know what I had learned. He seemed to think things were fleshing themselves out. So much for sanity.

Just as I was typing in a less-than-savory emoticon, my screen lit up with an incoming call from John. Friggin' satphone bill would be about a million dollars this month.

"Mark, I have engaged with the Sentinel." John didn't bother with formalities this time. "It seems that you, Mat, and the Sentinel share some common goals. The Sentinel has no desire to become known to you, though—or anyone else, for that matter. If you want him to speak to him, I can act as liaison and connect you via satphone. I'll be filtering the voice so it is unrecognizable. For you, it will sound Southern. Mat will hear plain American English."

Funny machine. I've never met anything, living or otherwise, that makes me want to pop someone in the windpipe like that son of a motherboard.

I told John, "Let Mat know, then. He'll be the primary contact. This is his shit show, I'm just a bit player along for the ride. And...thanks, John." However much the machine annoyed me, I couldn't deny the fact that I owed him one. John hummed, seeming pleased with himself.

"I will let Mat know posthaste. And you are most welcome, sir." Back to the butler voice. I rolled my eyes, clicking off and dialing in Tom's number to see how things were on his end. John had all of us secured from prying ears or tracers.

It turned out that Tom and company were en-route as we spoke. He seemed comfortable in his support role, even though plenty of people would have bailed by now. No surprise there. I knew the guy was tough as cut nails the first time I'd spoken to him.

Something Amber Lee said earlier had made me think we might be able to utilize an aquatic diversion—something I figured Tom and his crew would be more than capable of pulling off. Hell, nothing wrong with having a backup plan and a backdoor just in case. I asked if he could arrange to have a fishing trawler on standby, something able to drag a net around the point.

"A diversion—of course!" I could practically hear Tom's grin through the line. "Excellent way for a mini to enter and leave the scene without detection. One of my cousins has just the trick, I think. He works out of West Beach. I'll make it happen, you have my word. Anything else for now?"

I swear on a bottle of 60-year-old Macallan, I am well and truly getting too old for this shit. The guy had already finished the whole operation and was back home in Jillora Bindi's arms, safe and sound. And where was I? Still trying to get my fucking bag off the carousel so I could stagger outside to catch the ride up to the base.

Joe and I made it out to the curb and jumped into the older, well-worn Range Rover Tom had arranged. The driver shot us up 95, and in thirty minutes we were offloading our gear beside the de Havilland. He handed me a scuffed up, hard-shell case the size of a carry-on, we shook hands, and with a quick "Cheers!" he drove off.

Sirocco and Amber Lee were happy to see us, and we were equally excited to see them. We climbed aboard the rig with them and the pilot whirled up the props on the twin 1,450 horsepower Pratt & Whitney R-2000 Twin Wasp radial piston engines. Amber Lee's sub was snugged in and strapped down forward, while Sirocco's chopper was resting nose to the rear on a low-slung wheeled trolley. The landing gear had been popped off, the rotors snugged and laid back in order fit into the available space. It would take about five minutes to get the bird flight-worthy once we landed in Esperance. The trip would take about two and a half hours cruising at three thousand meters over a few hills comprising Mundaring State Forest, then nothing but sparsely populated farms, ranches, and open grass and woodlands.

We donned headsets and strapped into the fold-down jump seats set into the wall of the fuselage. This was going to be a utilitarian ride. I set the case the driver gave me at my feet and popped the latches after we had leveled off, revealing a collection of Blackhawk tactical gear neatly laid on top. There were eight cutouts under the black webbed units, four Glock 19 Gen 5 G34 Competition 9x19mm pistols. A bit large at nine inches overall length, but most handy if the range extends out to 80 meters or so. Close range, it can be your best friend. Further out, it's about as reliable as they come.

The other four cutouts each held six standard 17-shot magazines, loaded with Federal Premium 124gr HST JUP rounds. I passed out the webbed gear, guns, and ammo like it was lunch on a picnic table in the park. Each of us triple checked our weapons—magazines slid into the locked position and released before deeming the guns ready for use. Belt and holster rigs were adjusted, spare mags were stowed in the side sleeves, extra ammo stowed in backpacks. Once everyone was comfortable with the way the rigs hung, they were stowed into backpacks as well. The chances of having to defend ourselves seemed extremely low, but there is nothing wrong with being prepared. It's a Boy Scout thing.

As we flew over the green fields surrounding Perth, I couldn't help but think back to some boys I met a few years ago in Perry, Florida. An old friend had invited me down to shoot bobwhite quail with him and his bird dog, Miller. I was shooting a Bettinsoli Overland ELS .410, full choke, with Winchester X41 high brass 7½ shot as ammo. Not a lot of lead in the air, but the power pattern to drop a bird at 50+ meters so long as you don't flinch.

The birds were still wild here—no cage-raised birds for Carlos. The humid air was filled with hints of palmetto and soft pine, the muggy stillness allowing us to hear the single-note call of a redheaded woodpecker, the shrill whoop of a Cooper's hawk talking with a friend. We made our limit in record time and thoroughly enjoyed the outing to boot. There is almost nothing that beats working with a dog that can hold on point, even as you walk the wild birds up. Miller held on point time and time again, waited patiently time and time again. He would sit stock still and watch the birds push out in a fan, either fading into the distance or exploding in a puff of feathers and plummet to the ground. On command, Miller retrieved the fatalities.

We had walked several miles through the open woodlands and savannah-like territory that day, and we had come upon trails of total destruction several times. Carlos, my old friend, and guide, told me that it was the work of feral hogs.

"What the hell are feral hogs?" We were back in his well-used gray and red '96 F-150 XLT 4WD, bouncing over ruts in the dirt track. Even though I was fairly certain I already knew, I thought it was best to ask in case I was way off-base. Turned out, they were pigs that had escaped captivity over the years and turned wild. Not that hogs aren't pretty fucking wild to begin with if you have ever been around the domesticated variety. But these guys could grow to monstrous sizes—600 pounds or so, even larger if hunters' tall tales are to be believed. According to Carlos, though, most didn't get to more than 200 pounds.

It wasn't the size that made the hogs so dangerous. Both sexes have tusks up to about seven inches long, sharp as a straight-edge, and they're not afraid to use them for self-defense. A pig might not sound like much of an adversary, but get on the wrong side of a wild hog, and you might see more of your insides than you'd like.

Thousands upon thousands of these things were loose in the South, causing untold damage to land around the area. They were a particular problem for local farmers, as they favored certain crops like peanuts, soybeans, and corn. But really, given the chance, those hogs would eat virtually anything. Their diet was simple. See food, eat it.

A short drive later and Carlos pulled into the pea gravel and oyster shell parking lot of Deals Famous Oyster House on US 98. To me, there is no better natural material with which to pave a parking lot than oyster shells. We settled ourselves at a four-seat square wooden table with woven ladderback chairs for support. The air was filled to capacity with the smell of brine-soaked oysters, fried catfish, boiling crab, hushpuppies, and soft conversations.

Carlos and I ordered small plates of everything in the air, including shrimp, scallops, soft shell crab, beans, coleslaw, and a full platter of hushpuppies. Two dozen oysters on the half shell arrived almost as soon as we sat down, and we immediately went to tuck in. Like I said—it don't get no better than this. Years ago, I was able to suck down oysters like there was no tomorrow--I still remember eating twelve dozen on the half-shell at Felix's on Bourbon Street, all in one sitting. Washed down with a few local drafts from a brewery no longer in existence. In more recent years, though, I have not managed to suck down more than eight dozen or so at a time. Must be getting older.

As we ate, two boys wandered in through the front door. I might not have paid them any mind if Carlos hadn't called them over. They were six foot, slim, maybe 25 years old, wearing tusks carved into necklaces, belt buckles, and sheath knives. Both were wearing roughout cowboy boots, and one had a denim pearl button shirt tucked into his jeans. We stood, and I shook a pair of firm, outstretched hands. Carlos got big grins and bear hugs.

"Tommy! Sam! Sit down boys, we just ordered," he said, slapping the seat next to him. "Mary, can these handsome young men order, please? One check, I'm feeling generous today!" Carlos was well known in these parts and highly respected as an entrepreneur, rancher, hunter—just all-around good guy. We waited for the boys to place their orders, after which Carlos leaned in and asked, "So, what mischief have you boys been up to?"

Sam laughed. "Got two hogs in the truck, taking them over to the ranch. Got a yank coming down tomorrow to take a look. We'll make a buck or two hopefully!"

Between the two of them, Sam seemed to be the talker. From what I could gather, both boys worked with Carlos, and while I didn't know in just what capacity, I could place a good bet judging by the tusk bone around their necks.

"So how do you hunt hogs?" I was thinking it might be a good way to spend an extra day in paradise, and I was sure that these guys were all more than qualified to show me the ropes. Tommy grinned, taking a deep sip of his beer.

"Well, we got two bay dogs—Lacy dogs—and two catch dogs, a couple of American bulldogs. First, we release the bay dogs and let them track down the hog. We're walking fast and running once those Lacies are yelping on a hog. They change pitch when they're up close on an animal, see? We get in there soon as we hear that, then release the bulldogs. They drive right in and try to grab the hog behind the ears. Allows them to hold the hog still, if we're lucky. We move in, lash the hog's legs together, and then pull the dogs off." Tommy could also hold his own in the talking department.

"After that," he continued, "we run a stout pole through the trusses and each shoulder one end. Haul it back to the truck and run it over to the ranch, release it on a twenty-five-acre wooded plot surrounded by buried and reinforced fencing. Then we'll rinse and repeat the whole exercise with the yank. Of course, the hunt will go fairly quickly on such a small piece of land. That's the idea. Get the hunter on the hog and let him do the trussing." He paused, and must have noticed the eager look on my face. "Do you want to hunt one of the hogs tomorrow afternoon Mr. Mark?" he asked, a smirk ghosting over his face. I shook my head and sighed.

"Damn, you know there is almost nothing I'd rather do," I said, "but I have to be in Houston tomorrow afternoon." Bullshit—but the chances of me tackling a fucking 200-pound wild hog hovered around zero. "You know, this whole thing seems a bit dangerous. What guns do you carry just in case?"

Both Tommy and Sam balked at the mention of guns, all but rolling their eyes at my American ass. To underline the potential dangers, both boys pointed out scars on their arms, legs, and even torsos.

"No guns go into the woods, Mr. Mark," Tommy said gravely. "Yanks will shoot the dogs, for sure. And we don't want to take the chance of hitting one either—or ourselves, for that matter. Besides, the capture is the ultimate rush. The hunt is $500. If the yank wants a kill, then it's an extra $1,000, mounted and shipped anywhere in the U.S. Half the price for locals and friends. Yanks don't seem to feel right unless you fuck them a little!" Tommy laughed.

The food was good, the company was excellent. We polished off every last bit of our meal before parting ways. The boys thanked me and hugged Carlos, while I picked up the tab.

Looking at Carlos, you'd never guess that a few years back his life had been hanging by a thread. He had recovered nicely from the near-fatal beating he had taken at the hands of some transient neo-Nazis several years ago. Apparently, only Aryan, Anglo-Saxon, pathologically warped shitheads should be allowed to walk the planet. He was in ICU when I got word. I flew halfway around the world, hoping to hold his hand one more time before they dumped him in a hole and shoveled dirt over his carcass. He would have probably lost everything, the ranch included, but I slid my black card into the right hands at the hospital. Rumor has it that the Nazi assholes were picked up by the boys and some friends for a hog hunting trip. I'm guessing the only thing left of them now is some hog shit—no arms, no legs, no boots, no teeth, no nothing. It always remained a rumor because there was no evidence. The Sheriff had tried to look for the out-of-town trash himself, to his credit, but he'd spent most of his time watching over his best friend fighting in Intensive Care. I suspected he knew about the boys' hand in everything—maybe even mine—but I also suspected he would have done the same himself if given half a chance.

After Tommy and Sam headed out, Carlos and I went back to his home in the countryside. As I was climbing into my Landcruiser behind him, an idea struck me. There was a favor I'd been needing to return for a while now, and I figured Carlos and his boys might just have the means to help me out. I told him about my friends John and John, how we met, and how they were left at the altar by a shithead of an investor. I also explained how, without John, I would not have heard about his plight—how things might have turned out differently for both of us. Being the blood-brothers we were, Carlos immediately caught my drift. He suggested a hog-hunting expedition, handled personally by him. If the guy was a Great White Hunter like the rest of Carlos's clientele, it would be easy. Send the asshole an anonymous notice that one of his vendors was giving him a hunting trip, keep the real mission a secret until after the fact. I told him he might hear from John and John, he might not—you never know with those two. Either way, I gave it a shot.

I climbed into my rig and headed for Texas, passing the info along to John as I drove. He seemed noncommittal. I knew it would be useless asking Carlos anything as well, because he would never utter a word if the event occurred. But about six months later, I saw a news piece about a big-time name from Buckhead who died in a tragic hunting accident. It seemed he got out in front of the catch dogs when they got hung up in some thicket. Apparently, the bay dogs had rustled up about a dozen hogs and pushed them into a fenced corner. The hunter thought it was time to dive into the fray. By the time the boys arrived with the catch dogs, there wasn't anything left of the guy except hog shit. Once again, the Sheriff conducted a thorough investigation, and once again, evidence came up short. He concluded the accident was the result of stupidity on the part of the hunter and left it at that. It's common knowledge that you never get out in front of the bay dogs. You never corner wild animals. Everybody knows these things. Right? According to the society pages of the Atlanta Journal Constitution, the deceased hunter's young trophy bride is still living high on the hog to this day. So it goes.

The pilot touched base with one of Tom's kinfolk when we were about twenty minutes out by clicking the mic three times. Two reply clicks meant come on in. Anything else meant we were fucked. We were to overfly the tiny terminal at 150m eastbound—a wakeup call before circling back west one km to a fully lit runway. The plan was to turn around at the east end of the runway and park on the 29, then out go the lights. A fuel truck and the ground crew would expedite offloading the equipment and refueling the bird. The airport did not typically operate after dark, but just in case, the chains were up at the entry and exit points off Highway 1. Slim chances of being seen by bad guys in broad daylight, much less after dark with only a new moon on the rise.

The landing was perfect. The pilot turned the ride on a dime, coming to a smooth stop on the number 29. The truck pulled in, and the driver began the fueling process. Simultaneously, the ground crew offloaded the bird and pumped the hydraulic jacks to lift it off the dolly.

With the landing gear snapped back in place, Sirocco executed her ground check before she and Amber Lee climbed in and took off. They would scoot east a few klicks, then head south off of Cape Le Grand. There, they would rendezvous with RRS Sir David Attenborough. It was still inbound—about twelve hours out, sailing time. The ladies would meet with the crew, get the lay of the land while they had the chance. Amber Lee was particularly excited about the prospect of checking out the ship's sub, even if she and Sirocco wouldn't be using it directly. One does not have the opportunity to see truly world-class, state-of-the-art equipment like that very often. If some sort of cave was down there, the sub was sure to find it. Its electronic capabilities included side-scanning and ground-penetrating sonar that could find a fly fossil sitting ten feet under. Amber Lee planned to rendezvous with the two-person sub the next day, hopefully at the ledge where the original Jillora Bindi was resting.

Later, Amber Lee and Sirocco reversed their flight while the ship was still over the horizon and stowed the bird in a closed, secured hanger. Tom had ground transport ready to bring them to the hotel as soon as they touched down.

Separately at the airport, the sub was offloaded onto an old deuce and a half. The canopy was drawn and Joe and I climbed aboard. The driver brought us down Highway 1, turned south on Harbour Road, and parked alongside the 25m trawler docked directly under the blue arms of the gantry crane. The sub was cradled, lifted, and secured on the deck of the trawler in five minutes. These boys were good. Netting was draped over the sub in a business-like manner, and it disappeared. No one on the highway would give us a second thought.

The driver dropped us off at the Esperance Island View Apartments, a set of cheery blue suites overlooking the bay. We checked in, walked to our connecting rooms, unpacked and stowed our gear, showered, and met on the deck. Food and grog had been placed in the fridge earlier, so we treated ourselves to a flight of seven different brews from Lucky Bay Brewing. A seven-course meal, if you think about it. Tom had managed to reserve the entire property, only displacing a few families on holiday. They were relocated to similar quarters nearby, recompensed treble, and promised a tour of the Attenborough. No one seemed to mind the inconvenience.

It wasn't long before Tom arrived and grabbed a beer, sitting down with us to discuss logistics. He pulled out a package and opened it.

"This was the instrument in the dashboard of one of the now-dead Rovers," he explained. "I brought it instead of shipping it to Mat. It's an Olympus Delta Professional XRF. X-ray fluorescence—an old mining technology. This instrument is a state-of-the-art, handheld unit. While the marble may not be in the instrument's identifiable spectrum, it should still growl if we ping it up close. I figure we put it in a waterproof packet, attach it to the sub's reticulated extension arm, and hope for the best. Siltation inside the cave may or may not be an issue, but still, visibility will probably be slim.

"Legend has it that Jillora Bindi kept her round stone laying in the shallow recess of a grinding stone, essentially a metate, on a low ledge at the back of the cave. That way she'd always know where it was, even as her vision started to go. Legend also has it that the cliffside opening was a tight one—we speculate no more than perhaps two meters wide, two meters high. Perhaps double that in depth. I understand the modified arms on Amber Lee's sub have a total reach of around four meters, so we should be good."

"Small opening, low visibility..." I mumbled, thinking aloud. "How are we going to find this place if we can barely see it?

"Well, we can presume there was a ledge for passage to and from Jillora Bindi's home to the outside world. The ledge would have probably been two to four meters above the high tide line at that time. There are many such identifiable openings, both current and ancient, all along the coast. So, the sub gets to the 100-120m depth, looks for a ledge, then looks for the stone with the constellation. Remove the stones that close the cave off, insert the arm, camera-scan, and find the metate. Then we can pull the trigger on the XRF, and hopefully get a hit with a unique signature. Vacuum, scan the vac container to verify it's the same signature, then get the hell out of Dodge. Thoughts?"

Tom had definitely thought things through.

"What about inserting deep divers?" I asked, studying the XRF in front of us. The depths we were looking at were well beyond normal SCUBA dives, but I still wanted to hear Tom's thoughts. He snorted, shaking his head.

"Yup. Two words. Great Whites. Lots of 'em about in these waters. Seem to be a bit territorial, even with experienced divers. Best not to get eaten during the hunt."

Solved that great mystery.

Tom continued, saying, "I recommend we use the sub from RRS Sir David Attenborough as a decoy. Lower it down with some fanfare, let the locals observe from land—or, for the folks we kicked out of here, from aboard the ship. Later, when we recover the sub, we can open the catch basin and display some shells, stones, a crab or two. Show what we find, and we've got nothing to hide, right? As advertised, just a test run. Meanwhile, Amber Lee will go overboard from the trawler in the net. Once submerged, she can traverse a klick or so and do the deed. The trawler will pull the net so Amber Lee can ride a tether below the boat back into the harbor. That way, we can haul it out away from prying eyes. My cousin that runs the Harbor will close it for the afternoon and through the evening to allow everyone to take in the show at the Point. Gracious chap—closing the Harbor only costs about $7,000 US an hour, plus wages, benefits, and bonuses."

"Tell him he has my thanks," I said, taking a mental note to send the guy a bottle of scotch. "Is there anything else?"

"I understand Sirocco will act as a sky ferry between the Attenborough and our ground unit—and perhaps for some lucky tourists. I have my lads spread around from the Harbor to the Point and beyond to Eleven Mile Lagoon, all eyes and ears. Another twenty locals are on the payroll as well—all family and friends. They have specific contact info for me, and we have John listening in to pinpoint trouble before it becomes trouble. We can mobilize and remob instantly as need be. Hopefully, the shitheads are unaware of our intentions—but best to be prepared, as they say. Oh, and ah—almost forgot. Just in case, remind Sirocco about the wind farm along the Point."

Tom wrapped the package up neatly indeed. With that, the plan was set and ready. The only question that remained was whether or not we were as well.

Dallas (Mat)

The view over the north side of Dallas was a bit monotonous. The shielded one-way windows cut out enough light to make it permanently feel like dusk, but the shielding was what we needed now. There was plenty of space for the three of us, with the fridge and pantry fully stocked. The kitchen area had a walk-in fridge/freezer that probably held enough food for several months, and the pantry also brimmed over with shelves and shelves of canned goods, pasta, cereals, and soups.

The apartment was large, about 3500 square feet, including a high-tech communications center in the back. All comms, incoming and outgoing, were 100 percent encrypted and shielded. Any signal leaving the facility was pinged around the world, then to hell and back again before it reached the other end. A person could hide here for months and still conduct business around the world without being found.

We were squatting six floors below Sirocco's penthouse, in an area leased via a string of offshore companies. The place couldn't be traced back to her, not on paper. And yet, tucked into the corner behind a false wall panel, was a small elevator that had only two stops—here and six floors up in Sirocco's place, behind a sliding bookshelf. It could hold up to four people in a pinch, if we ever found ourselves needing it.

The entire apartment surrounding us was originally built as a safe house and escape room. A real work of art. John had made the arrangements earlier in the day, though I was still unclear on whether or not Sirocco even knew we were here. She had split with Amber Lee for parts unknown. I was pretty sure even Mark didn't know where we were.

The safe house was fortuitous, since I had other reasons for wanting to spend some time in Dallas. Joseph told me about an ace genetics researcher he knew in the city—one who owed him a favor. I didn't know all of the details, but I did know it involved a large gambling debt. Joseph had evidently stepped in reasons unknown to me and taken care of the problem. Regardless of their history, Joseph said the guy had the knowhow and the equipment to deliver for us. I still fretted, but not because I was worried about blowing our cover. My real concern was the potential amount of money at stake. I could only guess at this point, but if our fluid sample was laced with some type of alien DNA, then the first to patent it could end up being a very wealthy person. I didn't know how much of a driver money was for this guy. Joseph assured me I had nothing to worry about, though, so I kept my thoughts to myself.

It had not taken long for us to get set up for my conference call with Houston. Joseph had configured the conference space so I would appear as a lone figure against a flat black background, with he and Jenara off to the side and out of sight. We only wanted to reveal what was absolutely necessary. Comms signals were shielded, but there wasn't nearly as much we could do about visual cues. John would be monitoring the interface on both sides, just in case.

I settled into the chair and shut my eyes for a moment to clear my mind. Joseph counted down on his fingers: three, two, one, and then, a thumbs up. Kristin and Jagat appeared on the other end of the connection, the two of them in their secure conference room just as I had requested. Kristin looked calm, but Jagat seemed distracted.

"Is everything OK on your end," I asked, and Jagat paused a second before responding.

"Mat, there have been some people here today asking about you," he said, his voice wavering just a bit. "They basically want to know where you are. There were two separate inquiries. One was just a single guy who appeared to be a hired investigator, but the second group—there were three of them, Mat. They looked like FBI, but they wouldn't identify themselves. They didn't have any warrants or actual papers to speak of. Just said you were a person of interest in an ongoing investigation."

I smiled into the screen. "By all means, tell them what you know about my location. Of course, they won't find out much more than I'm sitting on a chair in a dark room. But let's be clear—my current financial dealings are client privileged only, and even if they get a warrant, that situation remains. If necessary, you have my authority to challenge any access they demand to my investment dealings with your firm."

"We have already put legal on notice about that," Kristin said.

"Thanks," I replied. "But I honestly don't think you will have anymore trouble. I have a feeling that in a day or two, anyone targeting me is going to have more important things on their mind. I'm more interested in what you've managed to dig up for me about this deal of ours."

Almost instantly, Jagat seemed more at ease. He leaned back in his chair as Kristen kicked into the details. The deal was reasonably straightforward, she told me. The $100 million cash infusion would get me a 10% stake in the company and a seat on the board of directors. A good situation because while access to restricted technology was my primary driver, I still wanted to make sure any investment I made was solid.

We spent the better part of the next two hours going over the company's current financial status and their revenue projections for the next five-year cycle. While it looked like cash flow would be negative until the end of that cycle, forecasts from their current sales and patents pointed towards breaking positive after that. I was particularly interested in projections of patent-based revenue, seeing as ThreeRock Analytics was one of the largest patent owners in the field. They had a good record of acquiring or developing the right technologies at the right time.

Jagat, Kristin, and I finished the conversation with the outline of an offer, but I predicated it on a meeting with their founder and CEO. I told them I wanted the deal closed within three days—by 9:00 pm on Thursday. Legal would be ready on Wednesday evening to fill me in on the structure of the final agreement.

After we said our goodbyes, I took a break from the screen to talk with Joseph before my next call. He would be leaving in about two hours to meet with his contact, Harry Tonkins, and supervise the DNA analysis. This was the only part of my plan that concerned me; if I was correct and the gel I collected contained DNA, then there would be a scramble to control it. Thus far, the rest of the world seemed to be focused on the metal casing fragments. Shards were found in Australia and Greenland. There must have been several groups their hands on a piece; the technology was valuable and potentially strategic to various governments. God only knows what Dahlgreen and his group wanted with the fragments.

As far as I knew, though, only two groups currently had access to genetic material; our group, and the government crew that cleaned up the lab in Eugene. I was sure they would have collected the rest of the casing slices, probably some water too. They would eventually get around to testing those samples, I was sure of it. Still, I was placing my bets on the idea that the water was second fiddle to the casing fragments. No one but our group knew about the crystal marble, and I wanted to keep it that way. I was a hot item, attracting way too much attention—and I needed a diversion. In fact, I needed two of them.

We were outnumbered and semi-trapped in our current quarters, though we had a single advantage in executing the next stage of my plan—time to act before everyone else caught up. Still, I knew we needed to act quickly to keep our pursuers off balance. I had to let Joseph in on the plan; timing was everything, and he had a built-in atomic clock.

DNA, if that is indeed what we had, is an interesting commodity. Modern DNA sequencing has opened the markets to massive collections of individual DNA. While some agencies focus on research, many more are concerned with profit. For just a couple thousand bucks, you can find out how likely you are to die of a heart attack, cancer, Parkinson's—you name it. The sort of information the medical industry would kill for. Imagine insurers being able to analyze individual risk, whip up personalized insurance rates. Pharmaceutical companies with the power to know what kind of drugs they could sell you to ward off the bad juju in your genes. Other advertisers believe genetics is a way to refine their marketing of non-medical products.

In the medical world, patents on genetically engineered products have always been wildly profitable. They let you control the market with the illustrious position of being the first entrant. A gene patent gives you the exclusive rights to a specific sequence of DNA for the next twenty years. If that DNA holds a use, a cure, you're the sole profiteer. Patents on valuable or useful genes are priceless.

There is a caveat, though. In 2013, when handing down a decision on the Association for Molecular Pathology versus Myriad Genetics, Inc., the Supreme Court of the United States nixed the patenting of human genes. Companies couldn't patent something our body can essentially make itself. Synthetic genes or modified human genes still remained fair game, though. And that was where my plan came into play.

I pulled Joseph and Jenara over to a conference table in the central ops room and unloaded what was going to happen in the next few days. Joseph would leave in an hour and take an anonymous vehicle to the lab in White Plains Dallas where Harry Tonkins, Joseph's contact, worked. The full DNA sequencing process should take a few hours, give or take, but Joseph said we were good to use the lab until the next morning.

I was still nervous about Harry, but Joseph told me again not to worry. Unfortunately, the man's loyalties weren't my only concern. There was no way to ensure that all of the information uncovered could be contained in Harry's office network. It could easily wind up on other company computers, which was no small worry to me. Fortunately, John had provided us with some sort of code that would fuck up their system for about a day if necessary. Joseph had it filed away in several formats to ensure he could infect the entire network. I also gave him the URL, user id, and password for a digital vault at a law firm in Washington DC, along with an encryption password to use on the data before transmitting it.

Once I was happy that we had sufficiently covered all the bases, I flashed Joseph a quick thumbs-up. He grabbed the gel sample and headed out the door, leaving Jenara and me alone in the apartment.

My next call was to the law firm of Williams and Bitten in Washington, DC. Craig Williams was expecting me, apparently, and accepted the video conference invitation almost instantly. Again, I was sitting in a chair against a pitch-black background, nothing of note in sight.

I had only worked with Craig once before, but I knew his group contained the best patent attorneys in the country. Patents are not a quick process, even with the Track One program instituted by the U.S. Patent and Trademark Office. It can take up to eight months for everything to go through, and that's considered quick.

Unfortunately, I didn't have eight months. Before I could get any DNA patents I obtained approved, there would probably be multiple filings to slog through. I was counting on mine being first in the queue, and the only way that was going to happen was thanks to constant pressure from my lawyers.

"Craig, thanks for meeting with me on such short notice. I appreciate you working with my lawyers to set up the e-vault." I paused for a moment. "Are you clear on how I want to proceed?"

"Good to be working with you again too, Mat," Craig replied. "I think I understand the issues, but it is a bit of an unusual request. Usually, patent holders are looking to lock in profits—but it looks like here, you just want to lock out other people's profits."

I nodded my head. "In a nutshell, yes."

"You know that whatever you do, I would still advise not giving anyone else access to the product. Not until you have a final stamp of approval on the patent."

"I hear you Craig, and I appreciate your advice," I said. "Unfortunately, the current situation does not allow me that luxury. Let's proceed as per the plan my lawyers provided. We are still doing some testing tonight, but you should have the sequenced DNA files in the vault by morning. If the whole thing goes belly up, I will let you know." I paused before adding, "You are going to have people ready to run with this starting at 7:00 pm this evening, right?"

Craig gave me a nod over the video. "We have it covered."

I gave him a smile. "Thanks, and one last thing. Late Thursday afternoon, there may be some breaking news that could put pressure on your firm. Nothing bad from a legal or criminal standpoint, but pressure nonetheless."

"Don't worry Mat, we're big boys and girls; we can handle it."

I thanked him again and cut the line. Call number two was finished, and now I paced around preparing myself for conversation number three. Before placing the call, though, I pulled John in over the apartment intercom.

"John, are the surveillance measures we discussed earlier in place?"

"No sir, but they will be by tomorrow morning," he replied.

"Thanks," I said. "And the courier?"

"Done. One hundred percent reliable. She will pick up the package tomorrow morning at 9:00 am from locker #6 in the front lobby, just as directed."

"Who is she?" I asked.

"An old acquaintance of yours—Eva." Jenara glanced at me and raised her eyebrows, an indiscernible look on her face. I'd had a brief affair with Eva several years before I met Jenara. It was Mark who introduced us, so it came as no wonder that her business was tied into the shadows. Even after an intimate relationship, I still only knew her as Eva. No last name.

"I'm sure she will be perfect for the job," I replied, though I wasn't sure how I felt about the whole thing on a personal level.

"Also," John continued, "I suggest you let Ms. Solido take the sample down to locker #6. She is not as high profile as you, and—" he paused, letting out a chuckle"—I'd say she's also a bit more capable of defending herself than you are."

"John, you definitely don't know how to appeal to a man's macho roots." In spite of myself, I grinned. "Don't worry, I won't take it personally. Thanks for your help with this."

"One more thing if you don't mind, sir. Could you tell me what you want me to do with the tapes?" John seemed curious—that was a new one for me. I won't deny that it felt more than a little good, finally knowing something the machine didn't.

"Let's just say the situation is fluid and flexible John," I told him. "Rest assured, you'll know as soon as I know."

"As you wish, sir. Though I must say, I think Mr. Mark was right when he mumbled about you being a black hole for information."

That was John's parting comment. The only thing that I could come up with to say was, "Hmmm."

The next call was short and sweet. No video; just a voice call. The phone only rang three times before a pickup. "Holy Mission Church, River Oaks campus. Megan speaking."

"Good afternoon, Megan." I put on the most charming voice I could muster. "I am trying to reach Pastor Dahlgreen."

"I am so sorry," she said. "He is not available right now. Who should I say is trying to reach him?"

"The name is Mr. Dover, and I can assure you that he does want to speak with me now. There won't be a second chance."

"Mr. Dover, he is very busy and I…"

I cut her off mid-sentence. "Megan, trust me on this. He will stop whatever he is doing to speak with me. I don't want to be rude—but please connect me to him now."

She was clearly put out with me, but even so, I could hear the connections being made. His voice was magnificently pitched and modulated when he answered. It flowed like honey. "Mr. Dover. This is a surprise."

"Yes, thank you for speaking with me on short notice, Pastor Dahlgreen," I said, and he let out a hum.

"Yes, yes. And what would be the nature of this call, might I ask?"

I took a deep breath. "Well, Pastor, I believe I might have something you want." I waited to see what kind of response this would evoke, but it appeared that Dahlgreen had an excellent poker face.

"You do, sir," he said, seeming almost disinterested. "Tell me, what do you expect to get for this item?

I smiled. "You misunderstand me. I am asking nothing. Simply seeking to provide a piece of the artifact you seek. Nothing more, and nothing less. Consider it a small gesture of goodwill. The incident with your son and his mercenaries was unfortunate, but know that I don't blame his incompetence on you. I understand that everyone has recovered well from that incident?"

I could hear the strain in his voice. "Yes, Brent was overeager in doing his job. You seem to be well informed."

"Well informed enough to know that the Cardinal and the Imam will be interested in what I have to offer." This gambit was actually just an educated guess based on some surveillance tapes John had obtained from neighborhoods around the church. The River Oaks campus is located next to some of the wealthiest neighborhoods in Houston, all with top-of-the line door cameras to protect their McMansions. John had a whole wealth of home surveillance recordings that were ripe for the picking. I had a gut feel that all of the meetings we witnessed between the Pastor and his two partners weren't exactly public knowledge, and my instincts seemed to hit the mark. His voice had an edge of anger in it when he spoke.

"What is it exactly that you are offering, Mr. Dover?"

"Tomorrow afternoon at 5:00 pm, I will deliver an artifact sample to you at the church," I told him."We can meet in your private study. You, DelBassey, and the Imam Najdi will all sign a letter saying you received the sample, and I'll hand it on over. At that point our business is done, and I expect no more interference from your group. Do you understand?"

"I do," said the Pastor, however grudgingly. I went to hang up the phone, but before I did, I couldn't resist throwing in one last jab.

"I will say that by chasing the sample you seek, you seem to have missed the bigger picture," I said. "Tomorrow; 5:00 pm." I hung up before the Pastor had a chance to respond.

Let him mull over that, I thought.

I had one final call to make, perhaps the easiest of them all. My lawyers had done some initial paperwork and delivered a background brief to Andrew Jenkins at the Washington Post. Andrew was a seasoned journalist with some excellent investigative reporting under his belt. He had recently published a piece related to political interference in public works bidding, the fallout of which had several once-popular elected officials resigning from their positions. Two ended up getting indicted.

The brief I provided him documented the frantic search for artifact segments around the world, and put him in touch with others who could confirm the existence of these fragments. One of my orange-slice shaped samples was at a well-respected lab for analysis, with instructions to send Andrew a report documenting everything they could determine by Thursday at 3:00 am. The second fragment I had would be going to Dahlgreen and his crew. The third, I would hold onto, maybe as a keepsake paperweight.

When I placed the call, I got an answer on the third ring. "Andrew Jenkins, Washington Post."

"Mr. Jenkins," I said. "Mat Dover here. It is a pleasure to speak with you today."

"Call me Andrew." He sounded breezy, casual, like he was catching up with an old friend. Still, there was a hint of edge to his voice when he asked, he said, "Do you mind if I record this conversation? Standard procedure."

"That's fine," I told him. "And please, call me Mat."

"OK, Mat." Andrew chuckled to himself. "Gotta say, I appreciate you sending me those briefing materials via your lawyers. I've done my due diligence, of course, and you have great credentials in the world of geologic research. Also looks like you were prescient on the bitcoin craze. Nevertheless, it's a wild story you tell, and you've got zero hard evidence to back it up. I can't really publish this with what you've given me here."

"I understand perfectly, and I agree. It's not publication material—not yet," I said. "That's why I am making arrangements for you to receive some additional information from a variety of credible sources. I just want your word that if I give you enough for a story, you will publish it at 3:00 pm this Thursday. You will have everything you need by 3:00 that morning."

There was no reply, so I kept talking. "There are still a lot of balls in the air right now, so I can't guarantee the final results. But my instincts tell me there is a real story here. You already have three or four solid leads for backup on much of the current brief, and I assume you have checked them out."

"I have," Andrew confirmed, though he still sounded hesitant. "Your story about groups, possibly government-backed groups, searching for these...these artifacts is solid." He stumbled over the word artifacts, most likely because he couldn't bring himself to call them alien artifacts as I had designated them in the briefs. "But, beyond that," he continued, "the theft of samples and coverup on the discovery of non-human technologies is a bit out in left field."

"Yes, I hear you. But I have faith you are going to get the information you need to nail down this story. You are very good at what you do, and I respect the fact that you can't publish if there is no reliable information to back up the story. I have labs working on that hurdle as we speak. If things don't work out, so be it. We part ways with no hard feelings, and I will find another journalist to work with."

"I can live with that," Andrew said. "You have my word that I'll do my best to publish by Thursday at 3:00."

Even though I knew he couldn't see me, I grinned into the phone. "Excellent," I told him. "I appreciate your time today, Andrew. I'm afraid I won't be able to speak with you again before Thursday evening, so let me give you a few more details now. You should expect copies of some genetic analyses to arrive at your office by tomorrow morning. You should also expect separate but similar reports from several well-respected research labs to confirm the evidence."

"Genetic analyses?" Andrew asked. "But what about those fragments everyone is after?"

"You will receive a mechanical and compositional analysis of the artifacts from a research lab by 3:00 am on Thursday morning," I said. "I'm not telling you how to do your business, but you may want to have some expertise on hand to verify the reports you receive."

"I'll be ready," He sounded more sure of himself than I had felt in a long time. It was refreshing, but at the same time, I wanted him to be fully aware of the risk he was poised to take on. I continued, telling him, "One last thing—not all of the groups pursuing the artifacts are governmental. You may very well receive anonymous videotapes, and I'm sure not all of them will paint my work in the best light. Treat that information as you see fit—and if you decide to publish anything, it won't hurt my feelings."

"OK, Mat. Sounds good."

"Thanks, Andrew. Fingers crossed the data comes through soon."

With that I hung up, my final call for the day finished. The ten pins were all set up, and now we just needed the bowling ball to roll down the lane and knock them over. I looked over at Jenara, who was smiling back with a bemused look in her eyes. "You do like being the puppeteer, don't you?" she asked.

"It has its charms, my dear."

"Well," she said, "while you have been chatting with your acquaintances, I have actually been getting some real work done. The artifact shell fragment is in locker #6 and I have packaged the gel samples for delivery. Assuming Joseph gives us the OK tonight, they will be picked up tomorrow morning from another locker and delivered to each of the five labs at the start of business tomorrow morning."

"And the letter?" I asked.

"Your delightfully benevolent but threatening note is included with each delivery."

The note Jenera was referring to outlined the terms and conditions of the sample usage. Since we had no real flexibility to establish any legal agreements, I settled for the following message from a shell company I had recently set up:

"Please find enclosed a sample of genetic material. This sample is unique and requires your immediate attention. Hadian Group currently has patents filed on these materials. Hadian Group grants you the right to use these materials royalty-free and in perpetuity provided the following three conditions are met:

1.   You do not seek patents on any of the materials found in this sample.

2.   You provide a report to Andrew Jenkins at the Washington Post of your initial analysis by 9:00 pm on the day of this letter's date, and you provide a brief review to Mr. Jenkins on the significance of your findings.

3.   You shall not disclose your possession of the samples nor your analysis to any other third parties prior to 48 hours after your signed receipt of the sample.

Derivative genetics synthesized from these samples may be utilized at the discretion of your laboratory. Relevant contact information and legal conditions are outlined below."

The letter was designed to hopefully provide the right combination of carrot and stick to force some action. The promise of future discoveries and patents was the carrot, and the threat to withdraw usage rights if conditions weren't met was the stick. Who knew how any of this would hold up in future legal challenges. I had no doubt in my mind that there would be some, but for now, time, curiosity, greed, and fear would hopefully drive the actions I needed.

If my hunch was correct, then the materials we had would provide the basis for groundbreaking advances in genetic science. They may even lead to a plethora of new medicines, cures, and treatments, which have thus far been out of reach. Whatever secrets our discovery might hold, I didn't want them held hostage to a single commercial entity with patent rights. Even if my company, Hadian Group, was eventually awarded the patent, the legal setup of the company didn't allow for profit. The patent holder could only award usage on a royalty-free basis.

Medical and pharmaceutical profiteering from human lives did not square up with my view of the world. Medical bankruptcy was a social poison. Taking a person's entire savings in return for sparing their life smacked of feudal practices, where ninety-nine percent of the people on Earth lived only to serve the other one percent. I determined I would not participate in that sort of commercial trade of human life. In a country where wealth abounds, reasonable healthcare is a right, not a privilege.

"It's been a long day," Jenara said, breaking me out of my reverie. "I think that a soak in the hot tub with a glass of wine is in order. Perhaps followed by butter-sautéed king prawns on a salad."

I gave a thumbs up to that and closed down the communications hub. That night, at 1:00 am on Wednesday morning, the call came in from Joseph that the genetic sequencing was done and results transmitted to the patent lawyers. Company computers at the lab where the analysis was done would not be a problem for 24 hours, or longer if needed. The key phrase that stuck in my mind was what

Harry Tonkins said to Joseph, "Holy crap, this stuff is the stem cell equivalent of DNA."

Chief Gallery (Mark)

My satphone rang a bit later, and I answered on the first ring. "Hunter—talk to me, man."

"Shitshow again, I'm afraid. I was walking up the street around the time just about every friggin' cop in Dallas decided to show up, sirens raging, flashing blue lights all over the street. You can probably hear them screeching in from your end. Whole place smells like burnt rubber. My guess is someone tried to rob the Hooter's up the street near the Perot Museum of Nature and Science, but I can't get within shouting distance of the front doors to see what the fuck is going down!" Hunter seemed a bit perturbed.

"Just hang there a second, I'm pulling up John now," I said, hitting speed-dial on my phone. "John, talk to us about Dallas."

I was the purveyor of calm.

"Sir, Dallas' finest just crashed the gates, pulled rank, ordered the car lowered, and are dragging the yoyos out." Contrary to his usual overconfident self, John sounded like one seriously flustered computer. It felt oddly good to hear the cocky little bastard freak out. "Nothing I can do but surveil," John continued. "Hunter?"

"Just another fuckin' bystander with my hands in my pockets playing with myself," Hunter grumbled. "They got the firepower out today. I'm backin' off a bit to see what I can see." Hunter was apparently feeling a bit leery of all the zip ties, and understandably so.

"Where is the backup team, John?" I ask, and he lets out something sounding like a sigh.

"The team had to back off—no choice." For once, John was communicating in plain English.

"Get Sirocco tied in now," I told him. This whole situation was beginning to seem a bit weird, but I had been to weird once or twice before. I waited while John tapped into Sirocco's phone, and a second later, her voice flowed in from the other end of the line.

"Sirocco here. What's up?"

John and I filled her in on everything that was going down on Hunter's end. She gave me a hum, and I could practically see the cogs in that beautiful head of hers turning.

"Hang with me," she said. "I'm calling a friend of mine. Are the locals still on site?" Sirocco was all business.

"I saw the two shitheads tossed into the back of a tactical vehicle," Hunter told her. "Man, did they look like forty hells. They screeched off westbound about fifteen minutes ago. The rest are clearing out as we speak, all headed west or north. Strange operation. No apparent cleanup, interviews, news crews—none'a that sort of shit."

Hunter had apparently been to strange once or twice before too. I couldn't say it surprised me.

From Sirocco's end, I could hear a muted blip before the line began to ring. It barely had a chance to make it past the first chime before a voice answered the phone. "Donna Gallery, Dallas Chief of Police."

"Chief, Sirocco here. Your guys just crashed my building and made off with two of my guests. What's up?"

"Sirocco, great to hear your voice, love!" Ms. Gallery told her to hold for just a second, the line going dead before crackling back to life. "Sorry about that," the Chief continued. "I'm moving to my ops room as we speak. Background noises and names being called into action said the Chief was a woman of action. She seemed to forget all about us for a moment as she moved, until John cleared his nonexistent throat over the line.

"Chief, my name is John," he says. "May I feed you surveillance video?"

"Of course." I can hear her settling into a chair, and then, the quick clack of a keyboard. "Luis, give me a link for the gentleman on the line so we can see his video."

"It's on your screens now ma'am." John had already taken the liberty of tapping the feed.

"Damn. How'd you do that?" the Chief sounded somewhere between impressed and unsettled. "You know what? Never mind. Sirocco's friend. You could probably watch me take a shower every morning if you wanted to."

The Chief was also a practical woman; it seemed.

We were interrupted by a sharp crackle from Gallery's end, and a voice came barking through the speakers. "Chief, Lt. Sharp here. Those are not our guys. Repeat, those are not our guys. They look like our guys, act like our guys, smell like our guys, but they aren't ours. Bad tag numbers on the vehicles, no facial ID on any of them." Sharp was pointed.

"What the fuck?!?" the Chief blurted out before quickly backpedaling. "Sorry, sorry, people. Not like me to curse. I'm just a bit upset that we have someone out there impersonating my officers. John, please forward everything you have to me—if it is OK with Sirocco, that is."

"Perfectly fine with me. I'd like to know just as much as you about who these shitheads are and who they are answering to." Sirocco was in a mood to kill. Her tour of the Attenborough had been rudely interrupted by the same shitheads she had countered earlier, and she was less than pleased about it. They were supposed to be out of the picture. Instead, it seemed her instincts were howling that there was certainly more to come. Who the fuck can impersonate a bunch of cops, commandeer a whole city block in downtown Dallas fucking Texas, and then just slip away? They had attempted a direct assault on her sanctuary, and I knew that she took it as a personal affront. Chances of them succeeding had been slim to none, sure—but still, just the attempt itself sent the hackles up the back of my neck. Same as casually glancing to your one-eighty and seeing a mountain lion

196

calmly gazing at you from fifty meters away in the middle of exactly nowhere. "Send Gallery everything you have, John," I said. "Further, provide a direct line between you and the Chief. She asks, you provide. Keep Mat and me in the loop, but don't wait on us if you need to act—or even think you think you need to act."

"As you wish, Sir," John said. "Is there anything else I can do for you?"

"Yeah. Anything on the satellite you can tell me about that might give us a hint where these bastards slipped off to?" I was ready for another seven-course meal, but it was being held up half a world away. Damn, I could not wait to clock the next asshole that pointed the wrong finger in my face.

"The vehicles have managed to disappear into the clutter of garages and other commercial spaces just west of downtown. I suspect the Chief's folks will find the vehicles abandoned." John was apparently disappointed that he did not have ground-penetrating radar and air-to-air missiles. Huh. Now there's a terrifying thought.

"Well, I'm just glad all of you folks are safe." The Chief jumped on the line again, speaking curtly. "I will keep you informed as I go. For now, though, I have work to do." The Chief didn't bother waiting for a response before signing off. I didn't blame her for being short; officers universally hold police impersonators in the same esteem as child molesters. The Chief'd had her shoes pissed on in the heart of her domain, and that was something her force couldn't tolerate. If and when the bad guys were ID'd and picked up, I was sure the Chief would deal with them harshly. Makes you wonder if there are feral hogs in the Dallas area.

After the Chief logged off, a new plan started forming in my mind on how to deal with these assholes before they could strike a third time. "Hunter, change of plans," I said. "Can you camp at Sirocco's?" An itch told me this might be a good idea.

"Of course." Good man.

Sirocco chimed in, saying, "John, give Hunter clearance, codes, delivery services, et cetera. Smoke if he likes. Show him where the toys are kept." Warriors like their toys. "Hunter, make yourself at home—top floor, north or south—and familiarize yourself with the security systems. Everything you need should be there, but if not, John will have it delivered. Use the front desk for any ground transport, leave Uber out of this. Don't know what the fuck will show up these days. And Hunter?" she continued, a hint of laughter to her voice. "Have fun with all my toys. I hope you like them."

I hopped in, wanting to get in a quick word before everybody signed off. "I want to take the chance to thank you guys," I told everybody, Sirocco and Hunter, and the rest—even John. "Hard to know what you may be needed for, but I'm glad you're all there. Catch the sunrise and sunset, enjoy your Scotch, and hopefully, this will be the last you hear from me for a while. I doubt it, but what the hell; I'm an optimist. The whole shooting match should be over within a week, two tops."

We all said our goodbyes and clicked off, and I tucked my phone in my pocket for the evening. Joe, Tom, and I each had another seven-course dinner booked, all of us sat out on the deck where we could watch the surf roll in from the veranda. Seafoam rolled up on the beach with each wave, the salty air intoxicating in and of itself. The vague moon gave off enough light to highlight the tips of the offshore break and the islands beyond. We ate a variety of local fish, crustaceans, mollusks, seaweed, and the like, all delivered by one of Tom's folks.

"I think we're set for tomorrow." Tom was in a pensive mood as he chewed on his scallops. "Sirocco and Amber Lee should arrive back at the airport from the Attenborough in their chopper later. A driver will bring them here, and we'll get Amber Lee to the trawler before dawn without fanfare. The boat will be underway and should be clear of land by first light. She will steer to the south side of Observatory Island and drop her net and the sub, while simultaneously, the Attenborough will be going through her ruse on the northern edge of the island."

"That all sounds good," I said, taking a deep sip of Scotch. "What about Amber Lee?"

"The trawler will maintain a dead slow trawl westward, eastward, and westward again in half-kilometer stints until Sirocco gives the signal to bug out and head back to port. I'll be surfside end-to-end with me mates keeping a surreptitious lookout. Additional boys will be holed up in the port and at the airport keeping a look out—just because.

"And the stone?" I asked.

"In a perfect world, Sirocco and Amber Lee would find the cave, pick up the stone, draft back into port, transfer off the sub and collect the stone, amble back up to the airport, catch the STOL back to Perth, and head back to the States on the mil aircraft." Tom let out a humorless chuckle. "But, just between us girls, I have yet to experience this 'perfect world' shit. In a perfect world, half of our country would not be on fucking fire due to the climate change we all made possible, would it? So here's to sharp knives and quick draws! Cheers!"

Well, damn. It seemed Tom had gotten a bit sentimental on us. Tough old bird, you just had to hand it to him. He was a rare one—not many thoughtful people left on this desolate old island we call Earth. I raised my glass alongside him and took a deep sip.

"Alright Tom, how can we help?" I asked.

"GIVIT," he said simply. "It's the best way to help out the folks impacted by the devastation. Anything you can do is most appreciated. I've gotten word from some of my folks over in Sydney and down toward Melbourne that a lot of folks are in desperate need of the basics."

Time to mobilize some resources, I thought.

I rang up John, and before he could greet me with any lip, I told him, "Send $1 mil to GIVIT, anonymously, and let Mat know they need help too. Maybe some of your other clients as well, if possible. I'll let the ladies know. I'm damn sure guilty of leaving large carbon footprints wherever I go, so it's time to pay some hard dues."

"Yes sir, and I have standing orders from several of my clients to offer financial assistance when I come across a worthy cause. I can match your mil without asking. In fact, I'll have ten times that before the day is over." John and John, class personified.

"On another note," John continued, "I just obtained video from IAH. Private Cessna Citation XLS, tail number N8679. The number is deregistered and belonged to a plane sent to South Africa. Very weird, but I'll figure it out. The important thing is our two yoyo's disembarked into a Ford Expedition parked at the foot of the stairway. The car is registered to a shell company, everything paid for in cash. I cracked the shell and found Edward Dahlgreen's fingerprints all over that registration. I've already relayed this information to Mat." John had discovered yet another useful tidbit. I was sure as hell glad it's our side he was on.

"Clue in FAA, Immigration, Harris County Sheriff, City of Houston Police—any other entity you think may hassle them," I told John. "Let them know about the fake ID, and don't forget to mention illegal transport, smuggling drugs and weapons, sex-slavery trade, and loud rock and roll music for grins."

I was feeling jovial. During the recent hurricanes along the Gulf Coast, a mega-church had locked its doors against the needy hordes looking for food and shelter. So much for the teachings of Christ; apparently mansions and private jets trump charity. So if you ask me: fuck a mega-church.

Eva (Mat)

Eva topped out at 5 foot 8 inches and 140 pounds. For all practical purposes, she was the perfect combination of muscle, brains, and street smarts. Add in good looks and the ability to read people, and she was perfect for her job. That job was hard to pin down precisely since she worked as a bodyguard, private security consultant, freelance "problem solver," and several other odd jobs all rolled into one. Eva was good at what she did, and she charged a base fee of $8000 per day for her services. She had such a good reputation she found herself turning away clients more often than not, usually sending them on to other colleagues for a finder's fee cut.

She took this job because Mat was asking, or at least because John was asking on his behalf. Eva was one of John & John's clients, and she had learned from them that Mark and Mat were evidently up to their hips in some kind of high-stakes chase right now. She didn't know the whole story, but bits and pieces drifted her way through the grapevine. The job was short and sweet, and she planned on foregoing her usual fee as a favor to Mat—unless the assignment turned into a shit storm, that is.

Eva had picked up the package that morning and decided to drive her red Ferrari 812 to Houston instead of calling her driver. Granted, the drive from Dallas to Houston wasn't the most exciting of rides, but she was looking forward to being on the road with her car. She took I-45 South to Madisonville and then SR90 down to Navasota; from there, she picked up SR105 to Brenham and then SR36 through Bellville and down to Sealy, Texas. It was a hot, sunny day in Texas, and traffic was sparse, so she was able to drink in the empty road as she drove.

Eva picked up the I-10 eastbound at Sealy, running the final leg through Katy and down to the I-610 loop. She got there an hour early, left her car in a private parking garage, and picked up a non-descript rental vehicle. She found the megachurch and then parked to observe the church and await her 5:00 pm appointment.

John had provided her with the blueprint layout of the facility, along with the details of the pastor's study where the exchange would take place. He confirmed that the Cardinal and the Imam were already at the church, and that a discussion was in progress as she waited in the parking lot.

Inside, the three men were none the wiser to what lay in wait, not fifty feet from their front door. Still, Cardinal DelBassey's voice was strained. "I fear we are being played for fools," he said. "Why would he simply give us what we seek? How will we even know if it is real? And what of Dover saying that we are missing the most interesting part of the story? I feel like we could be walking into a trap."

Edward was also unnerved by Dover's comments, but he could not see any other course than to accept the artifact and move on. At the very worst, he figured, it could turn out to be a decoy. For his part, the Imam remained silent.

"Will Dover be accompanied by the Solido bitch?" the Cardinal continued, looking around the room.

"He didn't say," replied Edward. "He only said that he would deliver the artifact and require our signatures on a receipt."

"I have no intention of signing anything," grunted the Cardinal.

"Nor I," added in the Imam.

Edward sighed to himself. He was regretting his agreement to work with these two. "Gentlemen, let's be reasonable. If the decision is to sign or not sign in order to get the delivery, I think we should sign."

The Cardinal huffed. "Edward, I am sorry, but the Imam and I have agreed that Dover can't be allowed to leave here after his delivery.

He knows more than he's letting on. We not only need his artifact, but we also need access to whatever information he might be hiding.

"We have a separate team en route to retain him," the Imam continued. "He will be our problem then. Once Dover enters the building, our men will follow behind and cut him off. You should tell your two guards out front not to interfere, we wouldn't want anyone to get hurt."

Edward was incredulous. "You are threatening violence and kidnapping in my Church." He tried to keep his voice under control, but the anger spewed out anyways. "And what good is Dover to you? What, are you going to torture him for information?" he continued, with a sarcastic bite to his voice.

He was shocked into reality when the Imam replied, "If necessary."

The gravity of the situation suddenly hit him. The Cardinal had Vatican resources at his disposal, and the Imam clearly had a direct connection to Saudi government interests. Edward was in over his head. Crimes, both legal and moral, were in progress here, and he would be left holding the bag at the end of it. He needed to control the situation if he wanted to keep from getting thrown under the bus.

John relayed the conversation's basics to Eva as she hopped out of her parked car and approached the building. "I spotted the second security team in two SUVs winding their way through Memorial Park, just to the north of you," he said, "but something is amiss. The cars stopped to consult, but it appears one party ambushed the other. All I know is that gunfire was involved, and now only one car is headed your way, about ten minutes out."

Eva paused to take in the information. It looked like Mat was going to be charged full price after all. She simply replied to John, "Thanks for the information. Call the police in eight minutes and report an incident at the church. An active shooter. Also, kill the video feed to the pastor's office as soon as I enter the church."

She reformulated the plan. Based on the information John had just related to her, she could take a good guess that the ambushed car consisted of Vatican-sponsored security. The Imam was clearly the Saudi path in the chase for the artifacts, and the probability was that the remaining team was Saudi. They would be professionals, Eva was sure, and willing to use whatever amount of force they deemed necessary. On the other hand, the mega-church security was probably fairly lightweight. She was banking on the chance that they would use violence only as a last resort. Eva was good at what she did, but even she would have trouble taking on more than four armed professionals at once. The odds would not be in her favor.

Eva relaxed and pulled her fedora low over her sunglasses as she approached the front doors to the church. Her auburn hair was tied in a tight bun behind her head. She was wearing an off-white silk blouse, open at the collar. A tailored black linen jacket covered the blouse and blended perfectly with a pair of black linen slacks. She knew her hazel-green eyes and generous smile were assets, so she put them both to use as she walked through the entryway into the front foyer.

Two security guards stood across the foyer, both positioned between the reception desk and Dahlgreen's private study doors. The floor was polished white marble, providing a good grip for her rubber-soled shoes. An oversized, polished wood cross hung on the wall behind the reception desk. She couldn't be sure, but it appeared to be made of medium-dark oak.

"Ma'am, I'm sorry, but we are closed at this time." The closest of the two guards appraised her, though naturally, he didn't seem particularly intimidated. He appeared to be just over six feet tall, probably weighing in at 190 pounds or so. Fit, but poorly trained was Eva's assessment. She figured he was the one in charge.

She kept walking towards them, removing her sunglasses as soon as she was angled with the foyer security camera over her right shoulder. Eva flashed a warm smile, making the laugh lines around the edges of her eyes crinkle just a little bit. She could visibly see both of the guards relax as they smiled back. The second guard probably weighed in at 220, bigger than his partner, but too much of that weight was in his belly. It stretched his jacket, making the weapon in his shoulder holster bulge out conspicuously.

"Gentlemen, I believe I am the reason you are closed," she said, her voice honey-smooth. "I have a package here for Pastor Dahlgreen, I believe." She reached into her left jacket pocket and pulled out a black sealed bag, dangling it up in the air.

"We were told to expect a Mr. Dover," guard number one replied. His smile was gone, and he was back to business. Eva was close enough to read his name badge.

"Dave," she purred, still smiling. "Mr. Dover couldn't make it, so I am afraid you are stuck with the courier. I was instructed to deliver this package directly to Mr. Dalhlgreen, or else return it back to Mr. Dover. It's your choice; it makes no difference to me since I get paid either way."

The guard paused and thought for a moment. "OK, Jack will escort you in," he finally said, pointing to the second guard. "Do you have any weapons on you?"

She gave him a mock disappointed look, returned the package to its pocket, then slowly opened her jacket to reveal the moderately tight-fitting white blouse beneath. "Search me if you must, but don't get too touchy."

"That's OK, ma'am, no need," replied Dave. He noticed—but didn't mention—the tight black leather gloves covering her hands.

Eva didn't have a gun in any case, so there would have been nothing for him to find other than the thin knife stashed up her jacket's left sleeve. Of course, these two probably wouldn't have detected the knife even if they had done a proper search, and she knew there were no metal detectors to worry about at the church.

Jack escorted her through the private study doors. She took in the looks of surprise as she entered the room, with Jack explaining that Mr. Dover couldn't make it, and she was his courier. The Imam appeared agitated to see her, while Dahlgreen looked particularly stressed; DelBassey, on the other hand, kept a neutral face.

Eva knew the clock was ticking, and she saw the Imam looking at his watch. She had to put things in motion. She extracted the package and a letter for their signature, laying it out on the coffee table in front of the men. The package, however, she returned to the inner pocket of her jacket.

"I need three signatures before I can release the package," she said, playing the part of bored courier flawlessly. Dahlgreen immediately reached for the letter, but DelBassey stayed his actions with a wave of his hand. He mustered his best command voice. "Guard, restrain this woman."

Jack hesitated and looked at Dahlgreen—an unfortunate mistake for him. Eva was primed and ready after the details John had divulged to her. Jack was to her left and slightly back. She pivoted on her left foot, and the fingertips on her right curled over, leaving four knuckles at her hand's striking end. She planted her right foot in front of Jack and simultaneously drove her knuckles deep into the soft tissue of Jack's shoulder. The strike was perfectly placed, the knuckle of her middle finger crushing a pressure point nerve center that temporarily paralyzed his right arm.

He screamed in agony, but Eva didn't stop moving. Her left foot shifted close to his right leg, sweeping up through the gap and then back down again to take out his right leg. Her momentum and the loss of leg support landed Jack flat on the office floor, and he shrieked again as his shoulder slammed into the rug.

Eva followed him down, inserting her right hand beneath his jacket and extracting his pistol in one quick motion. Then, rolling off his chest and back up to a standing position, she raised the gun just in time for Dave to come crashing through the door. The clock was still ticking in her head. With him staring down the barrel, it was all too easy to convince Dave to slide his weapon across the floor towards her. She tossed him a thin bundle of zip ties in return, giving him strict instructions to bind the four other men's hands together. When he was done, she had him use his teeth to restrain himself as well. She then grabbed the letter from the table.

"Don't worry if the bindings are too tight, gentlemen; the police will be here to untie you posthaste." Eva headed to the door, but before she left, she turned once more and said, "By the way, your whole conversation before my arrival is on tape. And DelBassey? You might want to know that the good Imam's security team ambushed yours about ten minutes ago. He was going to steal the artifact for the Saudi government. Speaking of which—" She tossed the package into Edward Dahlgreen's lap with a smirk. "My work here is done."

Eva exited into the foyer with her fedora pulled low to avoid the security camera. She took an immediate left, heading into a hallway that led south to the rear of the building. As soon as she was blocked from the security camera, she took up a shooter position with a full view of the front door. The four-man Saudi security team was about ten feet from the entrance when she placed a shot through the front glass panel to the right of the doors.

Glass shattered, and the security team scrambled for cover behind some of the church's front support columns. She took out a second panel when they tried to move forward again. The security team saw the police at the same time Eva did, and they immediately started retreating back to their SUV. They barely made it five feet before she dropped one of the team with a shot to the leg, firing two more rounds into one of the columns to attract police attention.

With the exits from the church parking lot blocked by the cops, Eva wiped down the gun and left it on the floor. Even though her gloves left no fingerprints, cleaning up after herself was a force of habit. She sprinted about thirty yards down to the end of the hallway and quickly picked the lock on a maintenance door. Through the door was a flight of stairs leading down to an equipment room, where a three-foot square grate along the far wall opened to a service conduit.

She unscrewed the wing nuts, removed the grate, and scrambled on all fours for another twenty yards through the conduit. At the far end, she climbed a short ladder and exited through a floor grate into the church's utility building. Eva glanced out the front windows towards the church and saw no action, but she could hear the police chopper circling overhead. She waited until the chopper was hovering over the front parking before slipping through the rear window and into a thick grove of trees.

A thirty-yard walk along a tree-covered path led her to the edge of one of River Oaks' residential areas. A small, nondescript Ford was parked by the road, waiting for her. She reached under the car, removed a black key box, and opened the driver's door. Her original car would go into police evidence, she was sure, but it was meticulously wiped clean—not to mention, she could write off the loss on her invoice to Mat as an operating expense. He was definitely getting her full charge, and then some. Leave it up to Mat to get himself into some weird shit like this, she thought.

Eva took a short drive to the Galleria Shopping Center and parked in a prearranged space, avoiding cameras as she entered the first available bathroom. The fedora and white blouse were disposed of, and she reversed the jacket so that when she exited, she was wearing a turquoise tee shirt under a white jacket with black linen slacks.

Eva did a little window shopping, exited the shopping center, and then took a short walk north across Westheimer to Morton's SteakHouse. She managed to get a table for one and ordered a petite filet along with a bottle of excellent Argentinian Malbec. She only really wanted a few sips, but it wasn't the kind of wine you could buy by the glass.

Eva lingered on the meal until darkness had fallen, and then caught a cab to a bar two blocks away from where her Ferrari was parked. A short walk from the bar and she was back on the road to Dallas.

Recycler (Mark)

In the early 1980's I found myself hiking about six miles southwest of Justiceburg, Texas, on a mesa that fell off a couple hundred feet or so into the Double Mountain Fork Brazos River. Justiceburg was home to perhaps 300 or so friendly folks and a few old soreheads. The population density dropped off precipitously once you left SR 84, as I had done a couple of hours earlier. It was a somewhat warm and sunny day with light to moderate winds out of the southwest, making it a perfect late March day. Sugar had run out ahead southbound, hoping to catch a kangaroo rat or coyote or world-class buck. It didn't take long for her to kick up a covey of blue quail. Most of the birds hit the ground running after a short flight, scattering through the creosote bushes and other prickly flora. Sugar did the half-sideways run and gave it a valiant effort, but the wily birds slipped away in plain sight from my vantage point. Interestingly, Sugar was not prone to barking unless something of significant interest grabbed her attention. She didn't bark at birds or coyotes or prairie dogs or jackrabbits and such. She usually just ran here and there, sniffing the wind and chasing whatever happened to be within chasing distance.

I mostly watched where I was walking, semi-successfully avoiding the pointy things that make one bleed out in the semi-desert. Besides—by looking down a lot, I usually found a sign or two of the old people, or perhaps a fragment of life frozen in time maybe two hundred million years ago or so. My intention was to slip off the mesa and down to the river and catch a largemouth bass or two in a couple of holes deep enough to hold fish. I had my old Zebco Ultralite spooled with four-pound mono and some #0 gold bucktail Mepps. The river was a bit low and a bit muddy when I crossed it earlier near Justiceburg, but still fishable. I had been along this stretch several times before. It was essentially a braided stream, the braids being either sand or water. There was a sinuosity between the two, alternating between inner and outer sandbars as the water changed direction 180° north and south while flowing generally west to east. The river nearly touched itself on some of these bends. Actually catching something was optional from my perspective; it was all about the process.

Sugar was headed in generally the same southward direction as me, trotting about a hundred yards ahead. She started barking and running toward the rim of the mesa about two hundred yards out from her. I stood stock still and scanned the real estate in front of her to see what had caused the announcement that she was in hot pursuit. Nothing large like deer, pronghorn, black bear, or mountain lion showed. None would have been unusual given the time and place in which we found ourselves, but not that day. After several seconds, movement at the rim caught my eye, and I saw one bobcat kitten, then another, both slipping over the rim of the mesa before disappearing from view. Sugar seemed to have her mind set on bobcat for dinner. The hackles leapt up the back of my neck and I shouted "Sugar!" several times before she slowed and looked back. I screamed again and she halted her headlong run into certain disaster. "Sit!" I shouted—and, yes, she sat. Good girl.

As I strode toward her, I admonished her to sit several more times when she turned her head back to where the kittens had dropped off the mesa. I continued scanning the rim and glancing at the dog until I touched her head and whispered, "Sit." At that moment, mama bobcat blossomed into sight from the vague trail she was on, positioned about fifteen yards from the rim. I say blossomed because even though I knew about where she was, I could not detect her until she decided to show herself. With the grace and fluidity borne of countless generations before her, she slipped over the rim and evaporated.

For the uninitiated, only moments before, mama had been lying flat on her back facing northward along the trail. Her claws extended from her deeply padded paws, her teeth bared. The cat would have disemboweled Sugar as the dog jumped over her. Thankfully, though, Sugar got to live another day.

The two of us followed the bobcat trail off the rim of the mesa and did the ole 'slide-down-the-face-of-the-mesa' thing to the river. We both managed to make our way to the bottom without doing the 'head-over-heels-down-the-face-of-the-mesa' thing. Over the years, we were about 50-50 between the two. The cats had headed west, according to the tracks in the sand, and though Sugar sniffed, whined, and waited to catch my eye, a firm "No" was all it took to get her refocused on the task at hand—Fishing. So it goes.

I would kill to be relaxing on that river right now, sipping a beer, casting a line. But I guess there's never any rest for the wicked.

"Sounds like a dirt bike driving around out over the Pacific," said Joe.

"That would be a bit of a sight." Tom grinned, chuckling to himself.

I'd heard that same sound not too long ago in a deep canyon along the Naches River in western Washington, east of Mt. Rainier. A fucking dirt bike on the near-vertical walls was just as unlikely as one skimming the waves out here. It was a small drone scooting up the canyon about a hundred feet above the river. I flipped the thing off and left it there. No idea if it was private, taking pics for postcards or that Youtube shit, or the government checking for poachers. I was westbound in my Land Cruiser on SR 12 in another few minutes without another though to spare for the drone. Until now, at least.

Tom pulled out his long-barreled Glock 34 Gen 4 and glanced through the X400UH-A-GN night scope. He scanned left and right, up and down for several seconds, and then finally said, "Got it. Wow, maybe two meters in diameter, square, with four rotors and a camera. Big son of a bitch, and it seems to be checking us out. My guess is about one hundred, maybe one hundred ten meters out and ten off the water. I can kill it, no problem.

Thoughts?"

"Probably not private," said Joe. "Kill it."

Tom clicked on his phone and said, "Watch on the perimeter for anyone leaving in a hurry. Keep an eye out in particular for anyone with a toggle and a computer or tablet."

He clicked off and locked the green dot on the body of the drone, squeezing off a +P round. We saw a brief electrical issue above the ocean, and then—nothing. Tom is a badass if there ever was one. He zinged another round and let out a rebel yell, followed by another round and another yell. I wondered where the hell he had learned a rebel yell before realizing I had shouted one earlier in the evening.

"Locals will just think we're happy. Nothing they have not heard before." Tom grinned and drained another beer. "The ladies should be arriving soon."

"I gotta hit the head first," I said, pushing off the railing. I crossed the deck in the dark, sea breeze-filled air and walked through the unlatched slider where the blackout curtains were mostly drawn.

I noticed the open front door across the room about the same time that I saw the friggin' 1911 Colt .45 come to bear on the end of my nose from about no inches away. The bore appeared to be approximately ten feet wide, and I swear I could see the tip of the nuclear warhead down at the bottom of the silo.

The fact that I was alive told me the dipshit on the other end of the weapon had not experienced a proper upbringing. When I was about six or seven years old, my daddy gave me my first weapon—a BB rifle. Before I was allowed to touch it, I was given the basic gun safety course that the NRA used to be known for. You know, back before the big dogs started shopping for hunting togs in Beverly Hills boutiques and essentially endorsing mass murders in the name of the Second Amendment. The one important point was to Never. Ever. Never ever point a weapon at another person unless you fully intended to kill that person. Instantly. Not that a BB gun was going to be lethal to a person, but the point was well taken. Apparently, nobody had bothered schooling Dipshit on this.

"No noise and turn around slowly." Huh, sounded more SoCal than Aussie. Perhaps a handy piece of information to have. I also happened to notice the guy holding the lethal antique was right-handed, like about 90% of the world. Me, though—I'm a southpaw. It comes in handy in times like these.

I pivoted slightly so my left foot was at nine o'clock to his twelve o'clock. My right foot ended up at ten-thirty. I glanced to the left as a second guy stepped through the door with what appeared to be a Beretta 92 FS 9mm. Shit was beginning to get serious. The guy advanced another step and held about two feet inside the door. Another right-hander. If I got the chance knowing which way to feint, left or right, it might make all the difference. In essence— would I bleed a lot, or not?

"How was your swim in Cali?" I had no way of being sure about who the guy was, but I figured a bit of casual conversation might help take the edge off, or not.

The guy blinked, saying nothing. Looking at him up close, I could see I had correctly surmised he was the guy that stuck Joe and me with a bug.

Both men were too focused on me to pay any attention to what was going on behind them—another rookie mistake. I caught a glimpse of Sirocco floating through the door behind hairball number two, her hands extending toward his head. In one quick movement I windmilled my left hand counterclockwise from my waist and hit the asshole in front of me, slamming my fist into his gun hand and sending the Colt .45 skittering away. I then swept my right foot up under his left leg, pushing against the back of his knee and forcing him to kneel. I had about a millionth of a second to glance toward the second guy, but it didn't look like Sirocco needed my help. She'd gone full Exorcist with his head, which had somehow twisted in a complete circle before Sirocco ejected it from her hands and let the asshole flop to the floor.

'Machine payback time,' I thought to myself. Just as my guy was on the verge of screaming, I pressed the first four knuckles of my left hand into a dull hatchet blade and buried it into his bare neck, crushing his trachea and cutting off his impending scream. I hate hearing someone scream as they die. Just die. Don't make a big fucking production out of it.

Boy, did I feel all of the pent-up pressure from dealing with a fucking smartass machine leaking from my pores, and I felt much better for the release. But now we had two dead guys on our hands that I did not feel like dealing with. Sirocco was staring down at the bodies with a look of distaste, while Amber Lee slipped in behind her and kept the parking lot scanned left to right with her Glock. I stuck my head outside and softly called Tom and Joe in.

"Well damn. How the hell did two dead guys get into your room?" Joe could be cool under pressure. "Looks like they got the drop on ya there, Butch. You are getting too old for this shit. Needing the cavalry to save your worthless ass and all." Joe could also be an asshole.

Amber Lee glanced over her shoulder, gun still lined up against the window ledge. "There's a guy down outside," she said. "He has a pulse, but he's asleep. I did not take the time to assess him. I presume he's one of your guys, Tom."

Tom clicked in a number and got his crew converging on us. I punched in John and asked for eye-in-the-sky support. He reported that the only sat comms he could secure were coming around and would be available in about an hour. We were in a somewhat rural area, to put it mildly. So much for stealing time from top-secret government satellites. Sometimes it seems like you can't depend on anything other than yourself and your closest friends. Sirocco wandered over to me, still flushed from the fight, and I flashed back to mama bobcat from way back when. I was for damn sure glad Sirocco was on my side.

Tom stepped up, taking the lead. "I'll have the perimeter secured in no time. We'll take the trash to the trawler and empty it when we launch the sub. OK with you, Amber Lee?" The man had a plan. Amber Lee nodded, smiling.

"Tossing the trash out—or rather, recycling—sounds good to me. Assholes tried to take Mark and the rest of you out. I have zero tolerance for that kind of behavior. Heads on a pike is the way to go."

Damn. Two mama bobcats is even better than one.

Several guys held a brief meeting in the parking lot and two came on up, one of them greeting Tom with a nod. "William has a bump on his head, but will be fine now that you cured what ailed him," he told us. "I'm setting up redundant perimeters out to one klick. No one in or out without the code words."

I had to be a dumbass and ask, "What are the code words?"

"Fuck off."

Yup. I just had to ask even though I was 99.97% certain I already knew the answer. I wondered if John could figure out the code words, and so out of curiosity, I rang him up. "Fuck off," was the first thing he said. Damn machine. Back to square one, I suppose. Now I had to hunt up someone else with kneecap issues.

Sirocco and Amber Lee freshened up, and we reconvened on the deck. A few more beers and a final review of the plan, and we'd be all set to go. Amber Lee and I would be driven to the trawler well before dawn, where I would provide topside support for her mission. Sirocco would be driven back to the airport to head down south, where she would set down at Twilight Cove Car Park around sunrise. A landing area was ready to go at the south end of the lot facing Lover's Cove, and from there, she would ferry a few folks out to the RRS Sir David Attenborough periodically. The eight-meter tender would do the same on the water from the northern dock at the Taylor Street Jetty in West Beach. Joe and Tom were going to stick together on land. John was going to lock us all in on the same comms line, including Amber Lee. Since she was riding tetherless, I presumed the telecom was magic or witchcraft or some such shit.

While it would have been nice to go into more detail on the plan, everyone seemed to agree that time was of the essence. Whoever the bad guys were, they would probably have professionals on the way. I could only assume that the amateurs we'd run into hadn't reported back, and I was sure they were due to be recycled. Presumably, they had an inkling about Jillora Bindi and the possibility that there might be another four-plus billion-year-old, marble-sized crystal holding the secrets of life hidden somewhere beneath the surface. Control of such a treasure would wield greater power than all of Earth's antiquities combined.

Hopefully, the fanfare around the docks, including stations set up with free food, beverages, and prizes for all ages, would dissuade any bad guys from misbehaving. There were similar stations located at several strategic points along Twilight Beach Road. These included Salmon Beach Car Park, Observatory Point, Observatory Beach Car Park, Ten Eleven Mile Lagoon, Eleven Mile Lagoon, and even one up at Eleven Mile Beach Wind Farm Car Park. Naturally, some of Tom's folks would be situated at each location just in case.

We called it quits for the night, and Joe and Tom headed for their quarters. The others, along the perimeter, either headed to their rooms or maintained their stations. Others were out there in the night checking code words if necessary. There would be no more intruders tonight. There had been no sign of the drone operator either, so I figured he must have been sitting tight in some hole. Maybe he had been outside the perimeter the whole time.

Amber Lee and Sirocco walked in through my slider and I followed close behind. Amber Lee braced a chair under the handle of the front door while Sirocco secured the exit out to the patio. I poured us a nightcap of some of Mat's Highland Park 25 I had nipped before I left Portland. Visions of bliss danced in my head as we climbed into the rack together, but instead, exhaustion from our recent travels conked us all on the head.

We rolled out at four and prepared for the day.

216

Tom and Joe were already on the deck with a restaurant-size pot of steaming hot Upward Spiral coffee and sacks of various fresh rolls and pastries from Cloud Eleven. Small but efficient lunch boxes had also been delivered personally by the proprietress, a young lady named Olivia. She was a distant cousin of Tom's, naturally, and seemed quietly excited about the day's festivities. She had personally prepared everything and brought it over at her insistence. Jim, her boyfriend, was along to help tote the essentials. One of Tom's guys had accompanied the two of them over, armed to the teeth just in case. Contigo Autoseal cups, in matt black, were handed out. A nice touch.

Some of Tom's folks helped Olivia set up small kiosks at each location, giving her prime front-row exposure. Tom had hit his black card for the whole thing, including logistics, materials, overtime for the help, banners, and prizes. Tom might be a practical guy, but he's got a big heart nonetheless.

Amber Lee and I slipped by the inner perimeter lads outside and climbed into the Rover. Sirocco climbed into a different vehicle as shotgun. Another gent rode in the rear seat for extra protection, which I was glad for. A cheerful guy named Dirk drove us the short distance to the gate at the Port, seeming unperturbed that we were being tailed by at least two sets of headlights.

"No worries lad, they are me mates," Dirk softly explained when he noticed my eyes on the shotgun side mirror.

The gates slid open to allow us in, immediately closing once our car had passed the threshold. In the mirror, I saw Dirk's mates meet nose-to-nose, effectively sealing the entrance and leaving Dirk, Amber Lee, and me alone. We rode another 200 meters, exited the car, and all climbed aboard the trawler aptly named Recycler. The skipper, Little John, greeted us. He was just over two meters tall and weighed perhaps 115 kilos in Kangarooland. For those of us from the good ole USA, the guy was about 6'7", roughly 250 pounds, and built like a tank. Tom's male kin seemed larger than life.

Three other deckhands were there to shove us off. We cleared the northeast-facing jetty with plenty of water beneath us, then turned due south and made it to the deep waters on the east side of Cull Island in about twenty minutes. Amber Lee and I were standing on the bow looking through the darkness at the lights of the Attenborough, about six nautical miles or so to the west. As we made the westward turn after clearing Cull Island, I heard two small splashes at the stern.

"Recycling," Amber Lee said softly. Damn—glad she was on my side. There's that multi-generational Texas Hill Country part of her that is unsurpassed anywhere in the world. "Let's get my ride ready for a swim."

Little John slowed the boat to a drift and brought the twin screws into neutral. The crew raised the netting off of the sub, and Amber Lee did her external visual pre-dive check under the dim glow of directed red lights. She climbed aboard and sealed the semi-globe plexi hatch, completing her pre-dive routine before flashing us a grin and a thumbs-up. One of the crew secured the bow rope in the clenched fist of the left arm. The sub was lifted and gently lowered off of the stern, Amber Lee giving another thumbs up before disappearing beneath the water's surface. Little John waited a minute for Amber Lee to back off and then engaged the props. He proceeded at a dead slow pace until the entire three hundred meters of slightly negative-buoyancy rope trailed and he felt a slight tug.

Amber Lee clicked her mike twice. Little John replied with one click and slowly turned the revs of the props up to give him about five nautical miles per hour. The still air was salty and fresh, carrying the sweet scent of kelp and the first sounds of sea birds preparing to fish and steal all day. The very first faint pinkish lines on the horizon behind the boat signaled another clear dawn. The seas were flat, a rarity according to one of the deckhands—and a plus for us, I hoped. Our wake dispersed in a broad and white-foamed V behind us, obscuring any trace of the sub running ten meters below and three hundred meters behind us.

Tom came in over the headphones that had been shipped down by John. We all had a set on.

"Joe and I will be at Twilight Cove in ten," Tom said, voice small and metallic in my ear. There was a crackle, and then Sirocco piped in from the other line.

"I'm pre-checking my bird. Depart in ten, meet you gents at Twilight Cove shortly."

Little John quickly added his prescribed lines in the dialog, saying, "We finished recycling and the fish is in the water. The fish will be released, and we'll be dragging nets south of the Attenborough in about twenty, as planned." Richard, skipper of the sub Boaty, clicked in and said, "We're being lowered overboard as I speak." His beautiful bride and submate, Eliza Beth, would meet up with Amber Lee in the depths within the hour. Time had become of the essence if we wanted to be lucky enough to retrieve the treasure. Mat was in dire need of some concrete proof for his wild-assed theory, and the crystal was it. Maybe by now he'd figured how to crack it open and send us all back to the birth of our singularity, for all I know. I just want to get it to him so I could be done with this shit and get back to my Land Cruiser. Back to some peace and quiet.

News Flash (Mat)

Jenara and I had pulled up stakes from Sirroco's safe house at 2:30 pm on Thursday. We were in a limo headed for a private hangar at Dallas Love Airport when a call came in from John.

"An interesting news flash was just published," he told me. "You may want to read it through."

I thanked him, hung up, and tuned into the breaking news article on a secure internet connection. It seemed that Andrew had held up his end of the bargain.

The Secrets of Life Emerge from Ancient Artifacts - By Andrew Jenkins

One of the unanswered questions about life on Earth revolves around the origins of DNA. In a bizarre twist of international intrigue, new evidence recovered from 4-billion-year-old rocks supports the theory that life did not originate on Earth, but was deliberately planted here.

Public announcements from multiple sources now confirm that alien artifacts were uncovered in ancient rock formations from a time known as the Archean Period. Geologists recovered a container from these rocks made from advanced metallurgical composites. Inside the container was a gel composed of DNA-laden material believed to represent the origin of genetic material on Earth. These findings suggest DNA did not evolve, but rather, was transplanted by an advanced civilization. A civilization that existed before life on this planet began.

During the past two years, geological fieldwork in both Greenland and Australia uncovered manufactured objects embedded in rocks, which originally formed on ancient ocean floors some 4 billion years ago. Laboratory analysis from the Metal Theory Lab in Washington State confirms these fragments, or artifacts, are built from a layered graphene-metal composite material. The metal is of unknown composition, though the composites point to the possibility of extraterrestrial technologies.

The lure of new technological advances has snared various government and private entities into a secretive chase to procure these ancient artifacts. Theft, kidnapping, and even torture were used or considered in pursuit of technologies that could revolutionize modern industry. Geological samples containing these artifacts have allegedly been confiscated or stolen by government security teams and commercial cartels seeking to profit from potential discoveries.

Despite these setbacks, one group of geologists managed to procure a rock sample containing more than just fragments. After discovering an intact metal sphere buried for millennia, they have managed to unlock its secrets working out of a facility in Eugene, Oregon. This research team reportedly discovered how to open the sphere and retrieve its contents, consisting of a DNA-based liquid gel. Preliminary tests indicate the gel acted as a stabilizer to preserve the DNA indefinitely.

Five separate genetic research facilities are analyzing the material, and all have confirmed it contains what two labs describe as "Stem Cell DNA." In the same way stem cells can be grown and transformed into a variety of other cell types, this newly discovered DNA appears capable of rapid transformation into any number of known and unknown genomes.

The CEO of LifeSearch Corp, Michael Dunkins, stated, "We have only been analyzing this new development for less than 24 hours, but already, the potential boost to genome-based medical treatment is obvious. Hadian Group holds the patents related to this DNA, but has distributed samples to four other companies and us for use on a royalty-free basis. Our group and our colleagues are now working on a fuller analysis of this newly discovered DNA. We have agreed to consult with each other about how to effectively spread this information for the advancement of affordable new medical treatments."

The Seed of Life

Until today, the how, when, and why regarding the origins of life's fundamental building blocks remained unknown, lost in our planet's primordial history. Some scientists have proposed the inception of DNA on a deep-ocean floor in the extreme pressures and hellish temperatures around a hydrothermal vent. Others postulated that the first replicable life occurred in a warm puddle of slime as electric current pulsed through the water from lightning strikes. An even bolder fringe of the research community made the seemingly prescient argument that life fell to Earth from outer space.

Deoxyribonucleic acid (DNA) is the virile seed of life shared by nearly all living organisms in our biosphere. The genius of DNA is that it embodies the "sine qua non" of existence. The quality that life cannot do without. Its mantra is, "If one of me is good, then two of me is even better." Without the ability to self-replicate, life could not thrive and evolve. There would be no biosphere on our planet. Humans would not exist.

When Did Life Begin?

Before today, the question of when life began on Earth was speculative. The most common answer was that the oldest uncontroverted evidence of life is found in fossilized bacteria, which flourished some 3.5 billion years ago. The evidence in question for establishing this date comes from fossil stromatolites in Western Australia. Considering the Earth is about 4.5 billion years old, this leaves a 900 million year period in which life could have formed.

If you aren't a stromatolite enthusiast, picture these fossils as big heads of cabbage buried in sediment and slowly turn to rock. When you break open the stone cabbage and look inside some 3.5 billion years later, you can still recognize layer after layer stacked up one on top of the other into what's known as a bioherm.

The original bioherm was composed of cyanobacteria, or blue-green algae, that trapped sediment on the mound's outer layers, giving it the layered, cabbage-like look. Stromatolites are one of the world's oldest life forms, and they have been in existence for at least 3.5 billion years. Shark Bay, Australia, is famous for its present-day stromatolites.

These observations on stromatolites are impressive, but they don't answer the question of when DNA, the seed of life, first appeared. Cyanobacteria represent a leap up the evolutionary chain from a mere DNA molecule to a single-celled organism. So it follows that DNA must predate the oldest known stromatolites.

Research into the Origins of DNA

Most research into DNA has historically focused on the idea that DNA development is purely in-situ to Earth. The famous Miller experiment of 1952 demonstrated that amino acids, the organic compounds critical to life, could be created in the laboratory. A mixture of water, methane, ammonia, and hydrogen was exposed to heat and electric current to artificially produce these amino acids.

Other similar experiments used high temperature and high-pressure conditions to create new amino acids using the basic Miller chemical mixture along with additional inorganic sediment. Zapping a clay and chemical soup with a high-powered laser also produces amino acids from where none existed before. The laser simulates large-scale impact events on the Earth's surface, such as a solar flare or meteor impact.

The production of human-made amino acids was impressive, but far from the holy grail of genetic research. While amino acids are essential organic components of proteins, and proteins are critical to the proper functioning of cells, what researchers have historically wanted to understand is DNA, because it is the "master builder," determining when and where certain proteins are produced.

The DNA of all organisms, from bacteria to humans, is made up of the same chemical and physical components across the board. The same six molecules control whether you develop into a jellyfish or a human being. The magic six includes a five-carbon sugar molecule called deoxyribose, a phosphate molecule, and four different nitrogenous bases known as adenine, thymine, cytosine, and guanine.

These six molecules are the key components of nucleotides. Each nucleotide will have one sugar molecule, one phosphate molecule, and one of the four possible nitrogenous base molecules. These bases pair up to form long, spiraling chains, determining whether you are floating brainlessly on the ocean currents or designing rockets.

The discoveries announced today point us towards an origin for life that is completely alien. An Earth, which was impregnated with DNA from an unknown civilization, billions of years before the seeds they planted grew to become life as we know it today.

A Trail of Secrecy and Greed

The path leading to today's announcements is crooked at best. A trail of interviews and documents reveals the onsite theft of rock samples containing ancient artifacts in two locations. Last summer, a shipment of samples disappeared from a field storage shed at an Australian geological excavation. German geologist Bruno Vandorff was in charge of the geological team onsite. Dr. Vandorff said he was unaware of the other thefts, but he confirmed that the stolen samples had densities greater than any known natural materials.

This summer, a sample container shipping from Greenland disappeared from the Atlanta airport without a trace. No official comments have been issued by U.S. Customs on the Atlanta disappearance. Tapes have come forth showing a third attempted theft from a rock storage facility in Portland, Oregon. The perpetrators, in this instance, are allegedly mercenaries of Eastern European origin.

The motives for the criminal activity surrounding these alien artifacts are unknown. However, the transformative new technologies represented by these discoveries are suspected to be a factor. Control of these technologies offers lucrative financial potential. Hadian Group, the holder of the DNA patents, has issued a public statement: "Genetic patents held by Hadian Group will be available to qualified research projects on a gratis basis. Use of all patents will be granted on a royalty-free basis." The status of patents on the graphene-metal composite materials is unknown.

An unexplained twist in this unfolding story is the involvement of a coalition of religious organizations in the race to control the alien artifacts. Shocking evidence indicates that Catholic, Baptist, and Muslim interests in the Houston area have been vying to procure one of these samples.

Chaos at Houston Mega-Church

At 4:56 pm yesterday afternoon, the Houston Police Department received notice of an active shooter at the Holy Mission Church in Houston's exclusive River Oaks neighborhood. This upscale neighborhood is located next to Buffalo Bayou in the uptown Galleria district of Houston. The Holy Mission Church is the largest independent church in North America. It's pastor, Edward Dahlgreen, built Holy Mission Church into a multi-billion-dollar business from the ground up. With two major Houston campuses and offshoot branches in five other large metropolitan areas, the Holy Mission Church runs its own syndicated TV channel with close to 100 million viewers worldwide.

The active-shooter call was from an anonymous source, but as the police arrived, shots were fired from within the church. Four armed men, all Saudi nationals, were taken into custody in front of the church, and unofficial sources maintain that a Catholic Cardinal, Lucas DelBassey, the Imam Ahmed Najdi, and Pastor Edward Dahlgreen were all questioned by the police and remain persons of interest in the ongoing investigation.

This news outlet has also received audio and video footage from the church. Three men believed to be Dahlgreen, DelBassey, and Najdi are seen discussing the kidnapping and possible torture of geologist Dr. Matthew Dover, one of the researchers involved in the discovery of the alien artifacts.

Brent Dahlgreen, the pastor's son, confirmed that the group of religious leaders believe the existence of alien artifacts is a hoax aimed at destroying foundations of their respective religious institutions and nullifying the content of both the Koran and Bible. Their goal is purportedly to obtain one of the samples and reveal the hoax.

Imam Najdi is closely associated with the Saudi Royal family, and the role of the Saudi government in the church shootout is under investigation. Other sources in the Houston Police Department believe the armed Saudi men are part of a security team tied to a separate ambush and shooting incident just prior to the church shooting. This breaking story will be updated as more information becomes available.

Jenara finished reading about the same time I did. She smiled and gave me a gentle squeeze on the leg, just above my knee. All hell was breaking loose now. I hoped it would provide enough cover to let me complete the final stage of my plan. It was then that my phone lit up. I let it ring three times before answering because I had my suspicions about the caller. I knew John would keep my real location hidden.

The voice was as smooth, calm, and mellow, as before. "Well played, Mr. Dover. I don't know whether to attribute your success to blind luck or exceptional skill. We have located you in Ms. Sirroco's condo complex. Rest assured, we have sealed the exits. My search warrant will be here momentarily, and then I am afraid our game will come to a close. We have reason to believe you possess a certain crystal. A whole crystal, not just a fragment. Your treasure from the Eugene lab has been declared a national security issue. You are under judicial order to release it to the federal government."

"Ah," I replied. "So you are the employer of Duncan Mercer. I wondered who paid him to chase the crystal lattice memory angle."

"You surprise me yet again, Mr. Dover, with how well informed you are. Nevertheless, we will have that crystal."

"I am a law-abiding man," I said, "and of course I will honor any court order, once it is served. I eagerly await your arrival—with proper documentation, of course." I terminated the call and looked over at Jenara. "The vice is closing on us. We still have some time, but it may not be enough. There's nothing we can do now but play it out and see what happens."

There was no doubt in my mind that once we were found to be absent from the safe house, my caller would put the pieces together.

We would be in the air by then, headed to Boston, or already landed with any luck. The private terminal was the logical interception point, the weakest link in the chain. If we could make it through that chokepoint, then we might just succeed. I raised John on the phone once more.

"John, can you hide our tracks on the upcoming flight?" I asked, and he let out a noncommittal hum from the other end of the line.

"I can try, Mr. Dover. But at this point, the odds are not in your favor."

"Do what you can," I requested before hanging up.

Delay only created more time for my pursuers. If they found my plane, they could simply track it to any change in landing location. The best thing to do now was to get on with the plan. I smiled at Jenara.

"Let's hope they have some good scotch stocked in the bar on this flight."

Jillori Bindi Lived (Mark)

John tapped in and said, "bad news from Perth RAAF Base Pearce. The de Havilland DHC-4 Caribou – STOL Master was destroyed in a suspicious explosion and fire, apparently, sabotage. I'm trying to come up with Plan B, but our options are limited at the moment for the return flight to Perth for Amber Lee's sub and Sirocco's bird. The base is on lockdown, but the culprits apparently slipped out before the explosion. They must have used delayed charges. Or they are still there. I tapped into some comms and am getting a bad feeling. I will stay with it."

"John, check with Hayden Airport, make sure I can refuel there. It is halfway between Perth and us. If they don't have the fuel, have it trucked from Perth now. Tom, can you get a ground crew there asap? My bird can handle most threats in the air, but I do not want to be naked on the ground. John, arrange for alternative transport for the sub. Amber Lee, where do you want it to land?" Sirocco was on top of her game. A good pilot always knows everything along the flight path, just in case.

"10/4." John did his neutral voice. A bit of tension, I guess.

"10/4." Tom.

"Houston." Amber Lee.

I piped in "John, find a jet, Gulfstream G650 or similar. It has a range of about 7,000 nautical miles or so. Check runway length needs and verify Esperance can take it in and relaunch it without making a hole at the end of the runway."

"Esperance runway is 5,906 feet. Last time I flew long distance the jet required around 5,900 feet," Sirocco chimed in.

"Six feet to spare. Make sure the pilot has a large pair," Tom was there. "So what's going on Mark?"

"Just had a short conversation with Mat. It seems the whole gig is closing in around us. We need to get the treasure into his hands sooner rather than later. He and Jenara are in Dallas with the hounds closing in. Adelaide or Melbourne would be best if you can find our jet John. Should be able to be in and out, refuel in Brisbane and make it to John Wayne or, if that's an issue, LAX. John, Mat has gone dark for now, so have Eva meet us when we arrive.

"Cancel the chopper trip back to Perth then?" Tom asked.

"Actually, let's make it a bit public as a ruse. Get a pair of your folks to fly Sirocco's bird there with some fanfare about the flight. If this ole' world is still spinning late tonight, we should be headed east into a dark sky and see the sunrise halfway to California. John, once upon a time, you told me you could make it appear our satphone was anywhere on the planet other than where it is. Does that still hold?"

"Yes sir." John was a bit machine and a bit Aussie now. "What do you propose?"

"We've discussed the fact that various jealous folks, agencies, countries, and others have tried repeatedly over the years to breach your security to no avail. Can you create an opening, dead-end, of course, and let someone peek in and see where Mat is?" I was playing three-dimensional chess with a pair of dice and a deck of fifty-one.

"Working on it now. There, hole dug, ready to deceive. Where do you want Mat to be?" The damn computer had all aces.

"Anywhere the fuck other than between Texas and Massachusetts. Send the assholes to Perry, Florida, and let the hogs eat them. Get Hunter on the line." He needed a heads-up.

"Hunter here," he seemed laid back. Must have something to do with being paid a lot of money to hang out in fabulous digs high over Dallas.

"Several of us are on the line. You still watching amazing sunsets toward Midland?" I asked.

"Yes sir. What's next? Mat and Jenara are hanging tight in their hidey-hole. A little while ago, I felt a change coming in the air blowing out of the southwest. They don't know I am keeping an eye out for them." No one seems to know Hunter's real name. He is called by what he does. And changes in a hunter's surroundings are noted and accounted for. "Change" could easily mean the difference between a sip of good scotch and being dead.

"Bad guys are headed your way with a bogus warrant. Probably time for you to split, find new digs." It's like I'm talking to the machine and know what I'm about to hear.

"Fuck that," he understated. "If it's OK with Ms. Sirocco I'll just stick around and be sort of a greeting party. I keep missing out on the fun. I'm in need of some wholesome release. Like bitch slapping some bad guys."

Sirocco came on "John, give Hunter access to the slide. Hunter, you are the only person alive with access other than me. If the end is in sight and the assholes penetrate my inner sanctum, go feet first and face up through the hatch and hold your feet together with slightly flexed knees and your hands together on your chest. Prepare for deceleration at the count of ten or so. I had the slide installed as a last resort escape plan. You will spiral very steeply downward and stop somewhat abruptly in the parking garage. The upper entry and the exit-entry will become indiscernible and inaccessible without explosives. Before you leave, please feel free to pull the safety's off of the various booby-traps John will show you. I can always redecorate once the blood is cleaned up—time to invest in some local artists again anyway. I suggest the '67 Shelby GT 500 as your ride out of town. The keys are hanging in the key box in the kitchen. It pulls a bit to the left, so I recommend compensating when you check it's top end. I had it updated. Let me know if you can top 207 mph."

"Got it, and thank you Ms. Sirocco. I'll let ya'll know." Hunter clicked off. Nice to deal with professionals. So few around these days.

Solved that issue for the moment. Time to visit Jillora Bindi's old haunt. Amber Lee opened the fist on the left-hand articulated arm and released the Recycler. She engaged the electric screws and descended into the clear, bluish depths. The Olympus Delta Professional XRF was tucked into the right-hand arm, on and engaged, ready to send out some mild x-radiation and hopefully get a return. She did a double click on her mic and received a single click in return. Even though they had secure comms per John, minimizing noise underwater allowed them to 'feel' the otherwise alien environment.

The deckhands winched in the tow line and secured the fluorescent orange capture loop on a hook. Tom and Joe could see the nets being lowered into the water from their perch onshore. Good. So could others. A simple diversion. Hey, look at this. What was not apparent was that the lower attachment ropes were released, but they were not shackled to the bottom of the net. Instead of dragging a huge open catch basin of netting the trawler was dragging essentially a sheet of netting. This resulted in a significant reduction in drag and, if necessary, two swings of the ax by a deckhand would jettison the entire system.

Amber Lee and I spent a memorable three days at the Inn On The Lake in Fall River, Nova Scotia a few years ago. She described the ephemeral nature in exploring the depths solo in a bubble while we shared local brews in the hot tub. She said she loved to kill the lights and the screws and listen to the pulse of the ocean. The word sensuality did not begin to describe the essence of her experiences. The word sensuality did not even vaguely describe the brief moments we have managed to spend together over the years. Sirocco joined us for a day and night. I caught some smallmouth bass on my old ultralite gear wading the shoreline of Thomas Lake early in the morning while the ladies caught up. To this day I do not know what I did to deserve experiencing the very essence of life. Perhaps it is because I never complain but instead simply enjoy every breath.

Richard and Eliza Beth reached depth and began scanning the submerged walls connecting Canning Island and Observatory Island. The sub emitted a faint greenish glow. Amber Lee honed in on the light and held off several meters from Boaty and clicked her mic. Eliza Beth clicked twice in return and gave a brief wave before returning her gaze to her gages.

"Lights." Richard made the request.

Amber Lee brought her green and red spots to bear, and the wall immediately displayed a ledge running essentially east to west and close enough to the anticipated depth for government work, as the saying goes. The subs moved in parallel westward along the ledge. Amber Lee spied the stone with the constellation first and gasped. She clicked once and received a double click in return. They had arrived on the doorstep of the twenty-thousand-year old home of Jillora Bindi.

"Contact." Richard provided everyone the word they had been waiting on. He eased into position and attempted to anchor the sub with the articulated right arm. The ledge crumbled a bit. He was successful in obtaining a firm grip on the second try. He brought the left arm in close and gently removed one of the pineapple-sized stones from the top of the wall the devout followers had erected 20,000 years ago. He swung the arm around and gently placed the stone on the ledge. The job could have proceeded much more quickly, but the intent was to not create silt inside the cave. So one by one the neatly stacked stones were lifted and stacked to the side. Amber Lee hovered on the perimeter, providing extra light and awaiting her turn. The current was light to moderate so she had to steer and thrust a bit to maintain position. Visibility was good.

Amber Lee clicked once, indicating she felt she had enough room to work. Richard released his grip and drifted off a bit. Eliza Beth engaged the props and adjusted the planes a touch to maintain a vantage point and provide extra light for Amber Lee. She used the left arm to grasp the inner left edge of the cave. The right arm extended and inserted the XRF into the recess and on to the back wall. Richard's lights came in from low to high throwing a perfect shadow that outlined the metate. Sure enough, the legend was holding. The working end of the XRF reached the upper edge of the ancient well-worn stone and slid further and downward an inch at a time. Silt had partially filled the shallow basin so the camera did not reveal anything laying on the bottom. But the XRF did. The sound indicator had been silenced, but the indicator light pegged. Bingo. Amber Lee raised the XRF and activated the vacuum line controller. The line slid forward and emptied the ancient grinding stone of its contents, pulling whatever was laying in the metate back to the sub.

She released the left arm's grip and slowly backed off of the wall. Eliza Beth came into position, and Richard used his articulated arms to hold Amber Lee in position. She needed to reposition her body in the snug interior of the sub to open the body of the vacuum. Using her tiny mag light, she peered into the one-gallon container and then put her hand inside to the bottom. She felt the small round object, grasped it, and held it up. She would not need the XRF to identify the wonder she held in her hand. A sense of enchantment came over her as she realized that the object was quite probably well over four billion years old and had come from some distant civilization. The purpose of the object and why it was here would be an interesting topic over tasty beverages in a more comfortable setting.

"Jillora Bindi lived." Three words whispered into the mic on the headset brought smiles to the faces of everyone intimately involved. She waved off Richard and Eliza Beth, grinned, and pushed the throttle to the peg. The treasure went into a zippered breast pocket on her Patagonia windbreaker. Time to get the hell out of Dodge. She throttled southeastward. Eliza Beth held her sub steady while Richard re-placed the stones into their original positions. The sacredness of the occasion escaped no one participating in the event.

Little John heard the good news and went into a slow one-eighty, coming about on an easterly track that would take him just south of the Attenborough. Amber Lee would bring her sub up to snagging depth. He yelled back for the deckhands to drop the umbilical rope and to wench in the net. He intended to snag Amber Lee and tow the sub southward and then come about northbound for the recovery. The sub could then be cabled back aboard out of sight from shore. He and I watched the Raymarine Axiom Pro 12 RVX MFD 3D sonar as we approached the pickup point. We had both subs on the screen and then a different ping from something the size of Amber Lee's sub but biological instead of mechanical according to the coloration. Damn. What the fuck?

"Great white, bearing down on you Amber Lee." Little John said. It came in slow but straight and bumped the sub.

"Well hello beautiful, I was wondering if you would show. Amazing creature, probably twelve, thirteen feet, fifteen hundred pounds. Just nudged me again, getting somewhat more aggressive. Circling. Thoughts anyone?" Amber Lee was amazed and maybe just a tinge concerned.

"If legend holds true, flash the treasure," Tom was on top of it.

"Just popped the Velcro and am pulling it from my breast pocket. Shark is inbound again, more speed this time. If it hits full speed I'm popping to the surface sixty feet up without my ride. Holding the marble up now, shark is still coming gaining speed. I think I better secure the gem in my pocket in case I'm a floater." Dead calmness now, concentrating on the business at hand.

"Hold steady girl, the power is there." Tom whispered, crossing his fingers just in case.

"OK. Still coming. Thirty feet, twenty, ten, five. Wow! Veered off, heading southwest. Has not looked back. Going, going, gone." Amber Lee seemed relieved, shaken, and exhilarated at the same time. What an encounter and what an outcome.

Joe, Tom, and Croc were standing together on the Twilight Car Park's upper northern edge, opposite from the designated landing area on the southern edge of the pavement. They noticed a guy sitting on the tailgate of his truck with an iPad and a joystick. The rig had a high-top shell. The back was packed toward the front end but mostly empty toward the rear. They separated, and Tom ambled over.

"What ya see mate?" Tom smiled and placed a friendly hand on the guy's shoulder.

"Not much right now. Just looking for the subs." The guy just fucked up.

"Subs?" asked Tom. "Really mate, I heard there was a sub. Do you think there is another one? How fascinating. How far out is your drone? Must be a ways because I can't see it." Tom was honey. Croc had come around the rear of the truck on Tom's side and looked over his shoulder.

"Near that trawler." The guy was oblivious.

"I see it," said Little John.

"Wish we had a gun," I said.

Little John told me to hold the wheel steady. He went into his cabin and returned momentarily. He held a Heym Model 89B classic double rifle, showing off a rounded action boxlock, with a solid crossbolt, chambered in the classic .450/400 3" NE. The 89B was made to kill anything you could hit that was smaller than a locomotive.

"Pop sharks if they fuck with my nets. A shark-tangled net can cost me fifty thousand or more." He propped the gun on the rail. The drone had drifted a little south so I pointed it out.

"So you had a second drone eh?" Tom watched the guy. The asshole looked up in surprise. Joe came around the other side of the tailgate and smashed the electronic equipment with his fist as Tom and Croc both punched the guy with uppercuts the size of bricks under the guy's chin. The guy was lifted from his perch like a blue quail coming up from under mesquite. He flopped bunched up in the rear of the cargo bed, sound asleep. They slammed the tailgate shut.

"Got it mate." Little John exhaled slightly and squeezed the trigger. The recoil hardly phased him. That same recoil had knocked me flat on my ass several years earlier when I tried to take out an armored personnel carrier with a similar shooting piece. The drone was there, and then it was ticker tape being blown about in the sea breeze. Still, we had to wonder who was receiving the transmission other than the guy snoozing in his camper.

Little John looked back, got a thumbs-up from the crew member at the rear. The net was in.

"We're dead slow Amber Lee. Can you see the marker glowing on the end of the tether?" Little John was a gentle giant. He would have gone overboard in a heartbeat if Amber Lee was in trouble.

"Just latched it, seems taut, ready to roll." Cool as a cucumber. Reminded me of an old song played by the Nitty Gritty Dirt Band. The song was about coon hunting. Racoons are hunted at night using coon dogs. The hunters built a fire and hung around it until the dogs bayed up a coon. The words I remembered were "…time to call in tha dogs, piss on the fire and head it on back to Bowlegs." So we headed on back to Bowlegs.

"John here. I've got the jet set to fly, needs two hours lead time. John Wayne it is stateside, Eva will be there. She has set up her own transport to Boston. Mat is in Dallas but heading to Boston soon. I arranged ground transport for the sub to Perth with Tom's guys, commercial transport back to Houston, arriving in two days. According to the cameras in Dallas the feds are serving the warrant to the guys at the front desk of Sirocco's place. Hunter is all set. If I may say so, he seems a little, uh, joyful. I hope he is OK. Have I missed anything? Next actions for me?" Full-blown Aussie. Computers do not have emotions such as pride or sympathy, do they? If so I'm sticking the 89B into my left ear.

"In one hour my boys will lash my boat to the docks. Sun sets in another hour." Little John knew his place and the needs of the team.

"The drone driver is sound asleep in the back of his truck. By the sound of Tom's and Croc's fist on the guy's face he just might sleep forever." Joe did not seem particularly concerned about sleeping beauty.

Tom said, "my boys will escort Mark and Amber Lee to the airport."

John came back in and said "the jet is airborne and will circle out fifty miles or so until we call it in. The pilot claims not to have a large set of balls, being that her name is Isla. She says not to worry though. She only needs what the runway offers in length. According to her, 'why waste a bunch of money on extra fucking concrete'. Further, she has followed Sirocco from afar and is looking forward to having her as first mate."

Tom came back on in a few minutes and said the boys were lined up to fly the chopper, and the refueling should go smoothly at Hayden Airport. A final stop in Perth, then aboard the civilian carrier to Houston.

"I'm still getting strange chatter in the background, but I can't seem to crack open the carrier. Definitely government or seriously serious private interests. Further, the satellite I anticipated appears to have lost power, so I'm blind in the sky over southern Australia. All in all, I recommend everyone keep your eyes open and stay locked and loaded." John was the concerned old man now.

The sub was pulled on-board without incident, secured, and draped with the netting. Sirocco left the last tourists onshore and flew her bird to the airport. Tom and Joe met her there. The new pilots were there. She was impressed with their obvious knowledge and laughed at their expressions when she showed them some toys that she had added during manufacture and also some after-market gadgets. Hopefully, the trip would be uneventful but being prepared often led to another local beer being downed. They did the precheck, wound it up, and headed west.

Little John eased the trawler alongside the dock, and the crew lashed it to the bollards on the dock. He jumped down onto the dock, turned and lifted Amber Lee like a child and lightly planted her on the dock beside him. She bent her outstretched index finger and bent it inward, displaying the universal sign for come here. Little John bent down and she planted a huge kiss on his cheek, turned and climbed into the shotgun seat of the Rover. I was in back beside a husky well-armed youth. The driver engaged the clutch, and we were gone. Much later in the day, the story goes, the deckhands slowly lowered Little John's hand from his cheek and gently took him home. I know the feeling.

The runway lights were fired up just before the pilot came by westbound, doused, then fired up again when the jet was on final approach about ten miles out. The Gulfstream touched down on the eight warning lines and turned on the east end warning lines with several feet to spare. Sirocco and Amber Lee climbed aboard, followed by Joe. I gave Tom a brief clasp and hug, then climbed up and pulled the door to and secured it. Sirocco donned a headset and climbed into the right-hand shotgun seat. Isla continued the preflight, grinned at Sirocco, they touched hands and she nailed the throttle to the stops while holding her foot on the brake. Just when the riders thought the ride would crumble, it came out of the gate like a two-year-old at Belmont. They cleared the creek and scrub at the far end by at least a foot or two. Isla gained five hundred feet and banked eastward and a bit north. She held the low altitude until they were over the desert interior, then brought the bird up to thirty-five thousand feet.

Hunters Time (Mark)

"Mr. Hunter, there are six gentlemen here to see you. They seem to have a warrant for someone named Mat." The signal was sent.

"Tell them to fuck off. No one here named Mat." Hunter was making a few last preparations. One of the assholes grabbed the landline. "Mr. Hunter, I'm here to search the premises. Do not interfere. We are coming up. We have overridden the external elevator controls, so there will be no yoyo this time. We'll see you shortly." The confident asshole, apparently one of the crew from Mat's very first encounter, rang off. Hunter had about one minute before the fun began. Way more than enough time to set the last trap. Six to one? Shit, he'd beaten those odds when he was a kid growing up poverty-stricken and having to fight with kinfolk and strangers alike for scraps of food. He had gotten pretty good at eating.

The 'hurricane' door was lowered in front of the elevator doors, effectively sealing the assholes in the elevator once it reached its destination. This was an add-on to the original construction. The door was two inches thick and was honeycombed with woven titanium and ceramic fibers. Little John's Heym Model 89B, fired at point-blank range, would put slight positive points on the other side of the door. Shaped charges placed properly could do the trick but would probably render the guys in the elevator dead. Torch-cutting the door was also an option, especially if you had all of the time in the world. The floor, walls, and ceiling of the elevator were conveniently enclosed in the same material. The seams were the most vulnerable areas but attacking them high or low or around the edges offered up the same level of danger. All in all, being invited into the living quarters was the only truly viable alternative for entry.

"911, what is your emergency please?" 911 answered John's call.

"Six pot-smoking long-haired bad outlaws are invading my apartment, and I need help!" John sounded like another stressed-out high-pitched Republican Senator caught with his pecker in the hired help.

"Address, please." 911 was cool as a cucumber—quite professional or perhaps just bored silly.

John gave the address and said to please hurry because he was scared and might get spanked with a Time magazine when daddy got home. That should do it. Dallas's finest were on the way. For good measure, John called in again and said there was a fire at the same address. There would be mayhem in the streets momentarily, and Hunter's plan was to exit via slide three minutes after initial contact at the elevator. Let the police and firefighters deal with the intruders.

There was a vague pounding emanating from the other side of the hurricane door and raised voices demanding immediate entry under threat of arrest and incarceration. Wow, was Hunter intimidated.

"Folks have come a-knockin' on the door. I can hear sirens through both balconies. I'm gonna hold for another minute, cause trouble for one more after that, and then skedaddle on out of here." Multiple clicks from far away acknowledged. Good luck and watch your ass.

"Show me your warrant," Hunter said to the door. About time he could enjoy himself. All this lollygagging had made him about half-stir crazy. Besides, he was bound and determined to beat Sirocco's 207 mph on a very clean stretch of SR 84 just above Justiceburg headed into Post. Lots of leg room there. Mark liked to fish. Hunter liked to hunt and go fast.

Sirocco phoned the private line of Dallas Chief of Police Gallery. She answered on the first ring. "Chief, Sirocco here. Hope all is well. I'm sorry to bother you, but the bad guys are at it again, and I'm out of town."

"Sirocco, I'm sorry, but this time it is out of my hands. Some black ops shit or something, but the Feds told us to back off. I truly am sorry." She rang off. Well damn.

"Everyone hear the Chief's message?" 'Yups' came from near and far.

"Open the fucking door, or we will shoot our way in." There were several reports followed by two screams of agony. Rude bastards had not even waited for a reply. Just gone and shot up the place. Served 'em right. Good ole Ricochet Rabbit could not have done better. Two down and four to go.

"Show me the warrant, you rude bastards. Or fuck off." We could hear Hunter's taunt. Almost time for his next act. "I can hear lots of sirens now. I also understand the sirens may be looking for me. I just sent a signal and the hurricane door started up. I rolled a smoke canister under the door and signaled it down again. Time is almost gone for me. I'm heading into Sirocco's innermost closet on the north wall and just sent a signal." Magically the wall opened like a kaleidoscope revealing the entry to the slide at floor level. "I signaled for the hurricane door to open and electronically turned off the safety features in the security system. Good luck to these assholes. I hope they survive to tell another lie. See ya'll soon." Hunter slid in face up and feet first. He held his satphone in his hands crossed over his chest. Much later, he would finally fess up to being scared shitless during the near-vertical slide. So much for his manli-manliness.

The old pony car cranked up with the subtlety of a male lion in heat. Hunter depressed the clutch, slipped the tight Hurst shifter into first, and made his way out of the garage on the south side just ahead of it being closed off. He left rubber in three gears. No problem though, because all the cops were inbound against his outbound leg.

"I'm clear. Gonna look for the top end out toward Lubbock. Cheers!" Hunter clicked off and was gone.

Hitch Hiking (Mark)

Richard, Eliza Beth, and the sub were winched back aboard the RRS Sir David Attenborough. Some tourists gathered with a handful of scientists to watch the event. With one of his coworkers' help, Richard opened the catch basket and emptied the contents on a cleaning table convenient to the sub's anchorage on deck. Various crabs, clams, and rocks intermixed with sand and typical reef debris were there for everyone to see—not much and definitely a bit of a let-down for the audience. They had hoped for a vast treasure of pirated gold and jewels and such. But it was an excellent show in case any bad guys watched and wondered if there was more to the Attenborough's presence than a shallow, warm water test run with new equipment. The skipper waved farewell to the last launch headed back for shore. He would head for Perth shortly, ending the brief respite from the hazards of sailing the waters off Antarctica.

Tom and Croc rounded up the local lads for one last evening at the hotel. Little John had shaken off the magical spell of Amber Lee's parting kiss, and he and his boys joined in the festivities. They would head back to Perth in the morning. It would be several weeks before all the repairs to the hotel rooms were complete. It seemed that this particular big adventure was winding down. Back to more mundane tasks like drinking and swapping lies in the local pubs back home. The local Constable, one of Croc's cousins, had responded to a call-out on the coast about an abandoned bad-smelling pickup with a camper shell. It turned out that a foreigner had died of an overdose of some bad shit. So it goes.

Tom had talked with his beautiful bride Jillora Bindi. She told him the present, past, and future were all well, and harmony reigned. The chain was unbroken, and the universe of the Aboriginals was in complete harmony. What is, was, and will be were as they had been for the last 20,000 years or so. Great news from my perspective because I had seen what could happen when someone threw the cosmos out of whack.

We were feet wet after refueling in Adelaide when John reported that Sirocco's bird had come under fire from drones on the approach into Hayden Airport. The armament and weapons array on the bird had quickly turned the attack into a rout. John had finally tied back in with the satellite and was able to find the controllers a bit off the beaten track. They were apparently the strange bit of chatter that had bothered John. Tom's boys crashed their ground party. Black-breasted buzzards would have a feast in a day or two. Refueling and the rest of the trip were uneventful.

Our flight into Orange County was long and restful. Joe and I mostly slept, and the ladies seemed to have had a delightful time in the cockpit. Amber Lee descended the stairs on the ground at John Wayne Airport, walked to the jet beside ours, and handed the treasure to Eva. A brief hug and Eva re-boarded her eastbound ride. John had taken care of Immigration. A red light on the panel held us on the ground for almost four hours. Finally, the ground engineer tracked down a faulty breaker. We were another hour getting queued and airborne out of Orange County. Mat might need us; he might not. Nonetheless, we were Boston-bound.

Mat and I thumbed across and around the big ole US of A when we were still kids. It forged an unbreakable bond and instilled confidence in us that has carried to this day. As previously discussed, if Mat said today is the day we die, I would ask when and where I needed to be for the event.

We flew over the Great Basin and Range section of the beautiful southwest and passed by Albuquerque. I could see the Sangre de

Christos and beyond it, to the north, the general area where Ghost Ranch was located. North and east, I scanned the upper reaches of the Rio Grande, cutting down into massive basalt flows and the southern edge of the Rockies up in Colorado. This country never ceases to amaze me in its vastness and its beauty. There should be a requirement for each and every person in this country to experience a window seat at 35,000 feet coast to coast. The opportunity always humbles me. We skimmed in across the eastern edge of the Atlantic just off of Boston Harbor and basically crash-landed on the short runway at Beverly Regional Airport. Five thousand feet was a bit short, but Isla nailed it, and we only skidded a few yards beyond the stops. OK. The jet would have to be towed back to the runway. But we were on the ground and rolling in a dark blue late model Expedition with dark windows before anyone really knew what happened. The runway 'mishap' would be laughed off on the local evening news. Lobsters and clams and stew would still be eaten at Roy's in Rockport long after the news was old. Eating lobster barehanded from a cardboard french-fry tray sitting on a lobster trap out back in the salt air on a brisk fall day is one of life's great pleasures.

I punched up Mat on the satphone.

Boston (Mat)

The night was creeping in, and the western horizon glowed with the last of the day's sunlight. Jenara and I sat silently together in an east-bound plane. She had the crystal sphere and was rolling it between her fingers, examining it against the light. She curled her fingers around it and shut her eyes as it rested, enclosed in her hand's palm. After several minutes she opened her eyes and handed it back to me. She said nothing, but she had a curious look in her eyes.

We were traveling on a Gulfstream g550 we had boarded several hours ago at the Dallas Love airport. The g550 is a workhorse business jet produced by General Dynamics Gulfstream Aerospace in Savannah, GA. It carries a range of 7,768 miles and a top speed of 585mph. These little beauties can be outfitted to accommodate up to nineteen passengers, but this one was designed to hold twelve. Tonight it just carried two: Jenara and me.

We were headed for the Laurence G Hanscom airfield, about 20 miles NW of downtown Boston. The airport was reasonably convenient to our final destination. But I was nervous. I felt like I was on the losing end of a time trap. Surely by now, my friends had checked Sirrico's safe house and realized we had flown the coop. It wouldn't take any real genius to track us to Love and then to our final destination at Hanscom. The timing was close, but the more I ran the numbers, the more certain I became; the odds did not favor me at this point.

We avoided mainstream news on the plan's passenger screens. Still, the stewardess had commented several times on the weird news that DNA was brought to earth billions of years ago by some unknown alien civilization. She wasn't sure whether to believe it or not and then she confided in us how she was nervous and creeped out about aliens watching us. I wasn't sure where she was coming from with that statement, but I commented they probably hadn't been sitting around, waiting for the four billion years it took Homo Sapiens to develop. She gave a curt "Umm" and got us another round of drinks.

After the drinks arrived, the pilot came online and told us that we were starting our descent and had about 30 minutes until landing. I shut my eyes and thought, "Here we go." Jenara messaged the base of my neck. "Don't worry, Mat. It will unfold of its own accord and in its own time. The path is beyond your control." The quality of her voice was like a drug, and I actually drifted off to sleep for a bit.

I woke back up as the wheels hit the ground. Airport traffic was heavy, and it took the pilot a while to get us into our final destination, a private hangar on the north side of the airport. As we wheeled in, my heart sank. I could see three black federal-looking SUVs parked on the far side of the hanger. I had played the game well, but not well enough.

As soon as the plane stopped, the pilot came through and informed me that I couldn't exit, since there were federal agents in the hanger who had a warrant for an object in my possession. I told him that this was not completely unexpected and thanked him for the trip.

The first two people to come aboard were my lawyers. I contacted them just before we left Dallas and requested they be here as a last stop measure. Justin Stoneman and a younger colleague I didn't know sat down across from Jenara and me. Justin introduced the second man as Jim, and I leaned over and shook his hand. "Pleasure to meet you, Jim."

"Same here, Mr. Dover."

"So, Justin, what are we looking at?" I asked.

"Well, Mat, it's pretty airtight. They have a federal warrant to search the plane, you, and your possessions. They have reason to believe you are in possession of an object linked to a National Security issue.

They are pretty specific. It is a crystalline sphere about one inch in diameter. It was retrieved from a container you to took to a lab in Eugene, Oregon, and proceeded to open using some sort of pressure device."

Justin stopped and opened his phone to a video. He started it running and then passed it over to me. I silently watched as the orb in the pressure bomb slowly unfolded like a flower, and its contents spilled on the floor of the container. I mentally kicked myself—another self-inflicted error on my part. I thought I had the only copy of the video, but I was wrong.

"Are there any legal grounds for me to resist this, Justin?"

He thought a moment, relooked at a document in his hand, and said, "not really, Mat. I am going to be frank with you. They have come here on a mission, and if they don't walk away with the sphere, then I am pretty sure they will walk away with you. As your lawyer, I advise you to play ball with them. "

I pushed back, sighed, and said," OK, bring them on board."

Only two agents came on board, and they sat down where Justin and Jim had been sitting. I looked them over and laid into the lead agent. "What do you people mean by entering onto my private plane and demanding possession of an object that was never yours to start off with?"

Justin was a little nervous, but Jenara was cool as a cucumber. She spoke in a silky hypnotic voice. "I have been involved from the beginning, and I can vouch for the fact that what Mr. Dover says is true. The thing you desire was never yours to start with." She sounded so damn convincing, how does she do that I thought?

"Mr. Dover and Ms. Solido I am not at liberty to discuss the issue since it is a matter of National Security," the lead agent said.

I rolled my eyes in my head and replied, "National Security, where do you guys come up with this kinda crap?"

The lead agent tilted his head to the side. He was clearly listening to something. He extracted a phone punched in a speed dial number and handed it to me. I pushed it up to my ear, and that same calm, smooth voice from Timberline came on.

"Mr. Dover, your righteous indignation will get you nowhere, and you know it. You have played an extremely good hand. I have been impressed, and I don't impress easily. You have played the game out to the last move. In fact, if your plane had landed 30 minutes earlier, you would have won. But we find ourselves here, and you know we won't walk away without it. So let's stop berating my agents and move on. Out of curiosity, where were you actually taking the sphere?"

"You haven't done me the courtesy of introducing yourself," I said , "so I shall refer to you as Jeff. Jeff, you have apparently won. Yes, I will give your agents what they desire and let them be on their way. As for my original plans, perhaps some things are best left unsaid.

"OK Mr. Dover, but I worry about your use of the words 'apparently won.' Is there more I need to know."

"You worry too much Jeff," I said. "You have what you came for. Take it and go. And we can let the winds of fortune blow as they will."

I handed the phone back to the lead agent and also handed him the felt bag with the sphere. He opened it up, examined the object, then motioned for the other agent to open his briefcase. It turns out it was not a briefcase at all, but instead a rather sophisticated piece of analytical equipment. The sphere disappeared into a chamber, and about two minutes later, the lead agent received a call. He simply listened and said, "Thank you Mr. Mercer."

Duncan Mercer, I thought, he comes back into play again. They closed the equipment case with the sphere still inside and exited the plane. I thanked Justin and Jim and motioned for them to go. Jenara and I sat in silence for several minutes. I finally said, "grab your bag, sweetheart, we still have a meeting to make tonight."

We exited the plane, crossed the now empty hanger, and went into the passenger lounge. There was one person there. A thirty-something woman in a dark suit, and she was clearly waiting for me.

"Mr. Dover?" she inquired. I nodded affirmatively, and she checked my face against a photo on her phone.

"This is for you, sir," and she handed me an envelope.

She had already left by the time I started opening it.

Mat,

Why don't you and your lady friend join me for a beer at Ricks, 251 Elm St.

Eva

Perhaps the winds of fortune were blowing already.

The driver picked up I95 South out of the airport and then cut off east on route 2. Route 2 eventually dropped us into the North Cambridge area, and soon after at Ricks.

Ricks was a skinny, deep, cavernous affair. A long dark-wood bar on the right wall stretched about halfway through the length of the establishment. The whole front area near the entrance was packed with drinkers, and while there were a few tables up front, most of the booth seating was near the rear of the bar. Jenara and I pushed our way through the throng of drinkers and headed to the back. There, in one of the last booths, was Eva. I gave her a kiss on the cheek and introduced Jenara. Eva was sitting eyes to the door, so we sat on the other side. We ordered some beers that almost showed up before we ordered them. Eva held sway here for some reason.

I thanked her for the favor she did me with the Dahlgreen incident just several days ago. She paused a moment before she lit into me.

"Routine job, Mat? Just a simple delivery? Those were fucking armed Saudi agents, in the country illegally and ready to use force. It became an active shooter incident at one of the richest churches in the USA. Houston police were swarming by the time I squeaked out of there. I billed your ass twice my usual fee."

"Yes," I replied," and I paid you another 50% on top of that."

She smirked a little bit. "Fair enough, sometimes bad shit creeps up on us unexpectedly, but with me, I always plan for it. So, all is well that ends well."

She looked over at Jenara. "You are doing a crap job of keeping him out of trouble."

"Trying my best Eva, but not succeeding."

I could see Eva sizing up Jenara. She didn't quite know what to make of her, which was interesting to me, because Eva could usually read a person like a book after about two seconds. Her job depended on it.

She sipped on her beer before starting up the conversation again. "I had some recent contact with your buddy Mark." The winds of fortune were blowing like a breeze on the back of my neck. "He asked me to do a favor for him."

I raised my eyebrows a bit before I replied. "Let me see if I remember this quote correctly Eva – If I never work with that fucking loose cannon again, then I will die happy. I believe that was in Rio."

"Umm," she said. "Sometimes, we do get a little overly dramatic when we are royally pissed off."

She slid a small felt bag across the table. I could feel the sphere as I slipped it into my pocket. "This is most fortuitous indeed," I said. "I was recently relieved of a substantially similar object when we landed at Hanscom. I thought perhaps the game was over, and I had lost, but I see now, I was mistaken. Eva, you are a bearer of good tidings, my dear woman."

She was listening, but her eyes were focused on the front door. "Mat, they tapped your ride. Don't turn around, but four feds walked in. I am going to take a stroll up to the front, and you two are going to leave by the back door. Go through the door 20 feet behind me, take a right, take the next left, and then exit the building. There is a Silver SUV waiting near the exit. Tell the driver Eva sent you. Go finish your little adventure."

She grabbed her beer and strolled towards the front. About twenty feet from the entrance, she bumped into some half-lit dude and spilled her beer all over him. He called her a bitch, and she proceeded to grab him by the right arm and flip him over her back, sending him skidding like a bowling ball towards the front door. He took down about six people, including two of the agents.

We were on the move, but I could see the guy pick himself up and charge back at Eva. When he arrived, he was met with a vicious nerve punch that numbed his right arm, and he collapsed against the bar. I could hear Eva leaning in close to him and ranting as we exited.

"What is the world coming to when a poor single girl can't even come out for a drink without rude men trying to push her around. You have a mother. Is this the way your mother raised you, to pick on little girls half your size. I just wanted a nice peaceful evening, but no, fuckwads like you just have to go around harassing and scaring women. You should be ashamed of yourself." He groaned again. The whole bar was focused on the scene.

The SUV was there, as Eva said, and we were back on track, albeit a few minutes late. I placed a call to Carl Jennings at ThreeRock Analytics and told him that I had a few unexpected problems, but that I would be at his office by 9:30. I also requested that he provide us direct access to his executive below-ground parking area. I did not want to take any chances on being unexpectedly intercepted again this evening.

As we rode in the darkness, Jenera asked to see the felt bag. She did the same routine she had done on the plane. Rolling the crystal in her fingers, holding it up against some light, and then cupping it in her hand and closing her eyes for a few minutes. The whole routine implied delicate and intimate familiarity. She finally opened her eyes, handed it back to me, and simply said, "It's the real thing." I didn't ask her any questions; I just nodded my head.

The ThreeRock headquarters were about a 30-minute ride from Ricks, and we arrived without incident. The building itself was a typical urban glass and steel affair. Eighteen stories high with beautifully manicured grounds and a small lake and fountain in front. When we exited on the eighteenth floor we were met by an assistant and taken to Carl's office. The south side of his office was a glass wall facing downtown

Boston and the evening light-show from the city was entertaining. The lawyers had worked out the details of the investment yesterday, and it was a done deal for all practical purposes, but I had this thing about personal contact when sealing a big deal. My signature in two places would finalize it.

Carl was a stout but fit guy in his early fifties. He was starting to bald on top but wore it well. Even though he had casual, laid-back mannerisms, I knew from my background work that he was sharp as a tack and had a reputation as an uncanny dealmaker. He and I opened a couple of beers, and he poured Jenara a glass of wine. It didn't pass me by that he happened to have my favorite Oregon beer, pFriem IPA, on hand in his private office bar.

We settled into some seats overlooking that gorgeous Boston light show. The papers were on a table in front of us, but I ignored them for the moment.

"Carl, "I said. "Let me tell you a story."

I proceeded to unload almost the complete story starting with Greenland. I even included the parts about hiding in Dallas and arranging a major news story that would provide me cover to slip into Boston unnoticed. I ended at the airport but didn't include the Ricks story.

"Well," Carl started, "I was as shocked as everyone about the news. It's fricking incredible. It's like science fiction, but it's real. You do know there are major religious groups falling into deep tailspins right about now, and there is widespread public unrest throughout much of the Middle East. Most world governments have remained fairly silent, but several have hailed the advances that may come from new technologies. There are, of course, a few governments declaring it a fraud. But the labs announcing the metallurgy and DNA analyses are all top-notch. Our investigators doing due diligence for our deal, said they thought you were the driving force behind the news cycle. They speculatively linked you in through the company Hadian Group."

I said nothing, but I pulled the papers over and signed them. "The deal is done Carl, I am looking forward to being on your board. But the first thing I want to do is finish my story. I had asked for your best tech guy to be on hand. Is he here?"

Carl got up and walked over to his desk, punched an intercom button, and said: "Jack, come on down to my office."

Carl sat back down, and I continued. "Yes the Federal Government played the game better than me and shut me down on my final gambit to get to Boston unnoticed. But the world flows in mysterious ways, and about an hour ago in a dark, seedy bar on Elm Street, the wheel of fortune spun back in my direction, and I was passed this." I held up the red felt bag. This was right about the time Jack walked in.

We introduced shook hands, and I asked him to hold out his hand. I dumped the crystal sphere out of the bag into his palm. "Jack, I have every reason to believe that this is an advanced crystal lattice memory device."

Jack sputtered a bit, "Holy crap, this is what Duncan Mercer described to me. He had a fragment of one."

My nervousness crept up a degree. "Well you may want to keep this to yourself since Duncan Mercer stole one of these from me just two hours ago at Hanscom airport."

"It all stays in-house, sir," he quickly replied.

"Carl, is it OK if Jack examines this now?" I asked. I was in no position to tell Carl's people what to do.

"Jack, I imagine you have the time for this?" Carl asked.

Jack was already moving, "I will let you know as soon as I have something."

As he exited the room, Carl said, "Jack is better than Duncan, a lot better. He will untangle the matrix memory and chase out the technology."

Two hours elapsed before Jack returned. He collapsed into one of the chairs and rubbed his eyes with the palms of his hands for a moment before he spoke. "The technology is incredible but mind-bogglingly complex. You can physically think of the sphere as having eight sectors. Imagine a ball sliced in two to create an upper hemisphere and a lower hemisphere, and then each hemisphere is divided into quarters. So essentially, you have eight sectors. It's not really like that, but the mental imagery provides a good visual prop."

"Four of those sectors are so foreign they are impenetrable at this point. The closest I can guess is that they are the output from some sort of quantum computing process. Three of them are packed with terabytes of binary data. This is something we can start investigating and unraveling. The last sector, however, is small in terms of data space and easy to read. Its audiovisual data, a movie essentially. There is no real audio information, just weird, slightly disharmonic background music."

This all made perfect sense to me. How do you send a message 4 billion years into the future to people with unknown languages, unknown cultures, and unknown technological skills? You gear it to the lowest bar, visual imagery. I guessed the message was visible across a wide range of light frequencies since there was no way of knowing the visual spectrum of your future target audience.

Jack continued, "I have constructed a reader for the sphere data, and it is set to play on your office wall display Carl."

Carl punched a remote, and two panels on the wall behind his desk slid apart, artwork and all, to expose a massive flat-screen display. Jack touched a second remote, and the display flickered to life. A rich and vibrant 3D animation started up showing a planet in an early stage of formation. Jack was right; the music was a bit disharmonic, but then, I had no way of knowing if I heard the intended full frequency range. The animation made sense also, simplify reality, making a more universal message.

The first thirty minutes of the message outlined the development of an Earth-like planet. It was more of a water-world than the Earth, with about 80 percent of the planet covered in oceans. Life evolved first at sea and then on land. There were active tectonic plates, and landmasses shifting geographic positions over time, but the plate tectonic activity was very low compared to Earth. Thousands of species came and went over time, but there was no real time scale, so I assumed the same several billion-year scale of Earth's evolutionary past.

No dinosaurs appeared, but equally wonderful and bizarre creatures were depicted evolving and dying off in the animation. Interestingly there were no mass extinction events detailed in the saga, and climatic conditions were remarkably stable. The polar regions remained ice-capped through the entire evolution of the planet, and equatorial regions remained tropical. Both of these aspects of the planet appeared to be related to the low plate tectonic activity level.

This low level of tectonic activity introduced several important factors. Many of the Earth's mass extinction events were intimately tied to massive outpourings of flood basalts when millions of cubic miles of molten rock spewed from the planet's interior onto the surface. The particulate aerosols from these volcanic storms filled the skies and temporarily blocked off the sunlight, sending Earth into a long winter. When the skies finally cleared, the degassing of the magmas had changed the atmospheric mix to create higher levels of greenhouse gases, and rapid planetary warming ensued. Noxious gases combined with water to create acid rains that further choked off life. Rapid change challenges the ability of species to survive, and at one point during the earths history, about 255 million years ago, 95 percent of all marine species disappeared.

The planet we were seeing never experienced this stress. The vast oceans of the planet, along with the continents' relatively stable configuration, created conditions for the development of stable long-term deep-ocean overturn currents like Earth's Gulf Stream in the North Atlantic. This development was a critical factor. These overturn currents are the heat dissipation engines that continuously move heat from the equatorial areas towards the polar areas. The stability of these currents supports stable atmospheric patterns. The world we were seeing didn't develop the intense glacial-interglacial cycles of Earth's past. However, long term solar cycles did appear to cause moderate expansion and contraction of polar ice—moderate changes compared to what Earth has experienced.

The rise of sentience capped off the early evolution segment of the message. A species with abstract reasoning capabilities strode onto the stage of life. Bipedal and equipped with the use of opposable digits on its upper limbs, these creatures took a familiar trajectory into the future. There was an early agricultural revolution where hunter-gathers became farmers, and stable communities became civilizations.

Wars were fought over many millenniums, affairs every bit as brutal as the ones on Earth. Regal depictions of fully-furred, flat-nosed creatures dressed in the regalia of medieval-like royal courts were stunning. Generals on the battlefield dressed like emperors commanding armies of peasants in rags. It was all so familiar but being played out on a foreign canvass.

Wars sparked technology, and technology, in turn, sparked innovation to usher in a true industrial revolution where the tricks of extracting stored hydrocarbon energy from the Earth provided the power to fuel these newly minted civilizations on a path of unimaginable development. There was only one world-wide military conflict depicted after the industrial revolution. It was nuclear. Over 20 percent of the existing landmass on the planet was laid to smoldering waste. They managed to step back from the brink of mutually agreed self-annihilation, and no further depictions of planetary-scale armed conflict appeared.

But technology raced on. Satellites filled orbital space over the planet. Interplanetary space was conquered, but there were no other habitable planets in their solar system. Rapid improvements in healthcare and access to food resources caused the global population to skyrocket until the planet reached a resource tipping point. Marine species were harvested to extinction, freshwater resources came under stress, and competition for farmable land became intense.

Food riots ensued, and global political tensions flared. In the background, the planet was changing. Increases in global greenhouse gas emissions raised global temperatures, both atmospheric and oceanic. The oceans acidified. Species already under stress from over-harvesting slipped away into the void of extinction. Relief finally came but at a price. A string of global pandemics wiped out 70 percent of their world's population.

The survivors pressed on, but the environmental damage was permanent. Polar ice had disappeared, and the vast thermohaline circulation engines keeping the oceans oxygenated shut down. The disappearance of deep ocean circulation created massive oceanic dead zones across their planet. Life was restricted to smaller and smaller areas of the sea. On land, the warmer climate created a hotter, dryer world with fewer places to live.

After the pandemic disaster, resources were focused on health and disease prevention, and no similar event was noted again, but the population stopped increasing. Whether this was by design or random circumstance was not clear.

Eventually, advanced geoengineering and biodome technology emerged and planned managed ecosystems became possible. Small inland oceans were created and managed. Land areas were locally re-forested, and their species started migrating to these controlled biodome communities. Environmental health improved locally but not globally.

This stasis continued for a very long period of time during which you could see the number of biodome communities rise markedly at first, then level off, and then slowly decline as one by one they blinked off the map. But science and technology pressed on, and the small scale use of wormhole technology developed. Small unmanned probes traveled through to other worlds, but our ancient benefactors could not transport themselves through the interface and survive.

The story ended with existing biodomes down to a tenth of their maximum extent—a dying civilization using their resources to do the only thing possible. They sent the mystical strings of life to fertile worlds where evolution could work its magic yet again. Sent with the DNA was a message retrievable 4 billion years later, the one we were viewing. A message about the intimate nature of life and the planet on which it exists. A warning that you have but one planet, live in balance with it or cease to live.

There was also a collection of high-resolution photos of our benefactors. Non-human yet sentient beings staring calmly and interestingly at us from 4 billion years ago.

I had Carl provided me with a copy of the message and a few of the photos.

His parting comment to me was, "Mat, you do realize that the sphere you gave us is probably of more value than your cash infusion."

I paused before I spoke. "I understand this Carl, but you are the man to make the most out of it, and I am happy with my 10 percent stake in our collective future. What Jack does with this will benefit the company, but it will also benefit the world we live in. Use the technology; just don't be greedy or stingy with the information passed on to us by our ancient benefactors. As a species, we need all the help we can get right now."

We shook hands and departed.

Somewhere around 5:00 am EST, a video started streaming from a remote corner of the internet. The video told the backstory of DNA's alien origin on Earth. It went unnoticed for about two hours until a large infusion of paid promotion kicked in. The clicks started picking up at 7:00 am, and by the time Jenara and I boarded the plane from Boston to Portland at 9:00 am it had gone viral. Evidently, there were some clumsy attempts to shut down the site, but it just popped up somewhere else.

Jenara and I sat on my penthouse deck, enjoying the warm Portland evening. We were sipping glasses of Champagne and discussing the past two weeks. Mark and Sirroco were expected for dinner in about an hour. Jenara slipped inside and returned with a box. "These are the things Maria gave to me when I last saw her."

She had some tears in her eyes. I had never seen her cry and softly rubbed her hand. She reached inside the box, picked up something, and told me to hold out my hand. She slipped a small crystal sphere into the palm of my hand.

"This is why I am so familiar with the crystal. I grew up with it. It is part of the mystery of the Solido women. It has been with us for more generations than even Maria knew. The sphere creates an energy connection with us Solido women. That's how I can handle one of them and know it is real. We had no idea that the sphere is an actual memory storage device; we just knew it had energy."

I handed it back to her.

"Speaking of which," she continued, "we need to be thinking about someone for me to pass this on to."

I sat back, shut my eyes, took a sip of Champagne, and thought about that.

Yaak River (Mark)

Well damn. It turned out Mat had made it into town, had his shit stolen, and then made the rendezvous with Eva in a bar. Eva had passed the ancient relic over to Mat, kicked the ever-loving hell out of a dumbass as a feint, and thus fended off the bad guys long enough for Mat and Jenara to slip out the back door just like an old Allman Brothers song. By the time we were offloaded from the jet and four-wheeling southbound, they had consummated some deal about saving humanity and were westward bound for Portland. Too much excitement for the likes of Joe and I and the ladies. So we turned the ride around and did the Bear Neck end of Rockport instead of killing a few bad guys and blowing up somebody's shit and scattering us across the universe. We had lobster and clams and chowder. Then we wandered out to the end of the stone jetty and watched the waves crash onto the rocks for a while. The briny air was tinged with seaweed and nostalgia. We strolled back landward, bought and ate some homemade ice cream, marveled at the red boathouse with the lobster trap floats and the fishing boats in the protected waters for a while, and then headed for Logan Airport. Amber Lee, Sirocco, and I climbed on board the Learjet John had procured for our ride westbound. The owner had called for it on the west coast, so it was basically a deadhead ride for us. Joe had other things in mind, so we parted ways with some hugs and see-ya'll-soons. Amber Lee needed to get back to Leakey for a few days before heading off to Africa. We set down in San Antonio and dropped her off, and then it was just Sirocco and I zinging on to Portland for a bit of R&R and decompression. It would be a few days before Sirocco's place would be cleaned up after the assault by the assholes. Time to take stock and sip a bit of Mat's scotch. Unwinding from our latest big adventure seemed like a good idea.

Sometime later, I finished up the day in my camp just off the East Fork of the Yaak River. The sky over the mountains was crimson and cornstalk yellow across the ridgeline. I was high up in the Rockies of western Montana, a few klicks south of the Canadian border. I had been off the grid for a few months. It was late August or early September by the feel of the air. The atmosphere was crisp and clean and full of mountain valley smells. Three small trout were frying in the iron skillet on the camp grill, a small fire burned in the pit surrounded by stones at the foot of my camp chair, and I had finished taking a hot shower thanks to the modifications on my old Landcruiser. I semi-dried off and slipped on a pair of faded Levi's and roughout boots. My long gray hair hung damply behind my ears and fell way below the back of my neck. My beard was a gray tangle. There were several small trout for breakfast sitting in the cooler. The icemaker provided a few chips and was up to the task. I had been fishing, writing, pickin' my guitar, and just marveling at the beauty of the seriously isolated surroundings I found myself in. The valley was long and narrow with quaking aspen and willows growing among fucked up rocks canting this way and that—begging the semi-scientist in me to figure the widely varying strike and pitch as I surveyed the land by day and pondered it by night. I had not seen or even heard another human since I left Highway 2 and made way to my current whereabouts unknown. I was a trustee of some land, a hundred thousand acres or so, and once in a while, I came up to clear my head. Only a serious adventurer and/or trespasser would ever end up in the small valley I escaped to a few months ago.

I dug two tators from the coals and put them on my warm pewter plate. The trout spilled from the skillet on top of the tators, and I topped it all off with some greens I picked along the river earlier. A cold Blackfoot Montana IPA rounded out my dinner. I was a bit low on beer but still had an ample cache of scotch. I sat in my camp chair by the fire and ate. Dust turned to pitch blackness except for the glow of my fire and my companions overhead. A definite chill was in the crystal-clear night air. The sky was filled with all of my old friends, both big and bright and dim and small. I left the skillet and the plate for the morning. I would wash them in the river during my morning dip in the deep pool just below camp. This activity usually ended up back by the fire with a quizzical what the fuck are you doing conversation with myself. I lit the end of a home-rolled and hit it a couple of times. I was worn out from wading the fast-moving river and hiking and thinking, so I closed my eyes a bit and savored the completeness in which I found myself.

As my mind eased itself into oblivion, I thought about the ancient ones from far away and the fact that they had managed to destroy themselves with their own bad habits. Later, in a dream, I think, I watched the dying ejaculation of a once magnificent civilization. Billions of orbs were sprayed down wormholes and skittered across the universe, skipping across the tops of ripples in time from one peak to the next, traveling millions and billions of light-years across the space-time continuum. Occasionally one or a thousand or more would hit home, and there on some distant rock or comet or planet, the orbs would offer up their bounty to anyone or anything inquisitive enough to figure out the proverbial message in a bottle. The dream was quite vivid and, undoubtedly, enhanced by the genetically perfected smoke. The universe hummed and glowed faintly and was most pleasing to me in the depths of my sleep.

The dream altered from galactic travels to a warm and liquid feeling on my hand and my left knee where my left hand was resting. Eventually, I was able to shake myself from my reverie and crack open my left eye. I was now determined to see exactly what had disturbed my nap before bedtime. Lo and behold, there was a full-grown female grizzly licking my hand. I blinked both eyes open, shook my head a bit,

262

and said, "hey Bear." I clasped the sides of her jaws in my hands and gave her a sloppy kiss on the nose. She made bear noises in return and eased closer to me. I asked her if she was hungry, and there went my breakfast. For dessert, I dug a Washington apple out of my rig and fed it to her. Soon she laid down next to the afterglow of the fire and started to snore. What the hell. I pulled my sleeping bag out of the rig and rolled up in it on the ground next to Bear. We cuddled and slept well. In the morning, we fished together and wandered the valley chasing small critters on the ground and butterflies in the air. She hung around for a few days, and one morning I awoke with a heavy frost on my brow, and Bear was gone. She was probably thinking about finding a hole in the ground for the winter.

Several years before, I had been slouching in my camp chair just the same as the night before, catching a little nap before turning in for the night. There was still a sip of Highland Park 18 in the glass on the camp table at my left elbow. After my shower, I had slipped into my lightly-laced roughout boots and nothing else. The fire did its magic and I closed my eyes and wandered off into the cosmos. Sometime later I was rudely awakened by mumbling and grunting and the rattle of bushes being disturbed. I opened my eyes and stared directly into the eyes of a female grizz cub about the size of your average refrigerator. Based on my years of experience living in the wild, I sat stock still and gathered my wits. If nothing else, my wits could serve as my last meal. I contemplated tipping my camp chair backward and scrambling off the ground and hitting the latch that would free the flush-mounted drawer where my .50 caliber Desert Eagle resided. By sticking the barrel in my mouth, the massively powerful pistol would allow me to die before the bear had eaten more than half of me. The reality was that I would probably tip my chair back and knock myself out on a rock, the bear would eat me, and the sun would rise in the morning none the wiser. So there I sat looking at this three-hundred-pound pup of a bear trying to think my way out of my current circumstances. No fucking way was I gonna get eaten by a bear after all the shit I had been through over the last umpteen years. Hopefully. What the fuck.

"You hungry Bear?" I asked.

"Muregrmmmuphm." The bear replied.

I reached into the cooler and pulled out a fourteen-inch breakfast rainbow trout and held it out to the bear. She sniffed and made soft noises that sounded like she was about to charge and kill my ass. What to do? I'm thinking fast and not receiving any clear answers from the parts of my brain that had never failed me before. I took a big bite out of the belly of the trout. And I chewed it and swallowed it. I held the trout in front of Bear and then went so far as to rub it into her face. She snatched the fish from my hand and inhaled it. I handed her my other breakfast trout, and she made short work of it. She sat back on her haunches and just looked at me. She had a sort of what next look on her face. In the back of my mind was the nagging question of where was mama? Because, as everyone knows, I was gonna die when mama showed up. Finally, I stood and dug an apple out of my larder and gave it to the bear. She gulped it down and then curled up by the fire and went fast asleep. I slept in the camp chair. In the morning, she was still there. I kicked her gently, named her Bear, and headed to the river. We swam together in the deep hole, climbed out and shook ourselves off, and returned to camp. I stoked the fire, cooked some coffee on the camp stove, got dressed, and grabbed my old fishing rod. We went back to the river, where I dragged several fish out for breakfast. I ate mine cooked, and Bear ate hers raw. Mama never showed, so I presumed she died of natural causes, or maybe some hunter had killed her and stuffed her and stuck her on a stand at the front door or some such. So it goes.

Bear hung around, so I taught her to fish by hooking a trout and then swatting the water until I finally tossed the fish onto the river's gravel bank. Bear would pounce on the fish and, eventually, after several weeks, she was proficient at swatting her own fish up on the bank. One morning I awoke, and she was gone. I tracked her to

264

where she had headed out of the valley. Mother nature had called. Over the next few years, when I had the good fortune to return, she would sometimes visit. We would fish and commune into the night for a day or a week, and she would be gone again.

I had turned off the satphone after leaving the pavement several months ago. As I cooked coffee and fish for breakfast, the breeze kicked up, and I felt the hairs lift on the nape of my neck. Perhaps Bear was right, and it was time to pack it in and head on back to Bowlegs. I swam one last time in the cold river and was drying when, I don't know why, I dug the old satphone out and hit the power switch. It powered up and there was the faint blinking of the message light. There are four people and one machine with the number. That's it. No one else on the planet has the number. I clicked on and heard Mat say, "hey buddy, wonder if you have time to stop by. I want to show you something." The message was five minutes old. Wonder if you have time to stop by and see something my ass. I wondered just exactly what the fuck kind of shit he had gotten himself into this time and, by osmosis, me.

I packed up my camp, pissed on the fire, and cranked up the Landcruiser. I tapped in Mat's number and clicked twice. I punched in Joe's number. He answered on the first ring.

"What the fuck do you want?" he greeted me.

"Where are you asshole?" I greeted him.

"None of your fucking business." Joe was an easy-going guy if there ever was one.

"Fine" I replied. "Contact Hunter. Ya'll are on call." I clicked off and a day later cleared the wilderness, hit the dirt road, then hit the pavement and headed toward Portland. Big deal or trivial, it made no difference to me. I was gonna sip some excellent, and free, scotch. I punched in Sirocco's number just for grins.

About the Authors

Rand Soler - Writer, environmentalist, and geologist living in the Pacific Northwest. His writing follows his travels around the globe, investigating the science and mystery of the world around us.

Y.A. Picker - Author, fisherman, player of the guitar and harmonica, lover of the outdoors, life-long member of the orgy-of-the-ologies club, all-around ne'er-do-well. Chaser of the crooked roads and the ancient ones.